The Alley

ELEANOR ESTES

The Alley

ILLUSTRATED BY
EDWARD ARDIZZONE

AN ODYSSEY/HARCOURT YOUNG CLASSIC
HARCOURT, INC.

Orlando Austin New York San Diego Toronto London

www.HarcourtBooks.com

First Harcourt Young Classics edition 2003
First Odyssey Classics edition 2003
First published 1964

Library of Congress Cataloging-in-Publication Data
Estes, Eleanor, 1906–   .
The Alley/Eleanor Estes; illustrated by Edward Ardizzone.
    p.   cm.
"An Odyssey/Harcourt Young Classic."
Sequel: The tunnel of Hugsy Goode.
Summary: Ten-year-old Connie, who lives in the Brooklyn neighborhood
called The Alley, investigates a burglary with her friend Billy Maloon.
[1. Alleys—Fiction.   2. Friendship—Fiction.   3. Brooklyn (New York,
N.Y.)—History—20th century—Fiction.   4. Mystery and detective
stories.]   I. Ardizzone, Edward, 1900– ill.   II. Title.
PZ7.E749Al   2003
    [Fic]—dc21   2003045290
ISBN 0-15-204917-7   ISBN 0-15-204918-5 (pb)

Printed in the United States of America

A C E G H F D B
C E G H F D B (pb)

To the memory of
Mama Sadie

CONTENTS

⚓ ⚓ ⚓

The Alley

I
⚡⚡⚡

THE VIEW FROM THE SWING

The Alley! To hear the name, you might think it an awful place to live—no sunshine, no light, with tin cans around, perhaps, and dreary old blown-about newspapers. Not this Alley, though. Gardens, flowers, pretty little red brick houses joined one to another; butterflies in summer, a squirrel sometimes in winter, and swings . . . that was what this Alley had. Connie thought the Alley the most beautiful place in the whole world to live in, and of all the little houses there, she thought hers the prettiest. They might look alike on the outside, but on the inside each one was as different as the people who lived in them.

From her jungle gym in her little back yard, where she was swinging, Connie had a wonderful view of the Alley, the best view of the Alley that there was.

There were twenty-seven little houses in the Alley. They all had blue-green picket fences between them, and they all had their own little gardens. At the end of each garden was a higher fence than the fences between the houses. Each

house had a gate into the Alley from its own back yard. These little houses were on the campus of Grandby College, in the heart of the city of Brooklyn. The Alley was shaped like a T, a T turned sideways, like this— ——————| . Eight houses were on one side, the long side of the ——————| , and they faced Story Street. The Ives—Connie and her family —were in number 175 of Story Street. There were eight houses opposite them, and these faced Waldo Place. That made sixteen houses, leaving eleven. These eleven houses made up the top part of the ——————| and faced Larrabee Street. Billy Maloon lived in the exact middle house of these eleven houses on Larrabee Street, and his view of the Alley was next best to the one from Connie's swing. From his bedroom window, or from the little roof outside it, he could see all the way to the Circle at the end of the long part of the ——————| ; and to his left and his right, he could see the two beautiful locked iron gates at the two ends of the top part of the ———| .

In the Alley there was more space than you might think to ride bikes in, and at the bottom end of the ———| was the Circle, excellent for turning around in and excellent for games.

Every yard had flowers. Now it was May, and the flowers were tulips, irises, lilacs. In the corner under the dining-room window of Connie's house, there were even a few violets and, under the rose bush, some lilies of the valley. On some of the fences, there was honeysuckle, but it was not in blossom yet. The lilacs were in blossom, though. There were purple ones in the Gwatkins' yard, opposite Connie's. In June the roses would be out. Almost every garden had roses. In Connie's yard, they were white. They were trying to spread all over the yard, and you had to watch out for the thorns, not let the little children crawl under the branches to pet the cats asleep there.

The Alley—the little houses on the Alley—was an oasis in a great city of good people and of dangerous people. In this city, there were some burglars. "But then, that is life," thought Connie. "In the old days, they had Indians, wild animals, pirates, and dragons. They had witches. Now— burglars. You have to take the bad along with the good." But Connie never thought much of the burglars there might be outside the Alley. She thought mainly of life inside the Alley, in the beautiful, fragrant Alley. Her life was made up mainly of school and Alley.

Connie was ten, and she was in grade five in school. She was known in the Alley as "the swinger" because, whenever she could be, she was usually swinging. "Connie Ives, the famous swinger," Katy Starr always said. Katy was a year and a grade older.

Connie loved school—all her studies, all her teachers, and every inch of the school itself. The school was an old one—red brick and five stories high. What a race there was to the gym, between bells, for the gym was higher still, in a sort of turret. It was a famous old school, ancient and with a long history. A poet had gone there once. Now Connie went there, in grade five, and also many of the other children in the Alley, big and little. When the sixth of June came, Connie would be promoted to grade six. She would take up decimals—not easy, not easy at all, they said—and problems —how fast one car would be going if another car was going forty miles an hour and if Mr. Grimes, the driver of the first car, got to the city ten minutes ahead of Mr. Cox, driver of the second. Connie had seen it in Katy's book and often tried to figure it out.

When she started in this school, Connie had been in grade two. Two, three, four, five, and next six. Grade six in this school! That meant that she had been living in the Alley for four years, almost a half of her life. She counted on her fingers to be sure. She always counted on her fingers. "Ts," Mama always said. "Counting on your fingers? Still?" And Papa, a professor, though of English not arithmetic, chimed in. "The way they teach arithmetic—by packs of cards, the numbers on each card having nothing to do with the numbers on the card before! This is why children age ten have to count on their fingers!"

"Yes," said Mama. "They should learn addition ('addition facts' they call them now!) by rote, not by cards. It's fun learning by rote, anyway. One and one are two, two and two are four, and so on. Some of the ways of doing things now don't seem sensible to me at all."

Connie had always loved to swing. Everywhere that she had ever lived—and that had been four places, counting this Alley in Brooklyn—she had always had a swing. Practically everybody in the Alley loved to come into the yard and swing. "Can I come in?" "Can I swing?" The big children and the little ones came to the gate all the time, asking to come in and swing.

"You have a regular playground there," June Arp's mother often said to Mama over the fence.

"I know." Mama laughed. She didn't care. She loved having the children in the yard. But she had had to post rules. Otherwise, there would be too many on the swing at once, and the little ones might get hurt.

Mama printed the rules on a nice thin, square, flat piece of wood, and she put these rules on the trunk of Mrs. Harrington's huge elm tree, the side of the trunk that was in Connie's yard. Next to Billy Maloon's oak tree, this tree was the largest in the Alley, and its branches spread over the jungle gym and most of Connie's garden. A lot of the little boys, like Nicky and Danny, couldn't read; but that did not matter. They knew the rules by heart. The rules were:

1. Always ask permission. Don't just walk into the yard and start swinging.
2. Always close the gate so that Wags (the dog) can't get out in the Alley.

3. No more than two little ones on at a time or three big ones.
4. Little ones under three must have a mother or a big person with them.
5. Don't go too high.
6. Don't jump off.
7. No reserving. (That is, you can't come in and swing and then jump off and say "reserved" while you go home for a cookie or something else. That would be hogging the swing.)
8. Don't stand up and swing.

Everyone knew the rules of Connie's jungle-gym swings and glider, and everyone obeyed them . . . at least, in the main they tried to, but some, Nicky especially, just couldn't resist going too high. And one, Katy Starr, often walked right into the yard, not asking first "May I?" and left the gate open, swung a short while, jumped down, and then went out, saying, "Swinging is boring." She did not close the gate after her, either.

"I wonder why she does that," Connie thought. "There are thirty-three children in the Alley, and Katy is the only one who leaves the gate open. Oh well, that is the way Katy is! She just is that way."

It was lucky that there were this many children in the Alley. There was always someone out, someone to play with. Connie didn't have any brothers or sisters herself—oh, how she wished she had one, a brother or a sister—but she didn't. However, this didn't mean that her family was a small one. Far from it. It was quite large and consisted of the following.

First of all, herself, Connie. She had long blond hair, which she sometimes wore in two braids and sometimes simply hanging straight. She had bangs; and very black eyelashes shadowed her frank blue eyes. Her face was serious, thoughtful. But when she smiled, her eyes and face lit up like moonbeams. She loved to read, she loved music, she made up songs, she took piano lessons, though she did not like them; she liked to play, simply play the piano, not to take the lessons. She liked to draw and often wrote a book and drew the pictures for it. She liked to think, just swing and think; and she loved animals. When she thought of animals, lost and out in the cold or in the snow, hungry in the nighttime, she cried softly to herself. She had a good sense of humor. It would be hard to say which of her favorite books her most favorite book was—*Alice in Wonderland, Floating Island, Charlotte's Web,* or *Half Magic.* She loved them all, each one being the best and most favorite while she was reading it.

Then there was her father, a professor of English. "Papa is the most distinguished-looking man on campus," thought Connie. "Next most distinguished-looking man might be Mr. Starr, Katy's father." He was a man with a beard like Van Gogh's, though Mr. Starr was a professor of archaeology, not an artist. Mr. Blackman, dean of the students and an oboe player, was very handsome, too. The Alley had many handsome inhabitants. Connie's father was from South Carolina and stemmed from the Rebels. Connie's mother, who, besides being a mother, was an artist, was from Connecticut; so she stemmed from the Yankees. Mama and Papa first set eyes on each other in a classroom right here at Grandby College. She was studying art, and he was already a professor of English; to be an artist, you must also study English, and he was her teacher. They met each other, for the first time, outside the classroom on a windy day in October at the cannon in Library Park, when she dropped her portfolio and her drawings blew all over the park. It was too windy to run around gathering up her drawings; she had to hang onto the cannon merely to stand up. Papa had run all over the grass picking up her drawings. They were not much torn, and she didn't care, anyway. What were lost drawings in comparison to lunching with Professor Ives? For they had had lunch together that day in the Grandby Drugstore—both had had tuna fish on toast—and then they had had lunch together practically every day thereafter.

Next came Nanny, Connie's grandmother, the mother of Connie's father, and likewise stemming from the Rebels. She loved to cook and was practically always in the kitchen. She always listened to the baseball games on the radio and knew every player on every team, and knew past famous players, too, and who won the pennant when. In her college in the South in her day, she was captain of the women's baseball team. She also loved horses and had been considered a dashing horsewoman, galloping along the country roads, sometimes bareback, or driving a little surrey, trot-trot, clop. "There goes Stacy," all would say; but she would be out of sight before anyone could really see her. That's what Connie's father told Connie. Nanny was in her seventies; but she did not sit in the corner and knit or anything of that sort. She cooked, listened to the news, wrote dozens of letters a week to her dear friends back home. She did not consider Brooklyn her home; she just lived here with Connie's father and mother. She dearly loved Connie, her only grandchild. It would be hard to imagine anything sweeter than her voice saying, "Yes, darling?" when Connie had something to tell. You could always count on Nanny's listening. You could not always count on Papa's listening; he had his mind on other things. He had so much to do—correct papers, have conferences with his students, go to meetings, read the paper, read books. But when he finally listened, he listened really hard. Mama was quite a good listener; sometimes, however, she had to listen to two people at once—Connie and her father, or even three, Nanny, too, plus Nanny's news report on the radio, with her comments about it—and that was not easy. Nanny did not like for you to let the cat out when she had just gotten her in, or in when she had just gotten her out—having beguiled her with a piece of kidney or a little scrap of something. She spoke crossly to Hugsy Goode and Billy Maloon—Billy was Connie's best friend—if they tracked in one drop of snow. They were both scared of her. It embarrassed Connie, the cross way Nanny spoke to her friends. But that was the only thing wrong with her. Otherwise, she was perfect and she loved Connie so. She loved Connie and she loved South Carolina. She had missed only one Christmas with Connie since Connie was born. That Christmas without Nanny had been awful; and Connie hoped she would never miss another one.

Next came Wags, nicknamed Wagsie. Wags was the six-year-old springer spaniel dog of the Ives family. She was dark brown and white with curly, shaggy fur and long, floppy ears. Ordinarily Wags had a melancholy look, wise and thoughtful; but when she rolled over on her back, she looked as though she was laughing, and she was. If Connie had any troubles, she buried her face in Wagsie's fur and told them to her. "Wagsie," she cried. "Listen." This wonderful dog was given to Connie by the wife of an F.B.I. man when Connie was almost three. Sometimes she was called "the F.B.I. dog." Wags was only eight weeks old then, and her hind legs were so weak, she could not get up on the sofa. Her legs never grew very strong, and sometimes, coming downstairs, she would slide on her stomach the last few steps as though she were a toboggan. Wags was a very timid dog. But she was a noble, wonderful dog and the most beautiful of her kind anyone was apt to see anywhere. That's what Papa said, and he had seen many dogs. Wags stemmed from champions, and Papa owned the family tree. Wags was quite nervous—her weak hind legs made her so—and did not like tiny little children, who scared her with their sudden movements and squeals. She had never bitten anyone, though, mainly because Mama was always on the watch—always.

Next in this family came the two large and fat cats named Mittens and Punk—Mother Mittens and Daughter Punk, to be exact, age two and one.

Mittens was a cat born in the Alley and given to Connie by Billy Maloon, who owned the father. Punk was one of Mittens' first batch of four kittens, her favorite and the one who slept with her mother's front paw around her. Punk was beautiful; but she was not as brilliant as her mother. She had been pampered by her mother, had never had kittens of her own, and still tried to gobble up her mother's food. Her mother let her. The reason Punk had such an odd name was that she was born on the Fourth of July. Connie named the four first kittens of Mittens after Fourth of July things—Punk, Rocket, Sparkler, and Pinwheel. Hugsy Goode owned Rocket now, but his mother had made him change Rocket's name to Smoky because she had just lost a cat named Smoky and she liked to think she had the real Smoky back.

That's all there was to the Ives family, unless you count Red Horsie, Bear, and Patricia. Connie still counted Red Horsie, her rocking horse, as a member of the family and still made him a Christmas card, even though he was up in the attic, being saved for her children when she grew up. Bear was a big teddy bear given to Connie on her fourth Christmas by her uncle Clare, and he still stayed in her room. Patricia had always been her favorite doll, and she still stayed in her room, too; sometimes Connie took her or Bear out to swing with her. So that was the family of Connie Ives, just one family out of the twenty-seven in the Alley.

2
⇟ ⇟ ⇟
CONNIE IVES

"The famous swinger." That was Connie's nickname. She was swinging now, and she thought of how practically everyone in this Alley had a special name: Katy Starr, the lawmaker, Arnold, the great R.A. boy—in the Rapid Advancement class, that means, in school—Mrs. Carroll, the rainmaker—so called because she sometimes beat on tin tubs, yow-yowed like an Indian to make rain come—Joe Below, the *boulevardier* (or Bully Vardeer, as it was pronounced)—too many to list them all.

Connie was watching what was going on in the Alley. Because it was Saturday morning, the iron gates were unlocked and the garbage truck would soon be here. The two pretty iron gates to the Alley were always kept locked except on the mornings when the garbage truck came in— Tuesdays, Thursdays, and Saturdays. Most of the littlest children were safely locked in their own back yards. They longed to get out to freedom in the big Alley, but they couldn't do this until the truck should come and go and the gates to the outside world be locked again. They waited for this happy moment by playing Superman, with sheets on for capes. One was Superman, another, a little smaller, was Superboy, and George Gwatkin, practically a baby, was Little Super. They flew from yard to yard on their side of the Alley, up one fence and over and so on all the way, shouting "Superman!" with capes fluttering behind them.

The Carrolls lived in the end house next to the iron gate on Connie's side of the Alley. There were four little Car-

rolls, and since each was born on or around Christmas day, they were all named in honor of Christmas. Their names were Stephen, the oldest, who was six, then Star, four, Nicky, three, and last, the littlest one, Noel—Notesy, her nickname was, and she was practically just a baby still and had to be held on the swings. All the Carrolls wanted to be garbage collectors when they grew up. The most interesting times of the week for them were the mornings when the garbage truck arrived. "Here it comes! Here it comes!" they yelled. They helped the men roll the trash cans down the Alley and were grateful for the privilege.

Then, the minute the truck went out, the gates were locked again. This made the Alley safe. The children couldn't get out of the Alley, and no wicked people could get in. There had been two burglaries in the Alley, though —one in the end house on Larrabee, the house of the Bernadettes, who had no children, and the other in the house of the Langs, who had no children, either. But the burglars did not get in through the Alley; they got in through the front doors. They just broke down the doors when no one was home, went in, and took what they wanted. These burglaries were long ago, historic burglaries, rarely spoken of now, mainly forgotten.

But sometimes, when she was swinging, Connie thought about those burglaries. From the swing she could glimpse the police station, a medieval-looking building—Precinct Number 9999. With all the houses torn down next to the Alley to make room for the athletic field, the police of Precinct 9999 could see the little houses in the Alley and foil a burglary now.

Even so, "Never leave the outer green door open," Papa always said. "Leaving it open is an invitation to burglars," he said. "They can get inside the outer green door, close it behind them, and then easily break down the inner door, with no one being able to see what they are doing. Always keep that outer green door locked!" Papa repeatedly warned Connie, Mama, Nanny—everybody. Still, Nanny often would keep the outer door open—she just would. "For the mailman," she said, so he would not have so much trouble getting her Chester, South Carolina, paper in the slot—it was too big, it and the Sunday *State*, to squeeze through the small mail slot in the outer door. "Tear them to shreds," said Nanny. "Tear them all to shreds." The Chester *Reporter* and the Columbia *State* were like home to Nanny. Then, the minute the mailman left, she tried to remember to lock the outer green door, not to be inviting burglars, as Papa said.

"Don't you worry, child," she'd say to Papa. (Though he was forty-eight, she still called him "child.") "No burglar is coming in while I am here."

Connie wondered if Nanny would think to use the tall Tiffany vase, which stood on the little marble-top table near the front door, to bop a burglar over the head with if one did break in. Connie doubted it. The vase was a famous one, given to Nanny at the time of her marriage by her dear friend, Becky Coker, Charleston, South Carolina. If a burglar appeared at the front door, Connie decided that Nanny, probably on account of the sentiment, would not use the Tiffany vase in this way. What would Nanny do in case of burglars? She would scream, probably, just scream. How Nanny could scream! She would scare the burglars away with just one scream, that's what Connie thought. In sorrow and in joy, Nanny was apt to scream; and when Micky Mantle hit a homer, you could hear her way down at the Carrolls' end house, for she loved the drama in life.

Opposite the Carrolls', next to the other iron gate, there lived an artist named Joe Below—nicknamed, Bully Vardeer. This artist had painted the portrait of almost every child in the Alley and of one or two out-of-the-ordinary-looking grownups. Katy Starr's father was one, because of his beard, and the President of Grandby College was another, painted with hand on stomach, mortar board on head—its tassel over his executive eye. If you were led blindfolded into any of the little houses and then allowed to take a look, you could tell which house you were in by the Bully Vardeer painting on the wall. The nickname "Bully Vardeer" stemmed from the French word *boulevardier*, meaning an artist who strolls along the boulevards near the River Seine in Paris, stopping to talk now and then with a fellow artist or a model, sipping an *apéritif* at a sidewalk café, and then sauntering on. Bully Vardeer had a jaunty, swinging sort of stride, wore his hat carelessly on the back of his head, and kept his hands in his pockets. It was Mama who said he looked like a *boulevardier* from the description Papa had given her of *boulevardiers*. Papa knew, having been to Paris in his youth. Mama had not been to Paris. But why go anywhere, living with someone who described things as well as Papa? Connie had thought *boulevardier* was a name—Bully Vardeer—and she called Mr. Joe Below by that nickname. Now, Billy Maloon and Hugsy—all the children and even some of the grownups—called him Bully Vardeer.

These two houses by the iron gates—the Carrolls' and Bully Vardeer's—had no windows on their red brick Alley side, so their walls were excellent for bouncing balls against

—the Carrolls and Bully Vardeer did not like that—and for writing on with chalk—the Carrolls and Bully Vardeer did not like that, either. When the four little Carrolls got a little older, they would probably begin writing in chalk on good places like their wall, too. Then their mother would have to yell at them, not at Arnold and June and Connie and Katy —some of the present chalk writers. "Who likes to read all those white and pink and blue chalk marks, such as the mark of Zorro and others?" Mrs. Carroll demanded. Children did not mind the writing on the wall; in fact, they pored over all the interesting news, as to who loved whom and who hated whom—Arnold had written his in Latin, H.G. *amat* C.I. But the grownups did mind, and once Connie and June Arp had to wash the writing off the Carrolls' wall. This was not fair, because Connie had put only one word on it—"Connie." "But that's life," she thought.

No one could live in this Alley except people who worked at Grandby College. That was fair, since the houses on the Alley belonged to this college. "Faculty houses," they were called. Everyone in Grandby College pined to live in one of the little houses. But there were not enough for all, and you had to get on a waiting list. Sometimes outsiders, children, looked through the gates and watched the children inside for a while, and then they'd rush away saying, "Poor things, they're locked up."

"It's as though we're in a zoo," said Connie to Hugsy Goode, age nine, and in P.S. 2, like Billy Maloon. The name of Connie's school was Morrison.

"Yeah," agreed Hugsy. "Once I heard a kid say—I think

he was a Gregory Avenue kid (Gregory Avenue was the name of the street outside the campus that ran along the athletic field)—I heard this guy say, 'There are tunnels under these houses, and they go from house to house.' "

"You did!" exclaimed Connie. "Do you think that is true?"

"No," said Hugsy, "because I looked in my cellar and in Billy's for secret trap doors. None! None at all! We tapped every inch. Mrs. Trickman thought we were burglars—called the police . . ."

Connie was disappointed about the tunnels. "Are you sure?" she asked. "You know there might be, there really might be tunnels." They both liked to think there might be and that one of them would be the discoverer of a tunnel, leading from Connie's house to Hugsy's, Billy's—or even to outside.

You might think the Alley was too small a place to have much fun in. That was not so. Ask any of the thirty-three children who lived there, and they would all say that was not so, even Anthony Bigelow, a small, bold new boy. The Alley was big enough for any game, even for sledding. Once, though, Connie had had a flying dream. In this dream she had flown out of her bedroom window, over her garden, over her fence, and down the Alley—not going high, just high enough to clear the grapevines on the Carrolls' fence—and then flying, like swimming in the air, around the corner to the iron gate. But when she reached the gate, she could not fly over it. She tried and tried, but she could not make it. She woke up, still trying to get out and over the gate. Perhaps she had wanted to fly out of the

Alley, fly all over Brooklyn and even over the Brooklyn Bridge. Did that mean she really wanted to fly out of Brooklyn? Fly back to Washington where she used to live? "Of course," she often used to say to Hugsy, Billy, or to anyone who would listen, "Brooklyn is not as beautiful as Washington. How could it be? That is the most beautiful city in the world. Still, Brooklyn is beautiful, too. It's quaint," she said.

Naturally, when the Ives first moved to Brooklyn, Connie had been homesick. But now, swinging high on this perfect May day, her heart brimming with joy, Connie thought with astonishment of those lonely first days. It was a little train busily making its way up the elevated tracks on Myrtle Avenue that reminded Connie now of them. Well, she had been only six then. Naturally she had missed beautiful Washington and her friend, Clarissa, who had practically lived with her, was practically a sister to her there. Connie listened to the little train go rumbling along. She couldn't see it from here, how it looked, like a little toy train; but she could hear it, saying, "Hello, Connie. Goodby, Connie!"

"The little train saved my life," she thought. "The Myrtle Avenue El."

"The Myrtle Avenue El," Papa said when they moved here, "is the very last elevated train in New York City! It will soon be torn down, too, I hear." But it was still up, it had not been torn down yet, and maybe it never would be. Maybe it would be kept as a souvenir of bygone days of old New York. "Save? For a souvenir? New York save anything? Why, they are talking of tearing down the house where Walt Whitman printed 'Leaves of Grass'! That's how they save in New York City!" shouted Papa.

Well, luckily the El was still up when the Ives moved here. Every day for the first few weeks, the minute Connie came home from school, she and Mama used to get on the little train and ride to the end of the line. Raining or shining, windy or what, it did not matter. The thought of the little train helped Connie to get through the long day in her new, big, strange Brooklyn school. She and Mama would climb the steep stairs up to the platform, and, no matter what the weather, they would stand outside rather than in the stale-smelling waiting room. They could see through the cracks of the wooden platform to the cars and people below; and looking way down the straight, silvery tracks, they could see the train come rollicking and swaying along—making their platform tremble, shudder, and steel itself for the swift onrush of the train—here now, at last, cheerful, inviting, and calm.

Usually, at that time of day, there were few people on the train; it was practically a private train. Sometimes Connie, her mother, the motorman, and the conductor would be the only ones on it. Jogging along, it was strange being able to look into people's second-story windows and onto the roofs where the pigeons were kept. Sometimes a man or a boy let his pigeons out to fly; and then when the train returned, the pigeons would be back in their little houses on the rooftops. "How did they know where to go?" wondered Connie. One man had chickens, real alive chickens—white Bantams they were, who squawked when the train went by and fluttered their wings.

Many houses, blocks and blocks of them along Myrtle Avenue, were being torn down to make way for new, big apartment buildings. The old, torn-down houses had no fronts to them any more; they were like rows and rows of huge dollhouses, or houses for stage settings that have no fronts to them, so that you can see in, see the characters inside. But these no-front houses had no characters inside any more, only rooms that had been lived in once and would never be lived in again. You could see the different colors the rooms had been painted and the different wallpapers. Some of the rooms were pale pink or blue or bright green; some were even purple. Others were coral or salmon. Perhaps, before their fronts had been ripped off, these houses might have looked awful—slums. But now with their ancient, crumbling wallpapers, they looked pretty to Connie as she and Mama went swiftly by.

They always went to the end of the line. Perhaps Connie hoped that the train would take her back to Washington, to drawing pictures there with Clarissa, to taking walks there with Mama, past the big and lovely ginkgo trees, smelling the violets and picking them—they grew right along the brick sidewalks and in between the bricks, practically everywhere, there, in Washington.

One day, however, walking home from the little train, Connie said to Mama, "You know, Mama, I don't think Washington is so beautiful any more, now that I'm not in it."

Mama agreed. "Yes," she said. "I think you are right."

In the nighttime, you could see the little train from Mama's bedroom window, prettily lighted; and in the nighttime—in the clear night crispness—the little train, lulling Connie, singing, "Hello, Connie. Good-by, Connie," reminded her still of Washington. But it was like a song remembered, part of a long-ago life. Life now was different. Now, they were living in the Alley, in one of the little Alley houses. Now Connie didn't miss Washington any more. She loved it here in the Alley. She never wanted to leave here.

3

♭ ♭ ♭

BILLY MALOON

Billy Maloon, who was Connie's age, a boy with large, sad hazel eyes, used to walk past Connie's gate in the Alley while she was swinging. He wouldn't turn his head to look at her, and she wouldn't turn her head to look at him. He would turn his eyes, though, to see her, just his eyes, and she would turn her eyes, just her eyes, not her head, to see him. Sometimes he would seem about to stop. But then he would go on up to his end of the Alley, to his house, climb over his fence, and go in. And Connie would go into her house and read to herself or to Mama.

Connie had many friends in the Alley. One was Judy Fabadessa, age ten, too, and in her class at school. But Judy was not another Clarissa—she would never take the place of Clarissa. Everyone in the Alley knew about Clarissa and Connie in Washington, the great friends they had been. You might say that Clarissa shone in their thoughts the way she did in Connie's. Still, Judy and Connie did become friends, and at first Judy came to Connie's house every day. Judy

33

liked to swing and to sled and to play in the deep snow, and so did Connie. Sometimes she and Connie and their mothers went ice-skating at Rockefeller Plaza. Connie and Judy laughed a lot, they gasped, they couldn't stop laughing. But sometimes Judy would turn her back on Connie and attach herself to the big girls—her sister Laura, Katy Starr, a very important girl in the Alley, the maker of its laws, and June Arp, the girl next door.

This was the way that Billy Maloon, instead of Judy Fabadessa, became Connie's best friend in the Alley. One day Connie was sitting in the kitchen, in the little red rocker, reading to Mama. Mama was cooking something that smelled wonderful.

"M-m-m," Connie said. "Smells good."

"Spaghetti sauce," Mama said. "Taste this for seasoning, will you?" she said. "What does it need? A little something or other—I can't think what. Thyme?"

Connie tasted. She ran her eyes around in her head like the dogs in "The Tinderbox." "M-m-m," she said. "Just right," she said. "Don't add another thing. You'll ruin it."

"I thought maybe a pinch more of salt," said Mama.

"Well, just a pinch, no more . . . you'll ruin it. It's perfect now. And now, I'll read."

Mama loved for Connie to read to her when she was cooking, and Connie loved to read to her. Connie planned to read every single good book that she had ever read out loud to Mama. On the day of Billy's first visit, she happened to be reading, *On the Banks of Plum Creek*. The "Little House" books were among Connie's favorites, and Mama had never read any of them. Can you imagine? This shows how old Mama was—these books had been written after Mama had grown up—not when she was a little girl like Connie. At least Mama had had *The Secret Garden* then, however. Connie sat back in the little red rocker and prepared to read. She said, "Where were we?" She knew where they were but said this to see if Mama really listened. Mama said, "We were up to the part about the grasshoppers, the horde of grasshoppers eating up all the crops and wheat, leaving everything brown as dust—nothing growing, nothing to eat, not a live stalk left—"

"All right," Connie said. "Now, I'll go on." She was happy. Mama always listened. "Now, don't run the water," she cautioned.

"Well," Mama said, "I am cooking, you know. Once in a while I just have to run the water. I won't run it any more than I can help, not leave it running."

Connie found the place, after the grasshoppers, where they had left off, and began to read. When Connie was in the kitchen rocking and reading to Mama, peace settled over the little house and quietude on Mama's face. Sometimes while listening, Mama would stop what she was doing for a moment and take in the view of the living room—bright rugs, the books, some still in their new paper jackets, the paintings on the wall, the accordion player, a lovely piece of sculpture, and the last late beams of sunlight, reflected from the windows of the school across the street, lighting all with a tranquil glow.

Connie stopped reading a moment and looked at Mama. She said, "You know, Mama, we could write a book. We could call it *The Little House in the Alley.*"

"Yes," Mama agreed. "We have a wonderful life."

"Yes. Well now, listen now—you are listening, aren't you?" asked Connie.

"I'm listening," Mama said.

"Don't stare any more," said Connie, "into the living room." She read one whole chapter, and she had just asked Mama if she should read another one—it was short—and Mama had just said she'd love it, and Connie had rearranged her legs comfortably—Papa was right, the red rocker *was* getting a little small for her—when the back doorbell rang.

"Probably some of the little ones asking to swing," said Connie.

But it was Billy Maloon. Connie was surprised. Billy had never rung the bell before. Billy Maloon was one of the shiest people in the Alley and not used to ringing people's doorbells. Although shy, he was thoughtful and considerate. Wasn't that a considerate thing to do—wait until Connie had finished the last of the chapter before ringing the bell? Who else would do that that she knew? Ring . . . just ring and ask to swing, that was what most would do. And never mind what was going on inside.

"H'lo," said Billy to Mama, not looking at Connie. "Can Connie play?" he asked.

"You ask Connie," said Mama, smiling. Connie could tell that Mama liked Billy Maloon. Mama was apt to like all children, and all children were apt to like her, too. She even liked Anthony Bigelow, and Anthony was not always a good boy. Sometimes he did not tell the truth. It was a shame. He was bright and could have been so nice. His tiny sister, Jilly, was so sweet, so good! "They are like sweet and sour pot roast," people sometimes said of the two.

Billy looked directly at Connie then. "Can you play?" he asked. His hazel eyes were large and shining, and a little frightened. In his slow, almost drawling way of speaking—a sort of singsong monotone—he said, "I brought this." He had a Dinky Toy, a lumber truck, in his hand.

"O.K.," said Connie. They went upstairs to her room. First they got some of her old put-away blocks out of the attic. Billy suggested it, so they could make a garage—it was low and modern—for the lumber truck. They also made stores, a whole village, with a lumber camp outside of it, and a super highway following the blue-green thread that wound along the border of the Chinese rug. Connie did not own any Dinky Toys, so Billy went home and got some more—his ambulance and his tractor. Besides these, he had a jeep. He also brought the catalog, to see what to buy next.

"Traffic is getting heavy," said Connie.

"I like the comment," Billy said.

Billy Maloon often used long and hard words. He was left to himself a great deal. But this did not matter to Billy Maloon. On the whole, grownups did not exist for him. They were obstacles to circle around. He tried to be unaware of their presence, even of Connie's mother, who liked Billy very much.

After that first day when Billy Maloon came to play with Connie with his lumber truck Dinky Toy, he came every chance he got. He and Connie became best friends. Judy Fabadessa did not like the idea. But Connie could not help that. She liked Billy, and she had more fun playing with Billy than she had had with anyone since she had left Clarissa and Washington. She and Billy never got into arguments the way she and Judy did. Billy didn't complain if he didn't win every time in checkers or chess. He never said, "Oo-oh, you cheated," the way Judy did when Connie was winning; and Connie had never cheated in anything in her whole life! She and Billy always agreed about what they wanted to play and what Dinky Toys each one should have for "his" in games, and how to divide things. Connie soon had some Dinky Toys of her own, a postal truck, a racing car, and a trailer.

Judy still often came over to play. But the more Connie played with Billy Maloon, the less Judy liked it. Judy had a habit of making a certain awful face, and now she made this face more and more often. She would pull the corners of her mouth way down and roll her eyes into a curious position that left only the white parts showing. She looked as though she didn't have any eyes. When she and Connie played checkers, or any other game now, she would soon get angry about something, make her awful face, and say she bet Connie was getting to like Billy Maloon better than her. Connie never answered, because it was true. Billy liked to play with Connie and Connie liked to play with Billy.

One day, when it was time for Billy to go and he had gathered up his Dinky Toys reluctantly, because he did not want to go home, Connie said, "Billy, you know that you can call me up and talk to me any time you want to on the telephone? And you can talk as long as you want." She

39

didn't know why she said this, because she did not like to use the telephone—she could scarcely remember when she had ever once spoken into it.

"O.K.," said Billy in his flat voice. But from his wide eyes Connie could tell he was pleased. One night he did telephone. Mama answered the phone and said, "Connie, it's for you."

"Me!" said Connie. At first she did not want to take the phone. Can you believe it! Here she was, a girl of ten, and she was still not accustomed to talking on the telephone; in fact, she was scared of the phone—don't ask why. Perhaps it was because many big people shout in the phone, and this hurt Connie's ears. Big people, even Nanny, must think all people on the other end of the line were deaf, they shouted so. It was a wonder that everyone did not become deaf, with all this shouting in phones. Connie just didn't like it. But, "Please, please say 'Hello,' just 'Hello,' to Uncle Laudy in Los Angeles," Nanny would plead with Connie. Connie would disappear upstairs and not say "Hello" to Uncle Laudy or anyone else. Papa was ashamed of her. He'd say, "Connie, it's ridiculous. You must learn to dial a number and ask for someone—talk! And also *answer* the phone when it rings, *make* yourself do that." And Mama said, "Yes. Practice on Papa, Connie. Call him up at the college. Dial the number of the college and ask for Professor Ives in the English Department. Is that hard?" Connie never answered. But some day, some day, she would surprise them —answer the phone every time it rang, talk to Uncle Laudy, Aunt Beasie, everybody, even the President.

Now, here was Billy calling her up, and here she was

talking! Maybe she would get over her fear of the phone now, if Billy kept calling her up. Connie was brave about practically everything else you can think of. She walked the high Harrington fence, and she climbed to the top of the jungle gym—Hugsy couldn't do that, not many people could—but phone? The phone scared her. She and Billy talked a long, long time together. He had a nice soft voice on the telephone—he was a pleasure to listen to; he never shouted, he did not hurt ears. But tonight he sounded sad, as though he had been crying. This troubled Connie. The Carroll children bawled and bellowed all the time over every little thing; but she could not imagine Billy crying. Still, she was sure he had been. As he and she were talking, he gradually sounded happier. Then Connie heard his mother's voice—from the upstairs phone probably—and this voice said, "Cut it out now, Billy. You have talked long enough." Then Connie heard him say to his mother, "But Connie said I could call her up on the telephone and talk to her as long as I wanted, any time, morning, noon, and night, whenever I felt like it—even the middle of the night."

Connie could not hear what his mother said next because Billy had hung up without saying good-by or anything. What had happened? Connie went upstairs to bed. His mother should hug Billy, just plain hug him, not scold him ever. "Never mind, Billy," she thought. "Never, never mind." And she imagined rescuing him from a horse's hoofs or from drowning.

Billy was a brave boy—he wandered all over the city— and he was not afraid of the Gregory Avenue boys; still, there were things—not the telephone, of course—that he was scared of, too. He scared himself thinking that someone might be looking in the window at him. Even the moon looking in the window scared him. He told Connie scary things that happened to him in Oldenport, the music colony, where his family spent their summers. He had to be on the watch all the time there, he said. Connie wasn't certain whether the things Billy told her really happened or not, nor was she certain whether or not Billy himself really believed them. Sometimes, while swinging or playing with the Dinky Toys, Billy told Connie such scary things about Oldenport that he and she would get tears in their eyes.

Billy was awfully afraid of burglars. He thought just any man walking up the street might be a burglar. This man might stop, sit on someone's stoop, and change his socks, probably plotting where he was going to burgle. "I saw a guy do this once, Connie. I really did. He came along, sat down across the street, and changed his socks." Another man might be muttering to himself. Mutterers were the worst sort, Billy said. "All burglars," he said, and his hair, which he always wore rather long, almost stood on end.

Now, Saturdays and Sundays were wonderful days for Connie, with Billy Maloon coming over and spending practically the whole day. He gave Connie a whole batch of old comics, ancient and crumbling at the edges—they had belonged to his sister first. Mama sighed—not when Billy could hear her, of course. Mama didn't throw them away, but she did say, "They are an awful waste of time!" "I love them," said Connie. They were her very first comics, and all about Mickey Mouse and Donald Duck. By coincidence, an old lady in California named Rosie Newell sent a subscription of Donald Duck comics to Connie for Christmas that year, so now Connie had some of her own and could trade. Mama sighed again. But, anyway, they were not horror comics. "At least, they're not that," said Mama. "Or . . . out they'd go!"

Sometimes on Saturday, Billy would be at the swimming pool when Mama took Connie there. The Alley children were allowed to swim in the college swimming pool on Saturday mornings. Once, after Mama had finally finished helping Connie dry her hair and they were ready to leave, Connie said, "Let's wait for Billy; he'll be ready soon. Are you almost ready, Billy?" she asked. Billy was out of sight in one of the little dressing booths. There was no sound coming from there. After some silence, Billy said, "Yeah."

"We'll wait for you then," Connie said.

After another silence, "Yeah," came Billy's slow, drawling voice again.

Connie and Mama waited. You would think he would have been dried and dressed a long time ago, not having long, long hair to dry as Connie did. Finally Mama stooped down to see, at least, what Billy's feet were doing. They were just standing there—with shoes on them. They gave the impression that that was all that Billy was doing—absolutely nothing—just standing there inside his dark little booth.

Mama made Connie look at the stand-still feet; her raised eyebrows asked the question, "What do you think he is doing in there?"

Connie frowned at Mama. "Say nothing, do nothing, just wait," the frown meant. So they just waited. Everyone else had left the dressing room by now, the Fabadessas, the Arps, everybody. Connie got tired of waiting then. She and Mama and Billy might get locked up here in the dressing room and never get out. So she asked again, "Are you nearly ready, Billy?"

"Almost," said Billy. His towel came hurtling over the door, and after some more waiting, Billy Maloon himself emerged, fully dressed.

"Where's your bathing suit?" Mama asked.

"I have it," answered Billy.

"But where?" asked Mama, bewildered. Billy didn't have it in his hands. He picked up his towel, which was not wet at all, and that was all he had.

"I have it on," said Billy.

"Under your clothes?" Mama asked.

"Yes," said Billy.

"Why, you'll catch cold," said Mama. "You better go in there, take off your clothes and your bathing suit, rub yourself down good, and dress again. We'll wait for you."

"No," said Billy. "It's all right. I won't catch cold. I always do this. It's easier to carry my suit this way."

Connie was afraid Mama would argue—make him; but she didn't. "All right, Billy," she said. "But you must run like sixty not to catch cold. It's below freezing out."

"I will," he said. And they all went out. But Billy Maloon, being the unhurrying type, unlike Hugsy, who always ran, did not run like sixty. He walked.

You never could count on what Billy would do—he was unexpected. One day Connie was outside with all the children. At first Billy was not there. But after a while, he came out of his house and solemnly climbed over his fence.

44

His mother always kept their gate to the Alley padlocked; and Billy always had to climb over his outside heavy, jagged wire fence—cut himself or not—to get out. On this day, although it was a really hot one in early May, hot as certain springtime days can be when you can't bear to go to school any longer—summer was practically here; why did school have to go on and on?—what was Billy wearing? A snowsuit! Imagine the sensation, with everyone else sweltering, and their faces streaked! Katy Starr exclaimed, "Billy! Whatever's the matter with you? What have you got that on for?"

"Because," he said, and you could see he had not put his snowsuit on, on this hot day, as a joke. "Because," he said triumphantly, in the voice of one who knows something, has an inside track that no one else has, "because I heard on the radio that a cold wave is on the way, that there's going to be a sudden, a great drop in the temperature. The cold wave is coming from Minnesota, and—yeah, smarty—they're having snow out there already. May, the month of May, and they're having snow! Snow may fall! That's why I have my snowsuit on. Any objections?"

Everybody jeered. Here it was—one of the hottest days ever—and now this! Then they said, "Phew!" mopped their brows, pretended to faint from the extra heat Billy generated with his snowsuit on, and Katy, the lawmaker, dissolved the game they were playing, a form of tag. "Everyone come into my cellar and sit out the coming storm!"

"Very funny," said Billy. And he and Connie went into her house to play and add to the village on the Chinese rug.

Though sweat was on his brow, Billy played in his snowsuit the entire morning. One thing about Billy was, he never wanted to take off his coat or his sweater, if he had one on, even if it were warm. And he did not like to put something more on than he already had on, if it were cold; he liked to stay the way he was.

Suddenly Katy Starr came into Connie's house. She swung up the stairs—she had not rung the bell—and she said, "Billy, you must not stay cooped up in Connie's house. Your mother wants you to come outside and play with the kids."

Billy Maloon did not answer Katy, and he did not go out.

"I bet she didn't," he said, after about an hour, meaning his mother, "say that at all."

Well, that's the way Katy was. She wanted everyone to be out with her. She made the rules, and she made the laws. All the laws of the Alley were made up by Katy Starr. "Katy's laws," they were called. "Most of Katy's laws are good ones," Connie told Mama. "Very good laws." Everyone thought so, Billy Maloon, as well as Connie, and they abided by them. If only outside-the-Alley people would abide by outside-the-Alley laws as well, the world outside might have been as good as the world inside.

4

⇟ ⇟ ⇟

KATY'S LAWS

"Where would the Alley be without Katy's laws?" That's
what Connie wondered all along. Now, while she and Billy
were swinging, they heard Katy's voice, "Everybody come
up to the Circle! Meece! We're going to play Meece." She
was cruising up and down the Alley saying, "Come
on . . . Meece!" in her clipped, shrill voice. At Connie's
gate she said, "Come on, Billy. We're about to begin."

Billy did not say anything.

"Come on, Connie," said Katy. "Come on," she said.
"Join in." She did not wait for an answer. She expected
everyone to come. And she had gone swinging up the Alley
toward Hugsy's house to get him. You could hear her now
from way down the other end of the Alley, near the gate,
probably searching for Arnold, too.

Before Katy moved to the Alley, it did not have any laws.
Everybody in the Alley did what he or she wanted to do
and did not think was he or wasn't he breaking one of

47

Katy's laws. Now they had Katy's laws in the Alley, knew what side to ride their bikes on—what to do and not do.

The Alley was paved with cement; the center part had small squares etched in it—that was where one of the laws said that the little ones must walk when the big ones were riding their bikes. It was called "the middle walk" and was also where the big ones must park their bikes. Another law said that people must ride their bikes on the right-hand side of the Alley and use the middle walk only for passing. This was so none of the little ones, to whom the middle walk ordinarily belonged, would get bumped into.

Katy invented "Free Day" and "Semi-Free Day." On "Free Day" you could ride your bikes anywhere, the middle walk included, and little ones just had to stay out of the way—in their own yards or else walk on the narrow curbing, known as "emergency walk," and cling to the wire fencing. On "Free Day" you could crash into people, have collisions. "Semi-Free Day" meant that you had to obey all laws but that there was no policeman to say "stop" or "go," so you could ride continuously. On days that were just ordinary days, not free or semi-free, there always had to be a policeman directing traffic. This policeman stood in the safety inner zone and said, "Green light," or "Red light." Usually he stood outside the Arps' yard, the one next to Connie's. Being the policeman was a boring job. To make it interesting, the policeman said, "Green light, Red light," very often, especially Ray Arp, when he had the job. "Red light," Ray would say right after he had said, "Green light," and the person would be caught in the middle and get a ticket. Then there would be an argument and possibly a fight, because someone might complain to Ray about having to stop every minute.

"All right," Ray would say in disgust. "You be the cop then, and let me ride your bike." Sometimes Ray would snatch the bike and make the person give him a turn being a rider instead of a cop. People really preferred "Semi-Free Day" to regular bike day, because no one liked the job of being cop for more than two minutes. This job fell to Ray more often than to anyone else, to him or to his sister June, because they did not own bikes. Although they did not have bikes, in their yard they had the best climbing tree in the Alley, known as "Ray's" tree. Ray made everybody ask for permission to climb his tree, the way Connie did to swing in her swing and all the kids did to ride their bikes. "That was fair," thought Connie. Katy said it was fair, too.

When it came to popularity, there was no one, big or little, boy or girl, who could compare with Katy. She would come to a back door and say, "It is I—Katy Starr—the most popular girl in the Alley." But she was nice about it—cute, gay, and bright. She would stick out her chest and beat it to show the comment was meant as a joke. But it was not a joke—it was true. Just look at "the laws" alone! All good, the laws were. Think of "Free Day," "Red light, Green light," the traffic laws. Think of Katy picking up the little ones if they were hurt, comforting them, wiping their noses, drying their tears, getting a Band-Aid or else the mother, taking out splinters, and telling them to be good; think of her telling Anthony Bigelow to get out of the way, not to hurt the tiny ones, not to kick Susie Goode, especially not to kick her on her sore leg, not to kick at all or to throw things. Katy also tried to cure Anthony of bad language. Over and over she told him not to crash into people, making them fall off their bicycles, unless it was "Free Day." Every day was "Free Day" to Anthony Bigelow, and he was the only child in the Alley who did not obey Katy's laws. Sometimes a trial was held in the Circle if a person broke a rule. The jail was in the hidy-hole of Hugsy's back yard. Anthony was banished there often. But he wouldn't even obey that law, and out he'd crawl. Off he'd go bawling to his mother, using bad language, not caring about little Janey, or Notesy, Nicky, or anybody hearing him, not even his little sister, Jilly.

Now children were gathering in the Circle. Some came running, some sauntering, some came in special ways, walking backward, eyes shut, to the Circle.

"I guess everybody'll play," said Billy.

"Yes," Connie said. But she and he went on swinging.

They *might* play. Connie watched Katy sorting people out up there, telling each one what part he'd play. "What a girl!"

Connie began to think about the day Katy Starr had moved into the Alley—two and a half years ago. Ten minutes after Katy had moved in, she was right at home. Compare that with Connie's first day here! Connie had spent her first day rocking on Red Horsie—they did not have the jungle gym yet—and Horsie gave Connie courage. But Katy! By the end of her first day, she had learned the names of everyone, had raced up and down the Alley dozens of times, knocked at people's doors, introduced herself, already had become important. The sight of such self-possession awed Connie, and she had gone into her house and, from her dining-room window, watched the new girl—where she went, how she spoke. Connie felt shy. You would have thought Connie was the new girl and Katy the old one.

Then, having caught a glimpse of Connie at her dining-room window, Katy came to Connie's back door, and she said, "I see you have different dining-room windows than we have." That showed how very observing Katy was, for Connie's windows were different. The Ives were among the few families in the Alley who still had the original little panes of stained-glass, turquoise and gold, in the top half of the dining-room windows. Papa washed them himself, not to let the huge window washer press too hard and break them.

Then Katy had gone on to someone else's back door, the Carrolls' perhaps. At home everywhere, everywhere. In one day! Why, it had taken Connie weeks—months—to get used to being here. But—"That was Katy," she thought. Look at her—in no time, roaming up and down the Alley, giving an order here where needed, thinking up laws already. There was never a minute any more when everybody did not have something to do. Before Katy there had been no real life. After Katy, then there was life. Before Katy, Connie had not known that one had to be doing something every minute with somebody, let alone with everybody. But, thank goodness, by the time Katy had moved in, Connie had her jungle gym with its swings; and swinging was doing something, alone or not.

Sometimes Connie thought that she had been happier before Katy Starr had moved into the Alley. But she grew used to her. "She is a great girl," thought Connie. "She is really a very great girl. And her laws are good."

There was Katy now, down in the Circle, having rounded up everybody for the game of Meece. Billy and Connie decided to join in, and they went down to the Circle, too.

"The game will begin," said Katy in her positive voice, "when Hugsy Goode comes. He's eating something." Everybody roared. Hugsy was a great eater; he wasn't the least bit fat though, just hungry—always. Now, here he was, and the game could begin.

Although the game of Meece was invented mainly by Katy Starr, it was Hugsy Goode who was responsible for the idea. One day the tree trimmer was working on Billy Maloon's enormous oak—it was old and getting dry and brittle. Hugsy picked up two huge leafy branches, held them—one on each side of his head—and charged up and down the Alley, saying, "I am a moose." He was a comical spectacle, and after the screams of laughter had subsided, Katy said, "I know what. We'll all be mooses—that's not right—meece—we'll all be meece. Everybody down to the Circle for the game, the brand-new game of Meece."

In this game, there was only one man—MAN, the hunter. All others in the game were meece, and they stood in a group at the edge of the Circle. Between them and MAN was the meece guard, who was supposed to warn the meece if MAN seemed to be about to hunt and prowl. One by one MAN would catch all the little meece, and they then must stand, frozen like statues, in the Circle. The last meece tagged by MAN would be the new hunter in the new game. Hugsy, the original wearer of moose antlers, was a fine meece, and he made a fine and sad death; he had beautiful, large round brown eyes, and they haunted you when he was a dead meece. In the game of Meece, it was no longer necessary to wear the antlers. They were to be imagined instead.

Today Billy and Connie were among the meece. They had a wonderful time, and they were glad they had joined in. Then, with everyone tired and hot from the game, the children began to go their ways. A number, Billy and Connie among them, sat down on the curbing and talked. Katy said something behind her hand in June Arp's ear.

"I wish they would not do that," said Billy as he and Connie settled themselves back in the swings, "talk in each other's ears."

"Well," said Connie. "They have a club, you know. And

if you have a club, you have to whisper in ears. It's a rule. Not to let the others know what is in the club. It's a girl's club," she added, in case Billy wished that he were in it.

"Hugsy is in it. Is he a girl?" asked Billy Maloon sarcastically.

"No, that's true," agreed Connie. "But a club," she said, "has to have at least one boy in it to be a good club. And, anyway, they hold the meetings in Hugsy's hidy-hole, so he has to be in it. Greggie Goode isn't in it, just Hugsy."

All the houses that faced on Larrabee Street had little hidy-holes under the dining-room windows to let light into the cellars. The hidy-holes were quite deep—it was a wonder no little one had fallen in and hurt himself. Hugsy's hidy-hole was the favorite one because squash vines grew over it, and no one would know you were in there. When more than two were down there, it was quite crowded. The club consisted of four, but they managed all right and could play "sardines."

Hugsy Goode (his real name was Hugo Goode) was one of Connie's favorite people in the Alley. She liked him next best to Billy Maloon. But Hugsy was terribly afraid of Nanny. He didn't like to have to get past her when she was in the kitchen—where she usually was—cutting up kidneys for the cats or cooking some good soup. But this he must do if he wanted to get into the living room where Connie was. Hugsy couldn't sit in a chair, any sort of chair, without a great deal of squirming around, tilting it, and winding his legs around the rungs. He couldn't help it—he often broke a chair. Practically all the chairs in his own house were broken one way or another; even his bed had to be balanced on bricks. This sort of sitting in chairs turned Nanny against Hugo. She knew that someday he would break the George Washington chair, which had come down through the ages in Nanny's family. She just knew it.

Billy Maloon was just as afraid of Nanny as Hugsy was. When he came in, he looked directly ahead. If there was mud on his shoes, he hoped Nanny would not comment on his feet. He wiped them carefully a long time, whether there was mud or not, to make a favorable impression; and he stalked straight past her, saying in a low voice, scarcely audible, "H'lo." Sometimes Nanny answered, sometimes not. How Billy brightened when he made it to Connie's room, where he and she could play! However, now and then Nanny surprised Billy and Hugsy by speaking to them in her gracious, Southern-lady manner—usually after she had had many letters from Chester. But how could Hugsy or Billy know the reason?

"You see," Connie said to Billy, although he had never complained. "You see, Nanny just does not like boys. She doesn't really like girls either, except for Clarissa in Washington, and little girls, like Linda May, who are related to her. Of course, she must have liked Papa," said Connie, "in spite of his being a boy. Still, she tells him not to eat that much raw food. 'That much salad,' she says, 'is not good for anybody.' You should see the amount of celery Papa eats at one time! Nanny tells him not to, and Papa does not like to be told. She says she does not like to hear the crunching sound, and he says, 'How can anyone eat celery without a crunching sound?' I've tried it, Billy, and it is true. To eat celery, one must crunch, but, of course, with mouth closed. Nanny says, 'Well, crunch somewhere else, not here in the kitchen where I am fixing the dinner. How can I think what I am doing?' Papa does not go, though. He just continues to crunch celery and lick salt and prowl around the kitchen. He loves to lick salt. It all sounds good to me. And it looks good. But Nanny pounds pot covers on the pots and bangs the stirring spoons on them, too, to show she's outraged."

Billy was silent for a while. Then he said, "Connie, that was quite a long story."

"Thank you," said Connie.

Connie wanted to excuse Nanny, to have Billy like her in spite of the way she treated him and all boys—even some girls. Oh, how she wished that Nanny would be nicer to Billy Maloon and Hugsy Goode, for otherwise, she was the greatest grandmother in the world. Sometimes, before she could think, Nanny would snap at the tiny ones. "Don't pick that flower!" she would say.

"They are not from South Carolina," Connie informed Billy. "That is the main thing wrong with the children here."

"You mean if I were from South Carolina, she'd like me?" asked Billy incredulously.

"And if you were a girl," Connie added.

"Zooks!" said Billy.

Nanny came out just then to air a mop—no one, none of the cleaning girls, did this properly. Connie and Billy gazed straight ahead—not seeing her. Nanny didn't care whether she was or wasn't seen by them—and went back in.

Then Hugsy came along by himself. Evidently the club

had not lasted long. "The name of their club is the G.G. C.," said Connie. "I don't know what it means."

"I'd say it means 'Girls' Goofy Club,'" said Billy. "Except that Hugsy is in it."

Hugsy had overheard this comment. "Nope," he said. "That's not what it is."

"What is it then?" Billy demanded.

"I forget what it is," said Hugsy.

"In a club and forgets the name of it! That's brilliant, really brilliant, I must say," said Billy.

Hugsy looked dejected.

Connie did not like arguments. She said, "Want to swing, Hugsy?"

"Well . . ." said Hugsy hesitantly. "I would like to come in."

"You can come in," said Connie.

Hugsy had something on his mind. At last it came out, and it had nothing to do with the G.G.C. "I didn't go to the club. I had to go to Myrtle Avenue. And I was robbed! My mother gave me a five dollar bill—in a little leather purse—and three kids came along, and they took it. I was robbed!"

"Hugsy!" exclaimed Connie.

And Billy said, "Describe them!"

Hugsy couldn't. He was still very shaken. "It happened on Story Street. I was almost to Myrtle Avenue. Suddenly I was surrounded."

"So you surrendered," said Billy. "I'd do the same thing. Better be a live chicken than a dead duck."

Hugsy smiled gratefully. Then Katy came along, and she

had to hear the story. This was the first modern burglary any of them had had—the other Alley burglaries being the old-time, ancient ones of the Bernadettes and the Langs.

Soon, Hugsy and Billy had to go home to lunch, and this left Connie and Katy. Katy sat in a swing, not swinging, though, and not saying anything—not even saying "boring" once. "Perhaps," thought Connie, "Katy is going to be a friend now and say, 'Want to join the G.G.C.?' Perhaps this great lawmaker girl, Katy, and I will become real friends." The idea had never occurred to Connie before.

Katy jumped down. She swung out the gate and she left it open, and she still had not said anything, not said, "Be friends," or, "Not be friends," and no mention of the club. Connie thought of impressing Katy with something, capturing a burglar, perhaps, bopping one over the head with the Tiffany vase that stood in the hall. Or maybe she should do something grand, be a prodigy of the piano; and she, too, went in to tell Mama about Hugsy's five-dollar-bill burglary and to have her lunch.

5

✝✝✝

CALM DAYS BEFORE THE BURGLARS

If only outside-the-Alley people abided by outside-the-Alley laws as well as inside-the-Alley people did by inside-the-Alley Katy laws, then there would not have been a burglary like Hugsy's five-dollar-bill one, or like the one about to happen in Connie's house.

The Ives's burglary happened suddenly and unexpectedly. In the morning, the Ives had not had burglars; yet by noon, burglars had come and gone. Looking back, Connie—all the Ives—could see that the burglary really had not been so sudden and unexpected after all. Looking back to the burglary, they could see that it was bound to happen. But going toward the burglary—*before* it had happened—one would not suspect that such a thing was going to occur in the Ives's family. These were the steps that led to the noontime burglary of Connie Ives's house in the Alley.

One day Connie and Mama were walking Wags up by the athletic field. Mittens and Punk were following along after them in the way that cats do—first running ahead a little, galloping, and then, lurking behind, furtively ducking under cars, making sure the path was clear, no enemies about. They'd crouch under the cars, their ears turned back, because they knew, and humans didn't, that trouble was always afoot. Then suddenly they'd gallop ahead, and just as suddenly they'd stop in their tracks, nervously clean a paw or their stomach for a second, and then go crouching on. They might be thinking that their enemy cat, the lizard cat, from blocks away, might be watching them—pounce out at them.

On this particular day—it was a sunny one in early May; Connie and her mother couldn't remember exactly which—there occurred a series of unusual incidents.

Connie and Mama were standing near the fence around the athletic field. They were laughing at Wagsie, who kept running up and down the fence trying to get into the field, a useless idea because, unless it was being used, it was always kept locked. But Wagsie remembered a certain time when she had seen a quail in the field—where it had come from no one could guess—and Wagsie hadn't been able to get into the field to chase it that day either; but she had never forgotten that quail and looked for it every time she was taken for a walk. Connie and Mama were also laughing at the two cats, who listened to Wagsie's anguished whining with disapproval and contempt, their ears flattened down. They did not like her noisy, emotional outbursts.

Suddenly up the Mall toward the athletic field strode Mr. de Gaulle, one of the campus guards whom the Alley people were supposed to call in case of burglary, fire, or any trouble. Mr. de Gaulle was not the real name of this man. The Alley children had nicknamed him de Gaulle, because in his gray-blue uniform, tall and handsome, he looked, stood, and talked like General de Gaulle. However, not really being de Gaulle, this guard spoke always in English, never in French. Paying no attention to Connie or Mama or the interesting animals, Mr. de Gaulle marched across the Mall, unlocked the gate to the athletic field, pushed it wide open, stepped inside, and said, "Get out! Get out!"

There was no one in the field at all, not even the long-ago lost quail. Mr. de Gaulle stood sternly within the gate, a few paces from Connie and Mama, who had gotten Wagsie back on his leash, just in the nick, and he repeated to the vacant field, "Get out! Get out!"

Connie and Mama were spellbound; they stood respectfully still. They need not have bothered. Mr. de Gaulle did not notice them at all. All he did was to address the empty field with his "Get outs!" Then he turned abruptly, put the key in the lock, banged the gate to, and strode away again—finishing his rounds.

"Just practicing," Connie said to Mama. "Imagine putting imaginary people, children probably, out of the athletic field!" she said. "Probably pretending the field is full of the Gregory Avenue kids—they do sometimes climb over the fence, bobb wire and all."

"I know," said Mama.

Connie and Mama slowly sauntered on their way when along came a lady, a poor old lady. Her stockings were black cotton and twisted in loose folds around her thin old legs. The skin of her face fell in loose folds, too, and was rather dirty. "Don't blame her, though," Connie admonished herself. "You know Brooklyn—all dirt and soot!"

Unlike de Gaulle, this lady had her eyes on Connie and Mama, and she came right up to them. She asked where Mark Street was. Mark Street used to be one block below Connie's street—Story Street—but since the Mall had been

laid out, there weren't any streets inside the campus gates any more, just walks, and except for those on the Alley, there were no houses on the campus either. So Mama said, "What part of Mark Street are you looking for? What number are you looking for? A house outside the campus on Larrabee or a house on General Street?"

The lady said, "I ask a simple question, and I expect a simple answer."

Taken aback, Mama explained that there were four gates onto or out of the campus, that Mark Street on the campus used to be a block below where they were standing now—she pointed down the Mall—but that now it was nothing but a little walk, and that she had asked the lady the number in order not to send her over in the Myrtle Avenue direction if where she really wanted to go might be toward General Street—in the opposite direction on the other side of the campus.

"I don't understand you at all," said the lady. "What you are saying makes no sense at all. I don't want people asking me numbers."

"Well," said Mama gently, "well, you know you can go out either of those two gates, the one on Larrabee or the other on General, and proceed to your destination on Mark Street—wherever it is. I thought I might save you some long blocks."

"You don't save blocks!" said the lady in disgust. "I ask a simple question—where Mark Street is—and you tell me to save blocks."

Since the lady still stood there trying to get her bearings and was now looking across the field, Mama gently pointed out that that street up there, on the other side of the athletic field, was Gregory Street."

"Who said anything about Gregory Street?" said the lady. "Mark Street was the name, Madam, M A R K Street."

Mama said, "Well, would you like to have me start you on your way?"

"When I need your help, I'll ask for it," said the lady

tartly; and she turned back in the direction from which she had come, where Mark Street used to be. But she continued on beyond it, crossed Library Park, slowly passed the cannon there, and vanished from sight.

"Maybe she used to live in one of the houses that used to be on Mark Street, before they tore them down to make the Mall," said Connie. "Maybe she is all mixed up, wandering around and wondering where her house has gone. Maybe she just wanted to sit on the step a minute and pull up her stockings—look for her old lost cat, maybe."

"Maybe she did," said Mama. Mama wondered if she should run after the old lady and somehow try again to set her straight. But the old lady would not like that—being run after—so she didn't.

"Well, quite a day for encounters," Connie said to Mama happily. And then there came still another one, a third one. This was a day when people felt they must talk to Mama and Connie, except for de Gaulle, who spoke only to people who were not there. The third person was a man, sauntering along, pleasant-looking, hands in his pockets, and he stopped and looked at the athletic field. Then he shouted in sudden passion, waving his hands excitedly, "Used to be mansions, beautiful mansions! Tore them all down! Down they tore them and planted bare grass! Bare grass where beautiful mansions used to be!" (There used to be more rows of houses like the little Alley houses where the athletic field was now, and the man was referring to the snug little gone-away houses. He looked hopelessly at where they had been.) "Bare grass, where the kids can't play. Worse—a fence around the bare grass," he went on, "so the kids can't get in! All this space and the kids can't play! Where can they play, lady?" he said angrily to Mama. "You know what will happen next? They will put a fence around the moon, that's what they will do next. You don't believe that, do you? Well, it's so—it's coming. Oh, the mansions that were here! Perfectly good houses. Tear them down, put up a fence, plant grass, and call it 'private'!"

Off he went, spitting in despair.

De Gaulle, old lady lost, beautiful-mansions man! You would think these were people enough to meet during just one walk with Wags and the cats. But along came another stranger, another talkative stranger.

Mama and Connie had not even seen this man coming. They were laughing and talking about the other three strangers and saying, "What a day this is—everybody stopping to talk—" when suddenly a man—he had a bullet-shaped head, was rather short and quite well-dressed—walked swiftly past Connie and Mama. Connie and Mama were really startled. They had not heard him coming and had seen no one until he passed by. Where had he come from? A few paces on, he stopped abruptly as if he'd had an afterthought. He turned back and very politely, in a well-educated voice, said, "Excuse me, ma'am. What a beautiful dog that is!"

Since the stranger had said something friendly about Wags and since every one of the Ives, Nanny, too, liked praise about Wags or the cats, Mama replied. "Yes," she said. "She is very beautiful."

"What kind of dog is she?" asked the man briskly. "Some sort of spaniel, is she?"

"Yes," said Mama. "A springer."

"Ah, indeed," said the bullet-headed man. "We had a spaniel—not a springer, just a little cocker. We had to get rid of her, though. She bit our little girl. On the hand, yes, she bit our little girl. In her high chair she was, just reaching down, and Goldy—that was her name—bit her."

"Oh," said Mama. "Too bad. But you were wise to give her away."

All this while the man was stretching out his arm and reaching toward Wagsie and saying, "Tluck, tluck." Wags cowered behind Mama—she did not like men, except for Papa. But the man kept right on reaching his hand toward Wagsie, as though he wanted Wags (Connie figured this out later) to smell his hand, to get used to his smell, also no doubt to see if Wags would snap or not.

"Now this dog, ma'am," said the man—Connie could sense that Mama thought the conversation had gone on more than long enough, for she had stepped back a pace or two away from the man as though to hint she was in a hurry to be on her way—"does this dog bite?"

"Oh," said Mama quickly. "This dog! Ts! I'd never trust this dog not to bite. Just let any stranger, grown or child, come up to her! With a jaw that strong? One bite and she could snap off a whole hand!" Again Mama tried to end the conversation.

The man, sensing he had outstayed his welcome, turned away, but he said as though in parting, "Hm, that's surprising. She seems timid." For there was Wags, still hiding behind Mama's skirts.

"Timid dogs, when they are frightened, are often the most vicious of all dogs," said Mama.

"H-m-m," said the man thoughtfully. He was determined to give Wags a pat on the head, and finally he accomplished this and even gave her a small dog biscuit—a pink one, which Wags enjoyed but had to swallow practically whole because Mama pulled her away. Finally the man tipped his hat, said what a pleasure, and briskly walked down Story Street and out the gate at Larrabee. He was whistling jauntily. He happened to be whistling "On the Street Where You Live," a favorite song that spring.

"He was nice, wasn't he?" Connie said uncertainly as she and Mama watched the man disappear.

"Talked too much," Mama said.

Connie could see that Mama was puzzled. She kept looking after the man—where he had gone, what direction —and she had fallen into a thoughtful and silent mood. To recapture their wonderful "de Gaulle" mood, Connie said, "Wasn't that funny, though? De Gaulle saying, 'Get out! Get out!' stamping his foot, waving his arm?"

Mama laughed again, too. "Yes," she said. "But come on. We better go home and have lunch."

At the word "lunch," Wags, who had been quite dispirited during the talk with the bullet-headed man, revived; she pulled at the leash, and her tongue lolled out of her mouth. She looked waggish, and the name "Wags" suited her. When she was a little puppy, Papa had tried to rename Wags "Heath." He said Heath was a more suitable name for such a noble dog. But everyone soon went back to

"Wags." Well, "Here, Heathie. Here, Heathie," *is* hard to say. Even Papa found it hard.

When Connie and Mama got back to their own little house, Mittens and Punk were crouching, one on each side of the top stoop, waiting for them. The cats were in identical positions, even to the curves of their tails. Everyone went in, and Mama thoughtfully locked the outer green door as well as the inner one. Few people bothered to lock the outside green door—usually never when they were at home or simply out for a few minutes, walking the dog or visiting a neighbor. Now Mama said, "We must remember to keep this outside door locked. Papa is right—it is an invitation to burglars to leave it open," she said.

For some reason, the thought of the bullet-head man popped into Connie's head. She remembered the sound of his voice when he said, "Does this dog bite?" Connie had a flair for imitating people's voices, and she said now in a high-pitched voice, "Does this dog bite?"

Mama smiled. "You got that down to a T," she said, and she began to prepare the luncheon, with Wags, as usual, hugging the stove in case a crumb should fall.

After lunch Connie went outside to swing. Billy Maloon was in the Alley, and he came into Connie's yard, carefully closing the gate so Wagsie would not get out. When Billy got settled in his swing (Billy liked the one near the house, and Connie the one near the glider—but they switched around—that was fair!), Connie told him about de Gaulle, the lady with the loose stockings, the man who said, "beautiful mansions," and last of all the man interested in dogs who asked, "Does this dog bite?"

Billy avidly listened to all.

"Mama said he was like the ancient mariner and would not letteth us go," Connie explained. "Except he had no beard—but did he or did he not have a little mustache? I can't remember; you know, Billy, I just can't remember."

"I sometimes can't remember whether my own father has a little mustache or not," said Billy encouragingly. "Go on."

Billy was a wonderful listener. Connie went on.

"You see, Billy," said Connie. "This man—his head was shaped like a bullet—kept talking and talking to Wags and trying to pet her. He kept holding out his hand and saying, 'There, girlie—what's her name? Wags? Pretty name, pretty dog.' He knows how to flatter dogs. 'There, there, girlie,' he said. 'Such a pretty doggie! I'm sure you wouldn't bite, would you? They are saying mean things about you, aren't they?' Finally, Billy, Wagsie let him stroke her head. It was so funny, I mean it, Billy—Mama saying Wags would bite! Billy, imagine Wagsie biting anybody! You see," Connie explained to Billy, who was enthralled with the anecdote, "Wags is a coward. But since Mama and I were standing right there protecting her, she finally let this man stroke her head. This was very unusual for her; she really does not like strangers, especially men. The man, the *only* man, she likes is Papa. She hates boys, too, you know."

Billy said, "I think she likes me a little."

"Once you are in the house, she likes you all right. But if she is standing on the top step of the back stoop and you are trying to get in, you know very well, Billy, that she growls even at you and bares her teeth."

Billy nodded forlornly. It meant there were two to get

69

by, sometimes, in order to play with Connie—Nanny and Wags! "Wags really hates Ray," said Billy.

"Oh, I know it," said Connie. "And Ray is terrified of her. Serves him right. When Ray comes banging out of his kitchen door, Wags barks at him. Then Ray, thinking he is safe on his side of the fence, imitates Wags. 'Aowf! Aowf!' he says. This upsets Wags still more, and she tears up and down the fence, barking her head off. Well, even though she is on the other side of the fence, Ray looks out of the corner of his eyes at Wags to make sure that Wagsie's big mouth can't get him."

"Once he threw something at her," said Billy. "An old piece of brick I think it was."

"Ts! Cruel, cruel and stupid! Wags will never, never as long as she lives forgive or forget that. Well, at least the bullet-head man, even though he did talk too much—I could tell Mama didn't like it—had the right idea about how you get to be friends with a dog."

Billy Maloon listened thoughtfully to Connie's entire account of her expedition to the field with Mama and Wags. "Very interesting," he said, "very interesting." He nodded his head; his lips were pressed tightly together, as they always were when he was thinking. His eyes were bright. Connie could see he had been fascinated by the story—it was like one of his stories of Oldenport, except that his stories were scary. And what was scary about hers?

"When we got home," she said, "Mama locked the outside green door. We almost never do that. But you know what Mama said? She said, 'That outer door is an invitation to burglars. It must be kept locked!' So she locked it. Oh, we know that man was just a dog lover—not a burglar—and the old loose-stocking lady, the angry mansion-man, de Gaulle . . . none of them, burglars! Imagine de Gaulle being a burglar, Billy!"

Billy turned his head slowly toward Connie. His eyes were wide and thoughtful. Billy was a very brave boy; but thoughts of burglars did scare him. All he said, however, was "Yeh. Just incidents on a college campus, that's all."

6

‡ ‡ ‡

THE DAY OF THE BURGLARS

Time passed. The day of de Gaulle, the lost lady with the loose stockings, the beautiful-mansion man, and the dog-loving man with the bullet head seemed weeks ago now. Nanny had gone south for a little visit before the weather got too hot. She wasn't here to leave the green door open to make things easy for the mailman. Sometimes, Mama herself began to forget again to lock the outer green door. She began to forget about its being an invitation to burglars. Of course, she locked it if she were going to be away for some time, down at A. & S. shopping or in town having lunch with her friend and the owner of her picture gallery, Melinda McIntosh. But just to go to Myrtle Avenue, to the A. & P. or to the More Better Food Store? Well, she didn't bother.

It was around the middle of May, on a day called "Alumni Day." Thoughts of a burglary were not in the minds of anyone in the twenty-seven little houses. Their minds were on the festivities. People who had graduated from Grandby College a year or more ago had come back to meet old friends, hear speeches, and wander around the campus. The campus was very pretty; a huge green-and-white-striped tent had been set up on the lawn of the Li-bary Park, and at first Connie thought a circus had come to the campus. She couldn't believe her eyes, and she wondered where the elephant was. But Mama said, "No, it's not a circus. The alumni are going to have lunch, the professors, too, under that tent. They will all, including the president of the college, have lunch there, make speeches, say 'Hello' to the old alumni, and see how the recent ones, last year's, say, are getting along—what they are doing, where they're working, are they being a credit to the college, are they married."

"Oh," said Connie. "Is Papa there?"

"Yes," said Mama. "Papa is there. Most of the professors are there."

So—that meant that practically all the fathers of the Alley were under the tent eating lunch with the alumni. The only father home in any one of the twenty-seven little houses was Mr. Fabadessa, who thought two dollars and a half too much for lunch. A few mothers had gone, too, joining the fathers under the tent, so the Alley was very quiet. Mama did not go because she had too much to do, getting some pictures ready for an exhibition.

"First, we'll go to the A. & P.," Mama said to Connie. "And then I'll get to work." They got out their squeaking cart. "I must oil this," said Mama for the hundredth time. But she didn't oil it; and they remembered not to forget the list. They told Wagsie, "Backson." (They had gotten this word from *Winnie-the-Pooh*, and they always told Wagsie, "Backson," whenever they had to leave her to go to the store or anywhere.) When Wagsie heard that word, she looked totally forlorn. She sat sadly in her tight little corner between the piano and the clothes closet and hung her head. Connie and Mama tried not to think how unhappy Wagsie was, being left. They tried uselessly to cheer her up.

"Mittens is here," Connie said. "You're not all alone, Wagsie."

Mittens had gone upstairs, and daughter Punk, looking like a tiger, was sprawled outdoors under the rose bush, one of her favorite sleeping places in the garden.

"Mittens will keep Wagsie company," Connie told Mama, hoping to console Mama as well as herself. "Probably she'll wash Wagsie's face when we're gone."

So she and Mama set out. They locked the two back doors and the cellar door. Then they locked the inner green front door. But—they did not lock the outer green front door. In fact, they left it wide open as they usually did for short periods of time.

They left at twelve, and they were gone a little less than an hour. Mama, who had said that she did not have much to get—that was what she always said—in the end bought about a million things—pies and pickles and everything—so the shopping cart was heavy, and she and Connie pulled it together. They soon reached the corner of their street, Story Street, and turned around it from Myrtle Avenue where the shops were—only one block away from the little houses, not far at all. From this corner one could plainly see

the little houses. They stood out, inviting and enchanting, in the midst of all this torn-down area with its no-front houses like stage sets. As Connie and Mama turned into their street, they noticed several men, four at least, and possibly five, leaving the front stoop of one of the little houses. Mama and Connie could not tell exactly which house they were leaving; but afterwards, recalling the scene, Mama said she had thought that they looked as though they were leaving one of the houses farther up the street, possibly either the Stuarts' or the Fabadessas'. Mama thought nothing of this because of the kind of weekend it was—Alumni Weekend. There were many out-of-towners, guests, on the campus, and she thought the clothes—for even from that distance she saw that the men had clothes piled over their arms—she thought that the clothes were probably academic robes or else just plain extra clothes. The men were also carrying what seemed to be little valises, further evidence that they were visitors.

Connie and Mama took their time coming up Story Street from Myrtle Avenue. The cart was heavy, and a loaf of bread kept tumbling out—lucky it was wrapped and not a French loaf. Finally they reached their house, number 175. They left the cart on the sidewalk because it was too heavy to drag up the four steps, and they were going to first unlock the door and then carry the parcels in, one by one, not to break their backs.

The minute they got to the top of the stoop, Mama said, "Hm, that's funny. The green door is closed. I thought I left the outer green door open—I *know* I left it open." Cautiously, she opened the outer green door, and immediately she and Connie smelled a strong whiff of smoke, cigarette smoke. In fact, on the floor of the vestibule lay a cigarette still burning.

("A clue!" said Billy Maloon, hearing Connie tell the tale later. "They could trace the burglars by the cigarette." "Clue . . . ha!" Connie said to Billy. "There were many clues, but they kept none, the police kept none. They took no fingerprints, not even . . . well, wait. You'll see what the policemen did and did not do. . . .")

So, there the cigarette was, lying there, still smoking. Connie's mother stepped on it automatically. She always stepped on burning cigarettes, not to start forest fires. Connie did, too. And then Mama let out a startled gasp.

76

"Connie!" she said. "Look at the door! The lock has been jimmied! We have been robbed! Those men we saw—but still—perhaps those men were not the burglars. Perhaps the burglars are still inside!" she said.

Tears popped into Connie's eyes, the way they always did when she was scared, though they did not roll down her cheeks the way they did Katy Starr's when she heard a scary story. Hastily, Connie and Mama went back down the steps and stood uncertainly by their cart. It is a terrible shock to see your house broken into.

Connie and Mama had cast one brief glance inside. The first thing that Connie had seen—she would never forget the sight so long as she lived—was Mittens crouching at the top of the stairs looking down at them, her eyes round and big, inscrutable and silent, and filled with disdain. It was too bad that Mittens could not speak English; but the mere fact that she was crouching there at the top of the stairs, and not in hiding, should have told Connie and Mama that the burglars were not still inside. Later they figured it out that probably Mittens had hidden somewhere throughout the entire burglary—in the attic or under a bed, in some secret, good place. She had probably enjoyed the unusual occurrence, for cats do like something novel.

In this one sweeping glance, Connie and Mama also saw Mama's big black handbag turned upside down—all its contents spilling out of it—on the George Washington chair. There hadn't been any money in it, fortunately, because Mama had taken her billfold with her to the A. & P. But if you have ever seen your own pocketbook turned upside down on a chair, the George Washington chair, and all your things—your eyeglasses, your pens and pencils, your Charga-plates—spilled out, you will know what a shock just the sight of that was to Mama and Connie.

("It's a wonder they did not take the Charga-plate and charge a lot of things at A. & S.—fur coats, hi-fi's, anything —your mother would have had to pay the bill," Billy Maloon suggested morosely later.

"O-oh, I never thought of that," said Connie wonderingly. She saw the possibilities. "How awful! They wouldn't do that. They were bad burglars, but they weren't that bad!")

So, there they were—Connie and Mama, standing bewilderedly outside by their cart, wondering were the burglars inside still or not—and Mama said, "Connie, go and get Charlotte Stuart as fast as you can. I'll wait here and see if anybody comes out."

Well, Connie had never done anything this important in her life before. It was like having to get help if someone has fallen, or calling an ambulance or the fire department or the police! Connie was scared, but she was happy. A burglary does not happen often, never that she could remember. And here it had happened to *them*. Her knees wobbled, but she was glad, anyway, that it was *their* house that had been burglared, not one of the other Alley houses. She ran to Mrs. Stuart's house, two doors down the street, and rang the bell. Thank goodness, Mrs. Stuart was at home. Keeping as calm and collected as Billy Maloon would, Connie said, "We have had burglars. Mama wants to know if you can come over right away. The door is broken open. Mama says the burglars may still be in the house."

"Burglarized!" exclaimed Mrs. Stuart. Her voice was rewardingly shrill. Hastily drying her hands on her apron and swallowing some snack she had been eating, she came.

"Oh, Jane!" she said. (That was Mama's first name.)

"Look!" said Mama. That's all she said, and she showed Mrs. Stuart the jimmied-open inner door. Even the pretty white wooden framework of the door was splintered, chipped, and broken.

"O-oh!" gasped Charlotte Stuart. She was one of Mama's best friends in the Alley—the very sort of person you would run to first in case of fire, burglars, or accident. She was very brave. Mama said that some of the burglars might still be in the house, that her sudden return from the A. & P. might have caught them in the act, that they might be in closets somewhere. Yet Mrs. Stuart, not thinking of her own safety—Mama was thinking solely of Connie's—tore right into the house, and she telephoned the police. (The phone was in the living room on the bookcase, just five feet from the front door, so Connie and Mama could have rescued her if need be, if a burglar, trapped and violent, came skulking down the stairs. None did.) Mrs. Stuart then came back out, and rather breathless, she agreed with Connie's mother that now no one should go into the house at all until the police came and assured them that all the burglars were out. She was inclined to agree with Mama also that the men Mama had seen leaving one of the houses were probably the burglars. "But, who knows?" she said. "They *might* have been alumni. And the Fabadessas are having a lot of company today."

"How strange it is," thought Connie, "to stand outside

your own house, its two front doors wide open for all the world to look inside, and yet not be able to go in. How strange that people, not people of the family or friends or neighbors, have been *inside* your house, have broken into it!" It was strange and frightening, but rather pleasant. Connie was inclined to agree with the cats, liking something novel. Then terror clutched Connie's heart. Where was Wags? Mittens had slithered outdoors and was crouching beside the cart, sniffing the bags, seeing if there was fish, enjoying everything. But, where was Wags?

7

↓↓↓

ARRIVAL OF THE POLICE

"Wagsie!" Connie called gently. "Wagsie."

Ordinarily, when Mama and Connie came home from the store, Wags was waiting at the door, ready to give them a welcome, partly loving, partly reproachful. How could they leave her? Never do it again!

"Wagsie!" said Connie again.

At last they heard a slow shuffling sound from way inside the house, the kitchen, probably, and a clinking of Wagsie's chain collar and license tag. She came to them with hanging head and, trembling as though she had chills and fever, she came outdoors. Her great moplike ears drooped and practically touched the ground. Not only was Wags frightened, she was ashamed. She sat down close to Mama, leaning against her legs for comfort. Her trembling continued off and on, as she recalled the terrible ordeal, no doubt. Mama looked Wagsie over carefully. She did not seem to be hurt. "Just her feelings," said Connie confidently. With heavy eyes looking down to the ground, blinking, she was a sad

contrast to Mittens, whose upturned, piquant little face said, "This is great, isn't it? What now? What next?"

Next, of course, were the police, and Mittens dashed in terror under the forsythia.

The police car came tearing into Story Street with sirens screaming; it stopped with a screech in front of the Ives's house. Two policemen, one large, one medium-sized, got out of the car, drew their revolvers, and roughly demanded, "Where are the burglars?"

Mama said, "I don't know. I don't know whether they are still in the house or not. We just got back from the store, and this is what we found." The two policeman cautiously entered the house. One pointed his revolver up the stairs, the other into the living room. "Come out, wherever you are," they said gruffly. "We have you covered," they said. ("It's just like a moving picture," thought Connie. "But it's not. It's real, it's real!")

No one came out. The two policemen went upstairs immediately; proceeding cautiously, haltingly, and with pistols pointing upward, they disappeared from the view of those in front of the house. Now there was silence, complete silence, except for a gruff remark now and then—"Look under the bed, Pat. Make sure they're not under the bed." Or, "Ippy! Did you look in the closet, there?" Or, "Come out, you rat. You're covered." Between these remarks was the same total silence. It was as though they were absent-minded actors, needing a bit of prompting.

Connie's heart pounded. "Wait 'til I tell Billy about this," she thought. She and Mama and Mrs. Stuart—Wags beside Mama, still shivering—remained in front of the house, talking and waiting for the two policemen to come out and say it was all right for them to go in now. Soon other neighbors came along; they wanted to know what had happened. To each of them, since they did not arrive at the same time, Mama had to relate all over again how she and Connie had been coming home from the A. & P. and how they had seen these four, or three men, or perhaps five—she had not thought to count them up; there seemed to be a lot of them, anyway—the whole story, including the burning butt, still lying on the floor of the vestibule, not to be touched, she cautioned, for it might be an important clue.

Suddenly Mama broke off, turned to Charlotte Stuart, and

83

said, "Charlotte! Does it strike you that those two police-men have been upstairs in our house an awfully long time? I thought that all the police would do right now would be—go up through the house and then, when they saw no one was there, tell me, and I would go and see what, if anything, was taken. After all, the burglars may have been those men Connie and I saw, and for all I know, they may not have had time to take one thing, seeing Connie and me coming back from the A. & P. They might not even have gotten upstairs at all. I was just scared to go in until the police checked to make sure it was safe. How do I know whether or not those men were burglars or alumni?"

"You're right," said Mrs. Stuart, who was very crisp and decided. "They've been up there for ages—now that you speak of it."

"Let's go in," said Mama. "Connie, you wait out here with Wagsie."

But at this moment, another police car came screaming into the street, stopped with a screech, and two more policemen arrived. They, too, wanted to know what the trouble was. Mama said that her house had been burglarized, that there were already two policemen inside looking for possible left-in burglars, that they had been in there for a long time, and that she didn't understand why they had not come out yet. Would the two new policemen go down into the cellar and see if there were any burglars hiding down there; because the two first policemen had certainly never gone down there—they had not even finished casing the upstairs. Was that such a lengthy thing to do, she asked?

The two new policemen did not say a word. Looking melancholy, they went into the house and back to the kitchen, and could be heard, soon, clumping down the cellar steps. They didn't wave their pistols around and say, "We've got you covered, rat."

"They are probably disappointed they were not the first policemen here," thought Connie.

"Well, we might as well go in, too," said Mama. "Quite a party there now," she said. So she and Mrs. Stuart went into the burglarized house, being by this time completely nonplused about the two quiet first policemen. The whole house was quiet.

"Can you imagine"—Connie rehearsed what she would say to Billy—"going into your own house—it burglarized, and with two policemen in it, you know not where? And with two other policemen down in the cellar?"

However, the minute Mama and Mrs. Stuart stepped inside and started up the stairs, the two policemen, the *first* two, hearing them coming, started down the stairs. They were muttering to each other saying, "Ts, ts, it's terrible." And halfway down the stairs, they and Mama met. One policeman said, "Ah, lady. They sure ransacked your house." "Ransacked it," echoed the other. "They sure gave your house the works from top to bottom," one said. "Yes —everything is a mess—" said the other. "Bureau drawers— ts. They left no stone unturned."

Mama was surprised. She couldn't believe it. She really thought that the burglars, seeing her and Connie coming home, had been interrupted at the very beginning of their work. But, being so scared of burglars—as who isn't? It's not cowardly to be scared of burglars; it's common sense!—she had not wanted to go inside the house until she was absolutely certain they had left. For a moment, she stared unbelievingly at the two policemen. Then she gasped, "Oh! My ring! My diamond ring!"

Usually Mama wore her diamond ring. But she had been planning to have it made a little larger. It was getting tight for her finger—or rather, her finger was getting a little too large for her ring. She had asked Papa to put the ring in a safe place—'til she could get to town—and he had. At least, he *thought* he had put it in a safe place. He had put it on the clip of a pencil, in its brand-new little pencil case, that some of his staff had given him for Christmas. And this—the pencil with the ring on its clip and in its case—he had put in one of the little drawers of his wardrobe, the drawer he kept his socks in, and also some ancestral jewelry.

Imagine! Only last night, Mama had said to Papa, "Where have you put my diamond ring, John? I feel funny without it on and not even knowing where it is. I have lost two pounds, and maybe it will fit my finger again now, and I won't have to have it enlarged." Papa showed her the ring. He showed her her diamond ring where it was on the little pencil in his wardrobe in his dressing room. And she had said, "Pshaw! It doesn't fit yet. Two pounds is not enough . . ." and off they had gone, just last night, to the alumni ball—she without her ring on. But, anyway, at least she knew then where her diamond ring was supposed to be.

So now, rushing past the two policemen, saying, "Oh, my ring, my diamond ring!" she tore into Papa's dressing room.

"Diamond ring? Diamond ring? Where, where?" the two policemen said.

Afterwards, Mama said she could feel their hot breath on the back of her neck as they raced after her to Papa's dressing room. They were almost shoving into her as she pulled open the drawer, the small one on the upper right, and of course—it had been rifled! Pencil case, pencil, diamond ring, gone! There were other things gone, too, but of these Mama knew nothing at the time. She knew only that her diamond engagement ring that had come down through the ages, from generation to generation, was most certainly gone.

Mama turned and looked at the policemen. They looked at her. The silence was heavy and deep. "Well, lady," said one of the policemen finally (his name was Sergeant Rattray—they found out later), "We can't spend any more time here. ("As though I had been keeping him!" said Mama to Papa afterwards, in disgust.) We'll list what's missing and then be off. What exactly is missing, Missus?"

Mama said she didn't know yet. She went into her room, and she saw that her bureau drawers had indeed been rifled, but in a neat and orderly way, not at all in the swift, reckless way that burglars usually turn things topsy-turvy. On the bed was a little package that she had wrapped in blue tissue paper, a present for somebody, and it had been unwrapped and was still on the bed in its loosened wrapping. Either the burglar did not want what it was—lavender soap—or had been interrupted or had no room in his pocket. Ah, but in Connie's room, her pretty little pink jewelry box had been roughly broken open, and although most of her little bracelets and pins were strewn all over the floor in true burglar fashion, her seven silver dollars that Aunt Lovey sent her—one practically every Christmas—were gone!

Then everyone went downstairs, where Mama listed things as best she could. The tall policeman—Sergeant Rattray—put in a phone call for the detective; and then he said he thought they'd go. At this moment, up from the cellar came the two second policemen. The first two policemen were rather surprised to see the second two— they had not known they were there nor how long they had been there. Now, could the first two look the second two in the eye when Mama explained to them that her diamond ring was gone? And that she didn't see how that was possible? Mama didn't say it, but she gave the impression that she thought maybe the two first policemen might have her ring! Connie was ashamed of her mother—and hoped the policemen would not arrest Mama for thinking such a thing.

The second two policemen looked at the floor. The two sets of policemen did not look each other in the eye. At this moment, Papa, summoned from the luncheon under the big green-and-white-striped tent, came in the front door; so the two fidgety first policemen had to wait until they had spoken to Papa, though they did say again briskly and with a hike to their shoulders that the detective would soon be here and they had to go. "No reason to stay," they said.

Mama whispered something hurriedly in Papa's ear— Connie heard her; thank goodness she was allowed in her own house now and could see and hear everything. "You know, John," said Mama, "I think those two first policemen have my diamond ring in their pocket! I don't think the burglars got it. It's as though someone whispered in my ear, 'Those two policemen have your ring.' It's as though I could see through their pocket, see it there, see that they have my diamond ring in their pocket, in one of their pockets."

"Sh-sh-sh," said Papa. "They'll hear you."

The four policemen were standing near the door, talking, making notes, clearing their throats. One of the first, Sergeant Rattray, picked up a screwdriver from the floor near the front door. "Here," he said, "here is the tool the burglars used to break into your house."

Mama took the screwdriver gingerly. The handle was partly broken, but gold letters on it were still legible— "Stanley." Connie said, "Why, this tool has a name, 'Stanley.' "

Papa went upstairs to see what things of his, if any, had been taken. He groaned, "Oh, my three brand-new suits are gone! Ding bust it!" This proved that the burglars really had been up in Papa's dressing room, and after they had taken the three suits, they might have, probably had, taken the ring as well. Then Papa made the discovery that his gold studs and cuff links inherited from his great-great-grandfather, a colonel of the South, were gone! Also, Papa's ancient watch and chain with his gold Phi Beta Kappa key on it were gone.

The two second policemen said they might as well go, and since no one could think of any reason why they should stay, off they went. They were very nice policemen—it's too bad they had not been the first ones on the scene.

Mama and Papa went back downstairs and sat down weakly at the dining-room table. The two first policemen muttered something to each other and said again they guessed they'd be getting back to the station to make their report. But Papa said they would have to wait for the detective and then go to make their report. The two policemen stood in the doorway, and they were obviously terribly anxious to get going. One whistled a bored little tune. In the dining room by themselves, Mama and Papa talked in low voices. Mama said, "John, I'm sure. I don't know why, but I'm sure the ring is in one of their pockets. What should we do? They look so guilty, and you see they want to be gone before the detective comes. When I said, 'Oh, my ring!' and they said, 'Where, where?' and I said, 'Here, here, in a pencil case that was in this drawer—that is where my ring was. . . .' My, how self-conscious they were! They may not even know they have my ring. They may think they have only a pencil!"

Papa looked bewildered. He had heard a lot about women's intuition. Still, can you imagine (Connie saw his dilemma) saying to two policemen—one would be more than enough—"Were you, by chance, the robber who took my wife's ring, instead of the real robbers? Otherwise, what were you doing upstairs all that time—twenty minutes, my wife tells me. Does it take twenty minutes to go through a little house like this and see if burglars are still in it or not? What exactly were you doing?" Papa sighed. "Oh, Jane," he said. "I don't see how we can accuse them on just a hunch, I really don't . . ."

Connie thought her mother could not be right. She was quite ashamed of her. Had anyone ever heard of a policeman stealing? She never had. Mama said hesitantly, "Ts, I suppose not, John, but don't you think—isn't there some way to tell my suspicions to the detective? Why, it's as though my eyes could pierce right through their navy-blue uniforms and see my diamond ring on its little clasp, in the pocket of one of them. The way they said, 'Where, where?' " Connie had never seen her mother more positive. "It's as though someone had whispered in my ear"—she couldn't get over it—"whispered, 'They have it, they have it. The policemen have it, not the burglars.' "

At this moment, a plainclothesman arrived. The two first policemen gave him a hurried report, and then, before you could say Jack Robinson, they were out the door, in their car, had stepped on the gas, and had sped off the campus. The detective sat down and talked to Mama and Papa. Mama, since she could see that Papa was not going to, told the detective her suspicions herself. He didn't say yes, he didn't say no. He said he would tell Mama's suspicions to the captain of the precinct.

Papa demanded hotly, "Do you really think that it is possible that two officers of the law would do such a thing?"

The detective said he would not like to rule out the possibility as being unlikely. "It is unfortunate but true that some policemen are dishonest," he said. "Oh, you don't run into them very often—but once in a while . . ."

"Oh, dear," said Mama. "I was sure of it, but what could I do? And now they are gone. My ring is probably gone forever. Imagine them, probably right this minute, taking a good look at it beneath the dashboard."

Connie was enthralled. Seeing Billy at the back door, she went out. "You know, Billy, that there may be two

91

dishonest policemen in the world—all the rest are honest—
and we may have had, we are not sure, the only two
dishonest ones?"

"Tell," said Billy, a happy shine in his eyes.

8

↓↓↓

TELLING IT TO THE ALLEY

By this time a lot of children had gathered in Connie's yard. Hugsy Goode, the Arps, Katy Starr, practically everybody —the entire children's population of the Alley—came gradually into the yard. They didn't have to ask for permission this time; they could all just come right in. Some sat on the ground, some climbed to the top of the jungle gym, some sat on the glider, but naturally what they all wanted to hear about was the burglary. Billy Maloon and Connie got in the swings, but they didn't swing. They just sat in them and they talked, or rather, Connie talked—it being her burglary. Connie soon reached the part in the story where Mama saw through the policeman's coat into his pocket. "But what could she do?" she asked Billy, or anyone else who would tell her what. "Nothing. She could say and do nothing."

Billy Maloon thought for a while. He was impressed with the story, and he was also frightened. "No," he agreed finally. "She could not search them, because it was just a

hunch, and you cannot search people, especially policemen, on hunches. Your mother could not say to them, 'You have my diamond ring!' They might have arrested *her*."

"Arrested *her!*" exclaimed Connie. "Oh, they could not do that! Arrest my mother? Just because she has hunches? But, you know, she might be right, that they—the policemen—had the ring. The way Mama tells things, you can't help but think that she is probably right. Even Papa looked as though he was beginning to think Mama was right. My mother is very persuasive."

"Well," said Hugsy. "What were the other two policemen, the second two, doing—the two in the cellar? Not much to rob down there, I guess," he said.

"Wait!" screamed Connie, who was doing her best, and doing very well, to tell the story in its proper order. "You have to wait 'til I get to them. The two first policemen wanted Mama to tell them everything, every single thing that was missing. They planned to take this list, go everywhere, and try to get back her possessions. They said, 'Sometimes thieves turn things in at pawnshops.' That was after Mama had looked in her bedroom and had found that all of her bureau drawers had been pulled out a little bit. But, the drawers were not dumped upside down on the bed or the floor, the way robbers usually do these things— Mama knows all about robberies. She was in one once before, before she was married. Papa—don't laugh—was a possible suspect, the policemen said at the time—he being her newest friend."

"Tell us about that robbery!" said Hugsy Goode, who was edging up more closely all the time.

"One robbery at a time," said Billy in his tense but quiet voice.

"Ts," Connie thought fondly. "Billy is really wonderful, the very way he says things like this—'One robbery at a time.' It makes your spine tingle." Out loud she said, "Yes. So, Mama looked in her bedroom, and she saw the little present that she had wrapped in blue tissue paper, and there it was—this little blue-wrapped present—on the middle of the bed, unwrapped, the ribbon beside it, more carefully than you would think burglars would take the time to do, for they always work in a rush. The present was still there, too; soap . . . no one wanted that; they had not taken it . . ."

"Too bad they didn't," said Hugsy, gulping in excitement. "Because then the burglars could be traced by their smell . . ."

95

"Just why they didn't take it, dope . . ." said Billy Maloon.

Hugsy said, "The burglars spent an awful long time deciding what to take and what not to take."

Connie said, "You're right, Hugsy. There were probably two burglaries that went on in my house today, not just one."

"Not just one measly one . . ." repeated Hugsy, "like mine."

"Measly!" exclaimed Connie. "Nothing measly about either one of them, our two or your one. Anyway, there was the first robbery, the real one that the real burglars did—they took Papa's three brand-new suits. Papa never had three brand-new suits all at once before in his life; but there was a wonderful sale at Pete Rogers, and he just bought three of them, all at once. Too bad the robbery did not happen before he bought the suits. And in that robbery, the first one, we think that probably my seven silver dollars were taken. When Mama went into my room, there on the floor was my jewelry box, smashed open the way real burglars do, not neatly unwrapped like the soap present was, but smashed to bits, and all my seven silver dollars were gone! Lovey . . ."

"Lovey! Who's that?" asked Hugsy Goode.

"Shut up," said Billy menacingly. Billy had the opinion that Hugsy interrupted too much.

"Lovey is an adopted cousin of my father's—I think," Connie said. "In the South, they adopt cousins and everything. Lovey is the one who gives me a silver dollar every Christmas. I *had* seven of them. *Now* I have none.

Well, after Papa saw that the ring was really gone and his jewels of his ancestors—his gold watch with the gold chain and the key for brilliance on it . . ."

"My father has one of those keys . . ." said Hugsy.

". . . also the cuff links," Connie went on, "that he had inherited from his great-great-grandfather—a colonel of the old South—studs, too, he was as stunned as Mama; he wondered should he or should he not believe what she had said. Mama was puzzled, you see, because so much had been stolen in such a short time—we were gone less than an hour —plus the voice she heard in her ear telling her that the worst, the diamond ring part of the robbery, had been done by the first two policemen and not the robbers."

"What about those second two policemen?" Hugsy reminded Connie. "Those two cellar fellars."

"Well, they came out of the cellar, and they said there were no burglars there. The coast was clear, they said, and they left. Forget them. They were never upstairs."

"Probably played ping-pong," said Hugsy.

"The Ives don't have ping-pong," said June Arp.

"No," said Connie, "No ping-pong. So then when Mama saw that the two first policemen were muttering together and wanting to leave, the whispering in her ear grew louder. She really wanted to yell at them, 'Let me see what is in your pockets, you!' "

"Joan of Arc . . ." suggested Billy Maloon.

"Joan of Arc!" shouted Hugsy Goode. "What's *she* got to do with it?"

"Hearing voices, get it?" asked Billy quietly. "*Connie's mother hears voices.*"

"Yes," said Connie. "Whispers. Mama suspected the two first policemen. These two guilty-looking first policemen said there was no use their waiting for the detective—you see a detective always comes at the end. But Papa made them wait, because Mama had said to him, 'It is odd that they should be in such a hurry to get away, when they were the first to enter the house.' So Papa asked the policemen to wait, and they did wait; and when the detective came, Mama told him all about our going to the A. & P. and coming home and seeing the men leaving the house—but of course she didn't know then that it was our house—with those three brand-new suits of Papa's; but she could not bring herself—neither could Papa bring himself—to say, 'Detective! I order you to search these two officers!' So they let the two first policemen go away. Off they went with the jewels, perhaps, we don't know for sure, in their pocket."

As different children arrived in the yard, Connie had to repeat parts of her story. To Judy Fabadessa, a latecomer, she had to repeat the part about the arrival of the two first policemen. " 'Stay back, stay back,' they said to Mama and Mrs. Stuart and me. And they went right in the house and up the stairs, one at a time, saying, 'Come out, come out, wherever you are, or we'll shoot!' "

Judy's eyes grew big. "I have an uncle who is a policeman," she said.

"Yes. But no one came out," said Connie. "Why should they?" she said. "The real right burglars had already left, calmly and quietly, as though they were going to the alumni luncheon, in broad daylight, with Papa's three brand-new suits over their arms and his little old portable typewriter that he had had since he was in college and had given me just last week."

"So, let's see," said Billy, counting on his fingers to be emphatic. "Those fellows you saw leaving the house were the ones who were the real burglars. That's one robbery. The second robbery—the jewelry robbery—you're not sure, but you think *it* might have been done by the two first policemen."

"Yes," said Connie. "Two robberies."

"What about those two guys in the cellar?" asked Hugsy again. "The second two policemen?"

"Hugsy," said Connie in disgust. "I told you they said everything was all right in the cellar and they left. What can you hide in your pocket from the cellar?"

"Your bike!" said Hugsy with a hoarse guffaw.

"Ha!" said Connie. "Anyway, there are probably only two dishonest policemen in the whole of Brooklyn, not four."

"World, probably," put in Hugsy.

"And those," finished Connie, "were the first two policemen, the upstairs ones. Now, we have two things left over from the burglary. We have a screwdriver that was used to break down the front door, a screwdriver named 'Stanley' —we have it in our own house right now—a screwdriver of a burglar."

"Let's go in and look at it, Connie. Could we?" asked Billy.

"I guess so," Connie said. She was terribly excited. You would be, too, if you ever had seventeen children listening

99

to you tell a story of a burglary that happened to you. They all trooped in. There, on the table near the front door, next to the Tiffany vase, lay the screwdriver!

"It sure is named 'Stanley,'" agreed Billy, examining the broken tool. "I never heard of giving a screwdriver a name before. It is an important clue. Any more clues?"

"Oh, yes," said Connie. "Look there," she said triumphantly. "The best clue of all, probably." She pointed to the floor of the little vestibule.

There, on the floor, right where it had been since she and Mama had come home, lay the burnt butt. Everybody gasped. What a clue!

"That," said Connie in disgust, "shows what sort of policemen those first two were, whether they stole anything or not. They left the important clue behind, the one named 'Stanley'—'Here, take this,' they said to us. And they left the cigarette butt on the floor. Oh, Mama had showed it to them, but . . ."

"Did they take any fingerprints?" asked Billy.

"Not a one!" said Connie. "Not one single one."

"Yipes!" said Billy Maloon. "What kind of police work is that? May I hold the two clues?"

"Yes," said Connie. "Yes."

Billy's eyes shone with pleasure. "Let's go upstairs. We may find more clues there. Anyway, I'd like to see the broken-into jewelry box."

"All right," said Connie. "But not the tiny children, just the big ones. Danny and Nicky, you better go out and wait for us outside; there are too many in here now."

"O. K.," said the two and ran out, whooping, "Bugglers, bugglers!"

The rest of the children—there was quite a procession, and all could not crowd into Papa's dressing room; many had to stand on the stairs—asked themselves and each other, "Any more clues? Anything else besides the butt and 'Stanley'? Good old 'Stanley'?"

A squeal from Connie was their answer. "Billy! Look!" they heard. Everyone wanted to see and crowded up the stairs.

"Yikes!" said Billy.

9

‡ ‡ ‡

CLUES

Connie was the first one to see the next important, perhaps *the* most important, clue of all. "Look!" she gasped. "The curtain!"

"What about the curtain?" asked the others excitedly. They were as hot on her neck as the two first policemen had been on Mama's.

"Look at that!" she said. "Bloodstains on the curtain. Oh!"

Connie drew back and so did everybody else. But then, fascinated, all drew forward again. Gingerly, Connie held the tip end of the curtain up so the others could see it. Sure enough, there were bloodstains on the curtain. A person with a hurt hand had lifted it to look out—for a sign or a signal from below, no doubt.

"You know," said Connie. "The burglar who broke the door down and then broke my jewelry box open to get my silver dollars probably hurt his hand, and then . . ."

"Then when he got up here in this little room, he had to

see if the lookout men were giving him the O. K. signal or the signal to get away quick," put in Billy.

"Mama!" Connie called downstairs. "You know what? There is blood on one of Papa's curtains."

"I know it. Ugh!" said Mama. "I'm going to throw the awful thing away. It gives me the heebies."

Billy, who rarely addressed an adult, called downstairs. "Mrs. Ives, did the police take tests of these stains on the curtain?"

Mama said, "No. They did not."

"Ts," said Billy. "They didn't take tests of the blood on the curtain. They didn't keep the broken screwdriver to trace it, where it had been bought—and think how easy that would have been, since it has its name 'Stanley' printed on it in gold letters. They didn't take any fingerprints off the door or anywhere—they took nothing! They did nothing."

"Nothing!" repeated Connie.

"That's the way they help to find burglars in this town—" said Billy. "Not at all like in the movies or in the Perry Mason show, in books or anywhere else that I ever heard of, even in Oldenport, and that's a small town. They have only three policemen there; but I bet Cop Hopper would take something, one fingerprint at least."

At this moment, there was a great commotion downstairs. It was Papa. He was fuming and shouting about how horrible Precinct Number 9999 was. He had gone over there to ask the captain if he thought—"And I asked in a nice way, Jane," he said. "I simply said, 'Do you think that the two first policemen, Sergeant Rattray and Officer Ippolito, might have stolen the ring and the jewels? Do you feel that they might have? Since they were upstairs such a long time?' Why, the captain was insulted! He almost clapped me in a cell. . . . 'How dare you think such a thing of those two fine officers, two of the best on the force?' he bellowed. 'Cited for bravery, time after time,' he said."

Papa's explosions continued. The children, upstairs, listened enthralled. There was no one who could surpass Papa in indignation, unless, possibly, Nanny; and Nanny was in South Carolina—in Chester—though her paper, the Chester *Reporter* was still coming here. Had Nanny been here, though, the house would be reeling with the double indignations, Papa's and Nanny's. Mama was indignant, too; but she had little chance of getting in a word to add to or stem—as the case might be—the avalanche of Papa's rage. She just said helplessly, "Sh-sh-sh," to Papa, not to upset the children upstairs.

"Connie," said Billy. "Do you think, since your mother is going to throw this curtain away anyhow, that we could cut out this bit that has blood on it and keep it with our clues?"

"Oh, sure," said Connie. She got her scissors, and Billy snipped out the little bloodstained piece of curtain. Now, Billy had in his pocket the screwdriver named 'Stanley,' the burnt cigarette butt—it happened to be a Mura—and a piece of bloodstained curtain. The children then all went back downstairs, streamed past Mama and Papa, who had fallen into an angry reverie, and went outside, where they gathered around the swing to piece the facts together.

"You know," said Connie, "that Mama says the two policemen, or the one of them, might not even have known that they, or he, had a diamond ring? They might just have seen the brand-new little pencil in its case and thought, 'Hm, here is a nice little present to bring home to Molly,'—or whatever their little girl's name is . . ."

"Or boy," said Billy Maloon.

"Writes good," continued Connie. "I bet that's what they thought."

Billy said, "We have three important clues. And we know that these three clues belong to the first, the real burglars. The real burglars were the ones who broke into the house, smoked a cigarette while breaking in, and lifted the curtain to look out to see if the coast was clear. But, you know the most important clue . . . most important but missing clue?"

"The pencil!" shouted Katy Starr, who always got A plus in everything.

"Right," said Billy.

"Yes," said Connie. "If we ever could find that, we would know whether Mama is right in hunches or not," said Connie. "You know what the pencil was named—it was a little silver pencil; it was named 'Eberhardt.' "

"Millions of pencils are named 'Eberhardt,' " said Billy.

"But this pencil has J for John and I for Ives in tiny little scrolls around the top of it. The J.I. doesn't look like plain J.I. at all; it looks like an ornament, a scrawling gold line."

"They probably will never see that the pencil has initials on it," said Billy. "Boy! If only that pencil would show up somewhere!"

"I know," said Connie. "But it won't. I know it won't. Things just don't happen that way in real life . . . or do they?"

"No," said Billy.

"Wowie!" said Hugsy in the pause that followed. "What a story! Can I tell my robbery now?" He wanted to remind them of his five-dollar-bill robbery in case they had forgotten.

"No," said Connie patiently. "One robbery at a time."

"How much," said Hugsy, who was terribly interested in money—he was always having fairs to sell his old comics and toys and pink cold drinks—"how much would you say the burglars got away with? In money, I mean, if everything were sold?"

Billy said he guessed a hundred dollars, easily.

"A hundred dollars, hah!" said Connie. "A thousand, maybe ten!" she said.

"Ten thousand dollars!" said Hugsy, and he fell down in a pretended faint.

"Well," Connie said. "Look at my seven silver dollars alone. They mount up, you know. And I had only just polished them the other day."

"Polished them!" said Hugsy. "I never heard of polishing money."

"Never heard of polishing money!" exclaimed Billy. "Yikes!" Sometimes he found Hugsy irritating.

"Oh, of course—polishing!" said Hugsy, ashamed of his ignorance. "I guess I didn't hear straight."

Then Katy, who had been remarkably silent during the entire reenactment of the burglary, turned to Hugsy and said, "Hugsy, if you can't keep quiet, you'll just have to leave the yard. Won't he, Connie?"

"We-ell," said Connie hesitantly. Although she found it pleasant to be appealed to by Katy, a most important person in the Alley, still, Hugsy was one of her favorite people, and she did not want him to be put out of her yard. So, instead of answering Katy, she said, "Well, do you all want me to go on, or don't you?"

"Go on, go on!" It was unanimous.

"Where was I, were we?" she asked.

"Well," said Billy. "You were up to the clues . . ."

"Oh, yes," said Connie. "You know that, although I think the 'Stanley' screwdriver is a very important clue . . ."

"Yes!" agreed Hugsy. "Stanley! It might be the engraved

name of the robber, a confirmation present. . . . I have 'Hugo' on my belt buckle."

"Don't interrupt," said Connie, but she added kindly, "Same idea."

Billy's eyes were dreamy, the pupils enlarged. ". . . fingerprints all over the place . . ." he murmured.

"Yes," said Connie. "Well, although 'Stanley' and all our clues are important, we should go back to the day long before the burglary, the day of de Gaulle saying, 'Get out, get out' to no one—the day of the bullet-headed-man dog lover."

"Oh, yes, Wags!" said June Arp accusingly. "Where was Wags during the burglary?"

"Wags! Yes!" said Hugsy. "Where was she?"

"Wait, can't you?" said Connie. "I'm coming to Wagsie. I'm getting to her right now."

Connie's head swam as she tried to recall the steps that might have led up to the robbery. So she said, although there was silence, "Quiet, can't you? I can't think."

Billy reminded her quietly—he knew how hard it was to tell such an important story in the right order—"You were on Wagsie. Why didn't she, well . . . bark? And you also said something about a bullet-head . . ."

"Oh, yes," said Connie. "Well, she probably did bark! She probably barked her head off—at first. You know that wonderful, deep, beautiful bark she has . . . ? She doesn't bark often, but what a wonderful bark when she does!"

"Then why didn't she bark that wonderful bark when burglars came?" asked Judy Fabadessa wonderingly. "She is an F.B.I. dog."

"Was," said Connie, "as a puppy. But listen, can't you?" she said, for there was some murmuring among the others, too—"Yes, why," said some, "didn't Wags bite or at least scare the burglars, arouse the neighbors?" and many other comments of that sort. . . . "When Mama and I finally had the chance to get into the kitchen after the police—the first two and the second two, and the detective—had all left, there, under the table we saw—a bone!"

"Bone!" exclaimed Billy. "What's strange about a bone?" But his eyes showed that he knew that what was coming was going to be good, and it was.

"Yes, bone!" said Connie. "Under the kitchen table was a bone . . . not one of Wagsie's real, right, regular old soup bones she keeps under there, but a strange bone that somebody, the burglar probably, must have given her. It was no bone of ours."

"O-o-oh," said Hugsy. "I see it all now. They tempted her with a bone—to keep her quiet. That is why no one heard her."

"And this bone," Connie went on, "may have had a sleeping potion on it. There might have been poison on it. We don't know, she might die yet. Papa's going to watch her carefully and take her to the vet's if she acts funny. But it might be a poison that takes a year to work; we don't know, we don't know. So Mama picked up that bone with a paper towel and threw it in the trash can . . ."

"Threw the bone clue away!" shouted Billy. "Your mother is no better than the police, who didn't gather up the other clues. Do you think the bone is still in the garbage can?"

"Sure," said Connie.

"O-o-oh, ugh!" said Katy. She had been sitting on the garbage pail, and she leapt off as though the bone beneath might bite or poison her.

"Good," said Billy quietly. "I'll get it out later."

"Ugh," said Katy again. "Who would want to touch a dirty old burglar bone like that, poison on it and all?"

"I would," said Billy.

("Ts," thought Connie proudly. "Billy is not afraid of anything. Not one thing. He's like Papa.") "I'll get it later," said Billy, "and put it with the rest of the clues."

"What for?" asked June Arp.

"You'll see," said Billy with a slow and meaningful nod of his head.

"Now I get it; now I get it all!" said Hugsy. "Take the bone to the drugstore, see what sort of poison is on it, see who has bought that sort of poison."

"You're brilliant," said Billy to Hugsy. He was a little put out because Hugsy had spilled the reason before he had.

To clear the atmosphere, Connie said, "You know how greedy Wagsie is; she's always hungry . . . always. She probably did bark her head off, but then the man . . . oh, you see—it's all coming to me now—I bet the breaking-into-the-house burglar was the man that talked to Mama and me that day, the bullet-head man who said, 'Does this dog bite?' Remember? The day of de Gaulle and the lady with the loose stockings . . ."

"And the beautiful-mansions man . . ." put in Billy.

"Oh, they're all probably in cahoots," suggested Hugsy.

"Oh, don't be silly," said Katy. Hugsy drooped.

"Anyway," said Connie. "When that bullet-head man put his hand in the broken-in door and spoke gently to Wagsie —who I know, I just know, was barking her head off—and probably said, 'Nice feller. You remember me, don't you?' Well, he probably had the bone in his hand then—it is the sort of bone that Wagsie loves; and probably then Wagsie, not knowing what else to do, just stopped barking and took the bone to the kitchen, crawled way, way under the table, close to the wall, and gnawed. It probably was like a friend to her—this bone. No family around, but at least—a bone. She tried to let the bone take her mind off the people in the house who did not belong here and had made such an awful noise coming in. It's like bad people giving a lollipop to a little child when all the while they are going to kidnap it . . ."

"Do you think, oh, you don't think they were planning to kidnap Wagsie, do you?" asked Judy, her beautiful gray-blue eyes wide with horror. Judy loved Wagsie and all dogs and animals—all. She owned hamsters, two parakeets, and a found dog. "Would they have planned to kidnap Wags?" she repeated.

Now, this was something that had not occurred to Connie at all. Tears of terror sprang into her eyes. "Perhaps," she said. "Who knows? She is a wonderful dog. Has a long genealogy."

All eyes turned to Wags, who knew she was being talked about. She was embarrassed and ashamed, and she looked aimlessly here and there, at her paws, behind her, at nothing. She dug at her itchy ear. With an enormous sigh, she raised herself—she was rather stout—ambled over to the iris, and lowered herself with an even deeper sigh to the ground. She closed her eyes and pretended to sleep.

"She doesn't seem poisoned," said Hugsy.

"Can't tell," said Billy. "Not yet." Judy lay down beside Wags and crooned to her. "Poor Wagsie," she said.

All eyes turned back to Connie, who went on, "Afterwards," she said "when we finally had time to pay a little attention to Wagsie, who kept looking at us as though she had so much to tell—imagine how terrified she must have been when they broke down the door, with none of us home to save her . . . well, we thought she was all right, only just scared."

"Still," June Arp spoke again, "I don't understand why she wouldn't bite them. Such a big dog!"

Judy defended Wags. "Because she is timid, that's why, very, very shy and timid."

"Yes," said Connie. "She is shy and timid, and she is a coward. She can't help it. She is even afraid of the minister's dog, though he is always on his leash. She hides behind the green door, in the vestibule, when the minister comes along . . . is dragged along, I should say instead, by his big black Doberman pincher. Wagsie peeks out at them, and she does not bark or growl at all—not to attract their attention—and she does not go back outside to sit on the top stoop and wait for Papa until the minister and his dog are way up the street. But what we wonder is—why no one, not one of the neighbors, heard Wagsie barking? She must have barked in the beginning, before the bone."

"Don't let me forget to get the bone, by the way," said Billy.

"I won't," said Connie. "But we wonder why nobody heard her barking. We know she would bark that deep, wonderful bark that means danger. June, didn't you hear Wags? Were you home? Living right next door, I'd think you would have heard Wagsie."

"Yes," said June. "Ray and I were home. My mother and father were out. But we were in the basement, we were all —Ray, Laura, Katy—all in the basement playing ping-pong. You know . . . I remember now . . . I *did* hear Wags. But I didn't think anything about it. 'Wags is barking,' that's all I thought. I don't remember anything else."

Billy reproached her. He said, "You should always think something when you hear Wags bark, because Wags is a thoughtful, quiet, silent dog, not like Atlas; and she barks only when something is really wrong."

"Well, I didn't know," said June, rather irritated. She looked as though she thought they were all accusing her of not having stopped the robbery. And she really could have stopped it, if only she had thought something was amiss when she heard Wags. She could have run upstairs, wondering what all the pounding—the breaking in of the door must have made quite a racket—was about. And the unusual barking of the Ives's usually quiet dog could have sent her to the front window, and she might have peeked out. Then, she would have seen those men across the street, the lookout men, and she might have thought something was strange about that, and she might have called—if not the police, at least Mrs. Stuart, next door to her on the other side. But she didn't.

"I just didn't think one thing about it," she said coldly to Billy Maloon, for he was looking at her with a certain amount of disgust. Here was June and also her brother Ray —they had had a chance to be heroes, and they had let the chance slip through their fingers. If *he* had been the one to hear Wags, he would have known right away something was wrong. "Some people have all the luck," Billy thought, "and they let it slide through their fingers."

"Well, anyway," said June's brother Ray. "It was lucky it wasn't *our* house the burglars burglared because *my* mother had six hundred dollars . . . *six hundred dollars in cash.* Cash is what they like, my mother says—they much prefer cash to anything else, suits, a crummy old typewriter; and here my mother had all this money, plain bills—greenbacks —lying loose on the top of her valise in her bedroom. The valise was wide open, too—they could have scooped the money up in a second and gone off with it. She had it for her trip to Spain next week. . . . Yeh, supposing it was *my* house they broke into! Supposing it was the six hundred dollars they got!"

Hugsy, always impressed with money, fell over in a pretend faint again. But Billy said somberly, "That can't equalize with the family jewels in Connie's house, including a diamond ring. You've heard of the Hope diamond, haven't you? Diamonds are worth more than any old greenback money. And you know that, Ray Arp. Think you're so smart, Ray," said Billy Maloon.

Connie was grateful to Billy for putting this slant on things, for reminding the others that money is not always the most valuable thing in the world. Old watches, rings, keys for brilliance are even more important. But she said, "Anyway, they did get my seven real silver dollars, not paper dollars. . . . And you can't blame . . . no one can blame Ray and June Arp for not paying attention to the barking. Mrs. Harrington, on the other side of us, paid no attention either, and she wasn't even playing ping-pong."

"Well, she's deaf," said Katy Starr. "You can't expect an old deaf lady . . . how old is she, anyway? A hundred?"

"Ninety-four," said Connie. "Exactly the same age as our school."

"Mean to say that Morrison School is nearly a hundred?" said Hugsy. "What an antiquity!"

"It's old, but it's a very good school," Connie said to Hugsy. "And maybe it's lucky Mrs. Harrington didn't hear; she might have died of old-age fright."

"No clues from her," said Billy. He had taken out a grimy little blue notebook and had made some entries. "No clues from Mrs. Harrington, and no clues from the Arps, except they did hear Wags barking. So far we have these clues— the clue of the man who got Wags used to his smell, his appearance, bullet head; the screwdriver named 'Stanley' that was used to jimmy the door; the cigarette butt . . . it's a Mura, that helps; the bone—I must remember to get that out of the garbage. Any more? Oh, yes, the piece of bloodstained curtain. Any more?"

"Not clues that we can hold in our hand," said Connie. "But maybe . . . let's see . . ." She was reluctant to have her story over, near its end.

At this moment, Judy's father, Mr. Fabadessa, came into the yard. Evidently he had been listening to the last words himself. "I may have further clues," he said. "Is your mother in, Connie, or your father?" he asked.

Judy's eyes grew big. Her own father! What did *he* have to do with Connie's burglary? That's what they all wondered—what did Mr. Fabadessa, and he the only man in the Alley home that day, know about Connie's burglary? They listened in amazement to what he had to say to Mama and Papa when they came to the door.

"Yipes!" said Billy.

For this is what Mr. Fabadessa said he knew about the Ives's burglary.

10
♯♯♯
MR. FABADESSA'S SLANT

Mr. Fabadessa said to Mama, "Jane," he said, "I'm sorry to hear about your robbery. You know something? At our house, this noon—I didn't realize it was important then— something happened that might help the police catch the burglars . . ."

"The police! they went! They left long ago," said Mama. "Thank goodness!"

"Well," (Mr. Fabadessa looked rather self-conscious, ashamed—he reminded you of Wagsie.), "I did ring your back doorbell while the police were still here," he explained. "But no one heard me . . ."

"Yes?" said Mama.

"Anyway, exactly when did the burglary take place?" asked Mr. Fabadessa.

"Between twelve and one," said Mama.

"Yes, that's what I thought," said Mr. Fabadessa weakly, as though he had been hoping against hope that it had happened any time but that. "Well, anyway, at that time, strangers rang our doorbell. I happened to be in the living room entertaining some old friends, missionaries just back from India. We were talking and reminiscing about old times when the bell rang. My wife was in the kitchen, preparing a little collation. You know you get a good view of the front door from the kitchen where she was. She waited for me to answer the bell because her hands were wet and I was nearer. So I did; but my mind was on the conversation my friends and I had been having, rather than on who was at the door.

"However, I was rather taken aback when I opened the door, because two men were standing very close to it—right tight up against it, in fact. Well, they did rather startle me. I sort of noticed, but absent-mindedly, you know, thinking of lamas, that three more men were standing on the side-walk, looking down the street toward Myrtle Avenue. One of the men at the door said, 'Does a Mrs. Hooker live here, sir?' He spoke briskly; he was polite and well . . . he seemed to be an educated man."

"That," said Mama, "is the first question those about to rob ask. They ask, 'Does a Mrs. So-and-So live here?' Meanwhile, they are sizing up the situation."

"Yes," said Mr. Fabadessa. "But my mind, as I say, was on our old friends and saying, 'Whatever happened to good old Al?'—not on strangers and *their* questions—and I said, 'No, she doesn't,'—expecting them to leave. They didn't leave, though; they were oddly persistent. They explained that this Mrs. Hooker had a lot of children—was I sure she did not live in one of these houses? I said, 'No, never heard of her, and it must have been a long time since she lived here or I would have heard of her.' Then I closed the door and went back to the living room. However, it struck me somewhere in the back of my mind that there was something unusual about these five men, especially as my wife, who had had a good look at them from the kitchen, asked curiously, 'Bill, what did those men want?' So I went to the living-room window. I didn't see *my* two men any more—"

("Oooh!" Billy whispered to Connie. "Those were the two that got into your vestibule, between the green doors, and broke in."

"Sh-sh-sh," said Connie.)

"But the three men," Mr. Fabadessa went on, "across the street seemed to be looking up at your upstairs windows, Jane."

("Already had broken in by this time," whispered Billy Maloon. "The three across the street were the lookout men, making sure your house was empty.")

"I still didn't think too much of it—it *is* Alumni Day, you know," said Mr. Fabadessa, nervously squinting an eye, a habit of his. "I thought they must be remembering someone from some long past day, and I forgot about them until I heard the police cars outside. Then," he said sheepishly, "I realized that they must have been burglars . . ."

("Brilliant," said Billy in Connie's ear. No one could hear him except Connie—a good thing because there was no sense making Judy and Laura ashamed of their father. Just the same, it must have occurred to everybody that had Mr. Fabadessa been on the alert, the men probably would not have broken into Connie's or anyone else's house, at least not an Alley house, that day.)

Mama said, to make him feel better, "It was the same thing with me. I thought when I saw them—I'm sure it was the same men—from Myrtle Avenue, I thought they were old graduates."

"I'd be glad to go to the precinct," said Mr. Fabadessa, "and describe the men, at least the two at the door," he said. "My wife said she thought they looked as though there was something wrong with them. She said so afterwards. From where she was standing in the kitchen, she said she thought that those men at the door were up to no good."

("Then she is really to blame, because she had the hunch and he didn't," muttered Billy.

"Sh-sh-sh," Connie said. She felt sorry for Mr. Fabadessa. He must feel awful to think he could have saved the diamond ring and the silver dollars, the suits . . . everything! Well, it was not his fault. He couldn't help it if long-ago missionary friends of his came from India the same moment burglars decided to break into one of the houses in the Alley.)

"What did the two men at the door look like?" Mama asked.

"Well, one of them, as I recall," said Mr. Fabadessa, "had a sort of a round head—a sort of bullet-shaped head. He was quiet, neat, looked almost like a teacher or something, spoke in an educated tone of voice. I think he may have had a slight mustache. The other fellows did not make so much impression on me. I think they were all rather well-dressed . . ."

"They're going to be better dressed than ever now," said Mama ruefully, "now they have John's three brand-new suits."

"Ah, yes," said Mr. Fabadessa, looking pensively at the ground. "Well, I'll go over to the precinct with John if he wants me to—describe them, at least the one with the round, bullet-shaped head . . ."

"Mama," Connie interrupted. "You remember the man who asked you and me, 'Does this dog bite?' the day of de Gaulle and the loose-stockings lady? He had a bullet-shaped head, too—you were the one who said that was what he had."

"Yes," said Mama. "That's right. He's probably been watching our house ever since. Oh, how awful!"

Mr. Fabadessa said, "Tell John I'll go to 9999 with him if he wants." And he went home.

Billy Maloon was more excited than ever. He asked for a sheet of paper. "Paper, I must have paper!" he said, like a man dying in the desert of the heat. Billy then drew a picture of a man on a piece of paper Connie furnished him. The man had a bullet-shaped head and a slight mustache. Billy was an artist, he might grow up to be a real artist . . . he might even be the sort of artist who draws pictures of people he has never seen, just imagining what they look like from little bits of information gathered from here and there—a detective artist.

"He might catch all the wicked people wandering around loose, put pictures of them in post offices—" thought Connie proudly. "Get the reward." Everyone was impressed with his drawing.

Then, who should come strolling into the back yard—to hear about the burglary—but a real artist, Joe Below, alias Bully Vardeer. He had eyebrows that went up in a point, bushily in the middle, and now his face expressed real concern. There were certain people you could rely upon in time of trouble to come forth generously to help, and Bully was one of these. He had picked ancient Mrs. Harrington off the floor three times when she had fallen and gotten her to bed.

Here then, now, was Bully Vardeer, looking over Billy's shoulder. First he scrutinized Billy's drawing close to, then backing off, the way artists do, he stood and squinted at it; next he studied it with his hand on his chin—"The Thinker." Then he turned practically sideways and looked at it almost upside down. Then he took it in his own hand and, holding it at arms' length, he looked down at it, eyes half closed. He was half making fun, half not. And then he said in a good-natured way, "Hm. That's very good, Billy. Is it somebody I know? He looks familiar. Connie, don't forget, I want to paint you again."

Then, without waiting for an answer, he went to the kitchen door and said, "Jane, I hear you've had a burglary."

The children looked at each other. Was he joking? Did he really know the burglar, recognize him from Billy's drawing? The drawing was an excellent one—a real artist had said so—it was a fine addition to the collection of clues. Everyone crowded around Billy to get another look at it before he put it away. They wanted to implant this likeness of the burglar on their minds, and if they ever saw him, either run or give an alarm. With clues of this sort—cigarette butt named "Mura," screwdriver named "Stanley," piece of curtain with stains of blood, and now a perfectly drawn likeness of the main burglar, the master mind probably, not to forget the bone—the children felt as though they almost had their man. Not that *they* wanted to have their man—they wanted the *police* to have him. What would they do with their man if they had him? Fall down dead, that's what they would do, they said, if they saw the bullet-headed man a mile away or heard his brisk, well-spoken voice.

"Any more clues?" asked Billy quietly, rolling up his drawing and putting it in his bulging pocket with the other clues, including the piece of curtain.

"Imagine," thought Connie, "wearing a piece of curtain with the finger-shed blood of a criminal on it, right next to you . . . in your pocket!"

123

Billy minded, too. He edged his body, as well as it is possible to do such a thing, as far away from what was in his pocket as he could. He told Connie the minute he got home he was going to put the clues in his safe, the one Connie had given him for Christmas. He was the only one who knew the code, how to open it. Connie was glad that he didn't recommend that *she* put them in *her* safe that Billy had given her for Christmas, the very same sort of safe. But, that's where she should have put her silver dollars. She alone knew the code to hers—and the burglars would not have been able to get them. But Billy was fair, and he was polite. He asked her if she'd rather keep the things. After all, it was her burglary, and these were her clues. Connie sort of did and sort of didn't want to keep them. Finally she said, "No, you keep them, Billy. You drew the picture."

Regardless of whose safe the clues were in, however, it was clear that Connie and Billy Maloon were the most important people in the Alley right now. The others soon respectfully left the yard. They trooped down into the Arps' cellar, all except Hugsy, who was not allowed to play with them that day—Connie didn't know why. "Not today," said Katy. "Another time," she said. In clubs they have these rules—not to play some days with someone, no one knows why.

Crestfallen, Hugsy asked Connie if he could stay and swing. "O. K.," said Connie. But Hugsy didn't stay long. He soon went home, and only Billy and Connie were left in the swings.

"I don't think," said Billy, "that I will take the bone clue home with the other clues, after all. It might poison Atlas.

He'd be sure to find it. You know Atlas—finds everything, and . . . was it big?"

"Oh, yes," said Connie, "a big round bone."

"It wouldn't fit in my safe then?"

"Oh, no," said Connie. "It would not fit in your safe, nor mine either," she said, not wanting it.

"We better leave the bone in the trash can so the trash collectors will take it away," said Billy.

"Yes," said Connie. "That would be best. Mittens or Punk might lick it, too, if someone took it out."

"And die," said Billy.

"Die," said Connie.

"That was a good idea of Hugsy's, though—take it to the drugstore, have it analyzed," said Billy.

"The police should have done that, but they didn't,' said Connie.

"No. We'll leave it then," said Billy. "We have clues enough to spare this one old bone one."

"Clues to spare is right," said Connie happily. "The most wonderful day of my life," she thought, swinging.

II
⇊⇊

THE TRIAL IN THE CIRCLE

A number of days passed. The burglary was rarely mentioned; it was half forgotten by most of the children of the Alley—not by Connie, of course, nor by Billy Maloon, who was the keeper of the clues. Even in their minds, the famous day was becoming a part of the past, momentous but nevertheless—past. The police must have forgotten the burglary, too, for they did not come back with the suits and other stolen things and say, "Found!" It was early June now. Vacation days would soon be here, and the nearer they came, the more impatiently they were awaited.

Down in the Circle, the games went on—Meece, a new knights-in-armor game, all the old ones; balls were being bounced against the high brick wall in the Circle that brought the Alley to an abrupt but convenient end—it made the Alley private, and you could bounce balls against it without anyone yelling. Some children began writing in chalk again on this wall and on Mrs. Carroll's and Bully

Vardeer's walls. In the main, Katy's laws were being followed with remarkably few in opposition.

Little ones and big ones came into Connie's yard, obeying *her* rules, just so they could swing, swing. It was truly a real playground. "Jane," said June's pretty mother. "How many sessions do you have there in your yard every day?" she'd joke. "Is this the second or the third? Oh, I see. This is the kindergarten session," she'd say, when Notesy and Jeannie finally got in.

Today Connie and Billy were swinging. At the moment, no game was going on in the Circle. Some children of Connie's age had trooped down into the Arps' cellar a few minutes ago. You could hear them playing ping-pong and laughing; and above everybody else's, you could hear Katy's quick-speaking, positive voice. "Now, Ray," she said. "You know you can't win every time. Well, get mad, if you want, so what!" Then there was quiet.

Connie caught a glimpse of Mama walking Wagsie down No-Name Street, the little street next to the Circle outside the Alley. The sight reminded her of the bullet-head man and the burglary. Suddenly, she had a wonderful idea. "You know what, Billy?" she said.

"No," he said. "What?"

The nice thing about Billy was that he never tried to take words out of your mouth; he waited for you to say what you wanted to say, and he did not guess, whether rightly or wrongly, and say, before you had a chance to, what you were about to say and spoil it all.

"I've been thinking," said Connie. "How about having a trial in the Circle? Some could be the burglars, and some could be the policemen—the two first policemen and the two second policemen. In the trial we would try to find out who got the diamond ring—the real burglars or the two first policemen. There would be parts enough for everybody," she said.

"O. K.," said Billy. "Let's tell the others."

"O. K." said Connie. "You call them. You tell them."

"Well . . ." said Billy. "It was your idea."

They kept on swinging because neither Connie nor Billy wanted to be the one to tell the others, to call them and explain the game. Anyway, it was Katy Starr's job in the Alley to call the others and to get everybody to do something, play some game. It was not Connie's or Billy's job, and neither wanted to say, "Hey, kids!" So, here they had thought up a great game, and they were stuck with it.

As luck would have it, at this very moment, out of the Arps' cellar streamed the others, Katy first. "Come on," she said. "Connie! Come on! Billy, come on! Everybody down in the Circle. New game! New game! We are going to have a trial, a trial of the crooks and the policemen crooks—crooks or not, we'll soon find out."

Connie looked at Billy and Billy looked at her. What a coincidence! Katy had thought up the same game that Connie had. Some day, thought Connie, she and Katy might grow to be really great friends, as she and Clarissa used to be. Katy and she had so many of the same ideas; they loved so many of the same books; they thought the same things funny. Naturally, Connie did not tell Katy of the coincidence of both of them having thought up the trial at the same moment. If they ever got to be really great friends, she'd tell her of the coincidence. Then, "Katy," she'd say. "Listen to this," she'd say. "We both thought up the trial in the Circle at the same time." Katy would smile.

Billy Maloon jumped out of the swing, and closing the gate behind them, not to let Wags out, he and Connie joined the others in the Circle. About fifteen children all told, so far, were down there—almost enough for every part that had to be played; besides, some could play more than one part.

First, everybody sat down on the curb and quickly reviewed the events of the day of Connie's burglary. Few had forgotten any of them. Connie, like Papa and Nanny, stemmed from a long line of good storytellers, and her telling of the burglary on Alumni Day had stuck in their minds for always.

"All right," said Katy. Everyone suddenly became more alive than usual—that was the wonderful electric effect Katy had on people. "We are now going to solve the famous Brooklyn Burglary Case called, 'Who got Mrs. Ives's diamond ring?' We'll hold court, right now, this very morning, June the third. Who wants to be burglars? Who wants to be policemen? Who the jury? I'm the judge."

There was silence, all parts being tempting.

"It was, or it may have been, a double burglary," said Billy.

"Yes, great! Two to solve," said Connie.

"That means that practically everybody—seven, anyway—can be a burglar, or rather, a possible burglar. No one, you know, can be called a burglar unless so proven," said Billy.

"I'll be the judge," said Katy again. No one could quarrel about that. With Katy, a born lawmaker, the judge, the trial would be a good one. "I'll get my father's acamadic robe," she said.

"Macadamic," said Hugsy. "Robe!" he said. "I thought macadamic a sort of nut. . . . We have them sometimes, for the president."

"Acamadic," said Katy. "Nothing to do with nuts," and she went into her house, which was on the Circle, the next to last one on the Waldo Place side of the Alley, and came back out with her father's robe. The full black robe was long on Katy and quite hot; but it was impressive and gave a real courtroom air to the whole proceeding.

"Oh, she's a great girl," thought Connie. "Knows how to do everything—everything!"

"Now," said Katy. "Silence in the courtroom. The judge —that's me, ahem—is going to speak. Oh," she said. "We need a whatcha-ma-call-it."

"Gavel," said Jonathan Stuart, the son of Mama's friend who had telephoned for the police on the day of the real burglary.

"Yes," said Katy. "Has anyone a gavel? I have to pound with it to keep order."

"We do," said Connie. And she ran home to get the wooden mallet that Nanny cracked ice with for her Cokes. In the South, they never serve Cokes without cracked ice and a piece of lemon. "That's the way they do," said Nanny, and she said that in the North, no one knew how to serve a decent Coke. "Too sweet," she said, "not enough ice," she said, "and no lemon. Ugh!" It was lucky that

Nanny was still in the South right now, or she might not have let Connie have her important ice mallet . . . she had brought it from Chester. Connie flew back with it, looking like an Olympics' torch carrier.

Now, with her father's academic robe and with Nanny's mallet, Katy was a real judge. "Silence," she said, pounding the trash can that was going to be her desk. "Silence in the courtroom. The judge is going to . . ." Katy was about to go into a long speech.

Billy interrupted. "The judge," he said, "doesn't talk much. He speaks when he charges the jury—that is the most important thing that he does, that and passing the sentence. He tells the jury what the penalty will be if the guy—I mean guys—are found guilty."

Connie thought that perhaps Billy Maloon, not Katy Starr, should be the judge—he knew so much. "Judge Maloon." It sounded fine. Moreover, have you ever heard of a lady judge? "Who knows, though," thought Connie. "There may be lady judges. I haven't heard of all the judges there are. If there aren't, let Katy Starr be the first lady judge!"

"Let's see now," said the lady judge. "Some of the jury can be girls. I've heard of lady jurors. They have ladies on juries now."

"And are they lousy!" said Ray Arp. "They're unfair. That's what they are—unfair. To men. Can't trust them."

"Oh, yeh?" said Billy. "That's not so, and besides, in this Alley, you're the unfair one, see?"

Ray's face grew red and angry. "Billy is stuck on Connie; that's why he defends ladies on juries," he shouted.

Billy Maloon flushed and looked down. Then he said—the words coming through clenched teeth—"You want to know something? Well, you're really stuck on her yourself. That's what."

"Yikes!" Connie wished she wasn't there. She rolled her eyes around to show she had nothing to do with anything.

Katy, ignoring the distasteful interruption, said that nobody could be a burglar or a policeman or anything if they were going to fight; and she said she would throw off her judge's garb, cast down her gavel, and go in the house if they didn't play right. With these words, Katy restored order.

Then Katy named the parts. Connie's was easy—she was to play the part of herself, Connie Ives, the robbed one. Billy Maloon was to be her lawyer, the prosecuting lawyer. This was fair, since Billy was in possession of all the clues, even carrying the piece of bloodstained curtain in his pocket—he often showed it to the kids in school, imagine! —also the burnt-out Mura butt, crumpled and in a piece of cellophane, and "Stanley"; likewise his drawn picture of bullet-head. Too bad he had not kept the bone. Billy was going to try to prove that the two first policemen, not the real, right burglars, had stolen Mrs. Ives's ring. His was a very hard part; but he could do it—Connie knew that he could do it—prove that ladies like her mother could see through pockets and hear voices.

Ray Arp, Hugsy Goode, Arnold Trickman, Jonathan's little brother known as Brother Stuart, and Stephen Carroll were to be the five real robbers, the ones who broke into the house in the first place, leaving clues everywhere, including fingerprints. Billy and Connie did not know how to get fingerprints off or their low-down on the robbers would have been complete.

Greggie Goode (he was a very good actor, which is why, though small, he was given this important part) was to be Sergeant Rattray. (They began, now, to call him "Ratty.") You couldn't imagine Greggie stealing anything, let alone telling lies. He was practically a saint and resembled Tiny Tim. Laura Fabadessa was to be the other policeman, Officer Ippolito. One of these two policemen, if Mama's hunch was right, was the stealer of the ring, and maybe of the ancestral jewels, too—though Mama's hunch had not gone that far. She had not seen cuff links or the Phi Beta Kappa key through the blue serge pocket. But then, at that time, she had not known they were gone!

June Arp and Judy Fabadessa were the two cellar policemen. They complained because they did not think the parts important. "You can both also be on the jury," said Katy. How well Katy managed everything! Kept all in order! For the two complained no more.

The jury consisted of the following: Jonathan Stuart, head man; Anthony Bigelow (to sit next to Jonathan, so that dependable Jonathan could keep him quiet) next, the three youngest Carrolls—even Notesy, who was barely able to walk. Being on a jury does not require much during most of a trial of this sort in the Circle, so the little ones could wander about from time to time if they got tired. At charging time Jonathan would gather the wanderers back and have them vote the right way—"Guilty" or "Not guilty." Trust Jonathan. Some of the burglars—whoever wanted to—were to fill out on the jury in the end, their parts being finished by then, except for hearing the verdict about themselves.

Judge Starr got her sixth-grade spelling book for the witnesses to take the oath on. There was a great deal of talk and confusion as there often is before a trial begins. Silence, however, settled over the courtroom when Katy again said in solemn tones, not giggling once, "Silence in the courtroom. The judge . . ."

"You mean 'monkey,' " said Anthony.

Oh, the pest! He was going to spoil everything. It was all right to joke ahead of time, but not *during* something important. Everyone glowered at Anthony, even the tiny ones, and Notesy put her thumb in her mouth. For a few moments, Anthony kept quiet, deciding whether he did or did not want to be put out of the game, or whether he could be more of a nuisance in it or out of it. He decided to be a nuisance in it.

"If you put me out," he bellowed so that his mother could hear—his house was not on the Circle. It was on Larrabee. But Mrs. Bigelow was usually in her kitchen or behind her rose bush, where she could keep track of unfavorable comments about her son—"why, I'll just tell my mother, that's what I'll do," said Anthony. "Moth-er!" He called his mother, not waiting to see whether he was going to be put out or not. For once Mrs. Bigelow did not answer, and Katy decided not to put Anthony out of the trial yet. He should have a chance to be in this trial and to remember it forevermore—tell it to his grandchildren, or at least his baby sister.

So she went on, "The judge is going to speak." She pounded the trash can with the ice mallet, and it sounded like Mrs. Carroll making rain.

"Monkey," repeated Anthony stubbornly.

It was too much. "Anthony," said Katy. "I accuse you of contempt of court. Go to the end of the Alley and stand in Hugsy Goode's hidy-hole. We may have to put you on trial instead of the real criminals."

"I'd like that," said Anthony. "That is more important than being a stupid old member of a stupid old jury."

"No," said Katy. "To be on the jury, to say 'Guilty' or 'Not guilty'—that is the most important part."

"Well," said Anthony, "I don't happen to agree, see? If there were no criminals, there would be no jury. *And* no trial, *and* no you, Miss Smarty Judge Katy Starr."

"We'll just put you in jail this minute!" said Katy, exasperated.

"My mother will fight you all," said Anthony.

"You won't be able to call your mother," said Arnold Trickman, his eyes sparkling at the thought. "You'll be in solitary confinement, in a torture chamber besides," he added. Arnold was reading the Dumas books, and they were full of torture chambers and the rack. True, they were rather old for him. But he was in the R. A. class in grade seven in his school, and his reading was that of at least grade nine, his mother said. Few mothers would be able to resist bragging a little about such a smart boy.

"Oh, come on. Get him to jail," said Jonathan Stuart impatiently. (Jonathan was always impatient—he couldn't

135

wait for you to make a move in checkers and would say, "Why not move *that* man?" or "Oh, come on," every second with a groan.) He said, "Isn't it about time to stop kidding around and get on with the trial? Otherwise, I'm going in to do something, fix my stamps, have a snack, something, I don't know, practice, play *The Mikado*, anything . . ." Jonathan was very fond of Gilbert and Sullivan right now, and often, as you passed by his house, you could hear him giggling over some song he particularly liked and even singing it along with the record.

So they hustled Anthony, bawling, clawing, and protesting, down to jail in Hugsy's little hidy-hole. "Yes," said Ray, looking down at him. "You'll probably have to stay there days, weeks, even years. We'll give you bread and water perhaps, if we think of it."

From the jail, they could hear Anthony howling now and then and calling, "Mother, Mother." His mother did not hear him, however, and bustle down to get him and scold the others; finally Anthony climbed out of jail and, outraged, ran home to report the injustice. "I should have been the bullet-head bandit," he shouted to all in the trial. "I have a bullet head."

"All right," said Katy. "Now we can proceed. Sergeant Rattray, take the stand please. Your witness, Mr. . . . Oh, my goodness, who's the defendant's lawyer? We have to have a lawyer for him. . . . Jonathan, you'll have to be the lawyer for the defendant until it is time for you to give the verdict as head juryman when I charge you."

"O. K.," said Jonathan obligingly. "I'll be the lawyer and

head juryman, anything you want, the whole works if you want."

"Well, O. K.," said Katy. "We should call the prosecuting lawyer first, anyway," she said. "So, your witness, Mr. Maloon!" she said. And she gave a resounding blow with her mallet that deafened everybody. Mrs. Carroll came out and sounded taps.

"At last!" said Billy with a pained sigh, and he approached Sergeant Rattray.

Ratty (Greg Goode) cringed.

"Now," said the lawyer, Billy Maloon. "Let's see. . . . I think," he said, "that you'd better give me the two first policemen at the same time, Rattray and Ippolito. If one is guilty, both are. They were together all the time."

So the two first policemen, Greg Goode as Sergeant Rattray and Laura Fabadessa as Ippolito, took the stand, two squares in the cement to the left of the judge.

Judy Fabadessa and June Arp, the two good cellar policemen, innocent of all involvement in the crime, stood smugly by—tinged with envy. Judy wished she had been picked to be one of the first, and, possibly, guilty policemen. But of course big sister Laura got all the good parts. It was so in their home; it was so outside their home, she thought morosely; she made her awful face, though she was trying to break herself of the habit.

Billy laid out his burglar evidence—the screwdriver, all of it, on the curb beneath the high brick wall where he and Connie had been sitting. "Mind them," he said, "while I prove these policemen guilty." He handled his clues fondly.

After all, for some weeks he'd kept them in his pocket; in school Miss Hoppeniemi, his teacher, said he should leave his screwdriver home because once it had gashed his leg, but he did not and she did not insist, for she knew boys like Billy have good reasons for what they do.

Connie moved away from the violent clues; but she said, "O. K., I'll mind them."

"Oyez, oyez, oyez!" said Katy. "Be it known," she said, swinging her robe around her with a grand flourish, "be it known and to all these presents, that these two policemen . . ."

Jonathan stood up. "Excuse me, Your Honor," he said. "I think we should try the real burglars first, the five burglars who we *know* broke into Connie's house. They were there first, and the policemen burglary—if there was one; I'm not at all sure there was—would not have happened if the first real burglary had not paved the way."

Katy was not to be shaken by the great checker player. After all, who was the judge? He or she? "We are trying these policemen first," she said, "because we are." And she went on, "Will the lawyer for the defense kindly take his seat until he is called upon."

Jonathan sat down. He knew she'd fork out one "Katy law" or another if he said any more.

"Oyez, oyez, oyez," said Katy again. "Be it known, and to all these sundries and presents, that these two policemen, defenders of the City of Brooklyn, and of our lives, and of our property, and of our wives, and of our children and dogs and poodles, are accused of stealing Mrs. Ives's diamond ring—an ancient ring, ancestral, and handed down to her from generation to generation, and be it known that they be accused likewise of stealing some ancient watches and cuff links and various other sundries of 'antiquay' and ancient value, handed down through the ages from generation into generation, by the ancestors of Connie Ives."

"It's lucky they did not take the George Washington chair . . ." said Judy Fabadessa with a gasp.

"Yikes!" said Hugsy Goode, half wishing such a thing might have happened, half devastated at the thought of the George Washington chair gone for good.

"O-o-oh!" Everyone gasped. They all knew the George Washington chair, not to sit in it. The Ives should have a rope across it, like in museums, some, who had been to museums, thought.

"Silence!" Katy shouted. Bang! went her gavel. "Your witness, Mr. Maloon."

Billy plunged in. He spoke the way Katy had been

speaking, that is, in the manner, he thought, of Shakespeare. "The awfulness of these policemen's crime," he said, "if crime they did commit, stems—stemmeth not so much from what they tooketh—though that ith—*is* bad enough—god wot," he said, "but stemmeth from the fact that they are *policemen* . . . a sergeant, Rattray, and an officer, Ippolito; and they are supposed to do no wrong, to set a good example. Also—consider the low nature of their crime, if crime it was—I know, Arp, not proven yet. . . . Well, they came into a house already broken into by those five real burglars, cowering there, shaking with fear, and swiftly—no, taking their time—pretending to see what, if anything had been stolen, they helped themselves to ring and hairlooms! What a cheap and cowardly thing to do! How low can one fall? The others, the real robbers, had already *done* the dirty and the dangerous work—mashing in the door, giving the bone to the sad dog, Wags. Then and only then, after the path had been cleared for them, then did these two scavengers take the leavings—the best of all as it happens—take what the five first and real robbers, who were really entitled to it, if someone were to have it, had not had time to find. These two fine . . . ahem . . . specimens of our police force should—if it be burglars that they be wanting to be and not officers of the law—strip themselves of their uniforms, their badges, and their clubs, and become real burglars . . . smash in their own doors, not go sneaking around after the smashing has been done and getting the best of it all!"

"Excellent," said the judge. "Do you admit your guilt?" she asked the first two policemen.

"No, Your Honor," they said.

"Your witnesses, Mr. Stuart," said the judge.

"I pass," said Jonathan. "Call the real burglars," he said. He really thought that first burglars should come first, Judge Katy Starr or no Judge Katy Starr, and seconds come second.

A murmur of disapproval ran through the courtroom. After all, why not at least *question* the two who were already on the stand? In trials like this, in the Alley, anyone might disappear suddenly for the rest of the day, have to go to the dentist, or to the doctor's for a check-up, or to visit a relative—a grandmother. Yet all that Lawyer Stuart could say was, "Call the real burglars!" He should have questioned the two policemen about lots of things—why they had stayed upstairs so long while Mrs. Ives and Connie were talking to Charlotte Stuart, why Connie's mother had had this powerful feeling, as though she heard a voice saying, "They have it, they have it." He should make excuses for them . . . he was their lawyer . . . see that they got off . . . explain everything convincingly . . . temporary insanity—something!

"Call the real robbers," Lawyer Stuart repeated, unshaken.

"He probably has a good reason," they all decided, though not being able to imagine what.

So Katy Starr called the five real first main robbers. "Five real robbers to the witness stand," she said.

The five hopped up eagerly. ("Shows they're guilty, or they would not have answered to the word 'robbers,'" said Billy bitingly.) Ray Arp, the bullet-head man, Hugsy

Goode, Arnold Trickman, Brother Stuart, and Stephen Carroll, all five filed to the stand. Some hung their heads in shame; others stared about belligerently with their lips stuck out.

"Do you solemnly swear to tell the truth, the whole truth, the real truth, and nothing but the truth?" asked the judge sternly.

Holding their hands over the grade-six speller, the accused five said, "We do. Aye, aye."

"You don't say, 'Aye, aye,'" admonished Lawyer Stuart. "You just say, 'Yes, Your Honor,' please. You are ignorant burglars. If you were not ignorant, you would not be in this sort of work. 'Aye, aye' sounds nautical, not like Brooklyn burglar talk."

"Could be burglars of the Brooklyn Navy Yard," suggested Hugsy hoarsely. "Picked up the language there."

Connie put in, "If the burglars prove to be related to the bullet-head man who stopped Mama and me the day of de Gaulle, they were not ignorant men, they were educated men; they had probably been through high school if not college—perhaps, Grandby. Who knows?"

"Might be professors here?" asked Hugsy.

"Come, come," said Mr. Stuart impatiently. "College degrees or not—that will come out in the trial—just try not to be nautical, try to be educated Brooklyn burglars," he said to the five.

"Nay," said they.

Jonathan sighed. He liked for things to be right—right language to fit a character—Brooklyn language for Brooklyn burglars, nautical language for pirates and sailors.

As for him, he tried to speak like Chief Justice Warren, to set the right tone. You could see that he was disgusted with the ayes and nays and with other stupidities—no Attorney General, for example. "Where were you between the hours of twelve and one on Saturday, May the fifteenth," he asked, "Alumni Day on the campus of Grandby College?"

"In the Alley," the five said. "Oh no, beg pardon, sir. We was on Story Street."

The listeners gasped. What could be more incriminating? Story Street was the street of the Iveses, the Stuarts—the Fabadessas, too, for that matter.

"Hm-m-m," said Jonathan. "This looks bad for you, Five Men, because Story Street is the seat of the crime."

"Scene," corrected the judge.

"Seat," repeated Jonathan firmly.

"Never heard of 'seat of crime,'" said Katy.

"Oh, all right, scene of crime if you must," said Jonathan, somewhat rattled. (He was rattled because, so far, his questions were proving these men guilty instead of not guilty as he was supposed to do.) To do better, Jonathan swung suddenly around. He knew to do this from watching the Perry Mason show. Then he grabbed the screwdriver from where it lay beside Billy, and he said, "You don't recognize this screwdriver named 'Stanley,' do you?"

"Nay," said the five.

"Your Honor," said Jonathan, addressing the judge. "You see? These five innocent men, dragged here to court in the prosecutor's hope of solving the crime speedily—politics! politics!—do not impress me as being guilty. Let them go, Your Honor. Let them go back to their peaceful pursuits and ways of life, their children, their wives, their trades, their work. They do not recognize the screwdriver named 'Stanley.' "

"Objection, Your Honor," said Billy Maloon, springing to his feet.

"Sustained," said the judge. "We shall now hear from the prosecutionating lawyer, Mr. (roars of laughter here) Maloon." (Well, Billy was awfully little for his age and once, on a broiling day, had come out in a snowsuit. No one had ever forgotten that.)

Billy blushed. Trembling with excitement, he said, "First of all, Your Honor, I want to point out that it is highly irregular (he had a television set, too, and knew as much as Jonathan Stuart about how to act in a courtroom) it's irregular for a lawyer on the other side to grab and hold up for the court things which the prosecution was going to present as evidence to prove his man, or his five men, guilty. I take time out from my prosecution of the five men to charge Mister Stuart, the state's lawyer, with contempt of court. Seizing pieces of evidence, right and left, before I can even present them," he added in disgust.

"You are *correct*," said the judge. "Consider yourself reprimanded," she said to Jonathan.

Jonathan said, " 'Let the punishment fit the crime,' " and he did a short Gilbert and Sullivan jig. No one particularly liked it; in fact, June and Laura, two G.G.C. girls, exchanged glances of derision.

"Be more careful," said Katy. "No more snatching evidence that doesn't belong to you, Mr. Stuart."

Then the trial went on.

"Now," said Billy Maloon in a cool voice. "Do you or do you not recognize this weapon?"

"That's right," thought Connie. "A screwdriver can be a weapon, you know. If the burglars had found someone in the house, they might have hit him with it. Supposing Nanny had been home? Dear darling Nanny! She almost always was here, and the burglar with the screwdriver might have hit her. Thank goodness, she had been in the South then, and still was, writing letters every day—or a card—about her silver, to count it and be sure it really was all still intact—not a pickle fork or anything missing. Wasn't it lucky that the burglars had not taken any of Nanny's silver? That would have killed her, just plain killed her. 'Oh!' she would have screamed (Connie could hear her now), 'Percy's silver! Dear Percy's silver!' Well, they hadn't. 'Too hard to get rid of flat silver,' the detectives had said when Nanny wrote to ask why no one—burglars, real or otherwise—had taken her flat silver. 'The silver is most unusual and very valuable—priceless!' she wrote. It almost sounded as though her feelings had been hurt because none of the burglars had taken such a valuable collection, as though they did not think it valuable at all, passing it over like that for suits and coats. 'Oh, but then,' she must have told herself, 'they had been interrupted, they had not finished; they might have been *going* to take the silver last, stuff it in some great bag. And the two first policemen, if they were also robbers, they could not very well take all that much silver, her father's loving cup—all. Still, they might have taken one spoon or one fork, a ladle even. 'Count it please.' Her complaints kept on coming. 'Thank merciful heavens they didn't, though,' she hastened to add in a P. S. 'As for the two second policemen—the cellar policemen,' she wrote, 'be sure they did not get into my trunk down there in the cellar—my big black trunk.' She had things there . . . put away there . . . dear Polly's things."

"Nay," said the five, answering Billy Maloon. "We told the other guy 'Nay,' and it's 'Nay' to you, too. We do not recognize the tool." Ray Arp did the talking for all of them —a miracle, for Hugsy Goode loved to talk.

"Well, remember," said Billy Maloon, "that honesty is the best policy." This remark did not sound like Billy Maloon; it sounded like Jonathan. But that was what Billy said, anyway—a comment made while collecting his wits probably. "Are you sure that you do not recognize this screwdriver?" he went on. He was needling them, trying to unnerve them. "Is it yours? Or yours, or yours, or yours? Yours? You are under oath, you know, to tell the whole truth."

"Is it marked 'Stanley'?" asked Ray Arp. (Perhaps he wanted the trial to get over with now, asking such a silly question, so that he could go to the athletic field and play soccer.)

"It's marked 'anley,'" said Billy. "But there is part of an 'S' and part of a 't,' and the bits of this screwdriver that Connie, my client, found on the floor by the door do show that the screwdriver's name was 'Stanley.'"

"If the parts fit and they are marked 'Stanley,' then it is ours," said Ray Arp.

Lawyer Stuart shouted, "Objection!"

"Objection sustained," said Judge Starr. "We don't have time for jigsaw puzzles in the courtroom."

Bellows of laughter greeted this witticism. "All right," said Billy, reddening. "But, Your Honor, this burglar . . ."

"Objection," said Jonathan, flushed with victory. "Character besmirched. Can't call Arp a burglar until it's proven Arp is a burglar."

"Sustained," said the judge.

"All right then," said Billy Maloon. "This 'guy' confesses that he had a screwdriver named 'Stanley' and that since the parts fit, he admits it belonged to him. Your Honor, I charge this man with breaking into Connie Ives's house on the fifteenth of May, a Saturday with the intention of stealing whatever he could steal."

"Objection," said Arnold Trickman, the second of the five burglars on the witness stand.

"You are not supposed to say 'objection,'" snapped the judge. "Your lawyer is."

Jonathan jumped to his feet. "Objection," he said. "Now, Trickman, what's on your mind?"

"There are many screwdrivers named 'Stanley,'" said Arnold with a few grunts thrown in, such as he imagined burglars (forgetting these were educated ones) might punctuate their talk with.

Everyone was astonished. No wonder Arnold was in R. A., knowing a fact that no one else had known.

"Objection sustained," said the judge. "Inconclusive evidence," she snapped. "Many screwdrivers named 'Stanley.'"

"All right, then," said Billy Maloon in a smooth and

confident voice that could be heard distinctly by everybody. He reached down for clue number two—the Mura butt. Holding it up carefully (he kept it in a plastic wrapping, not to ruin it), he said, "What sort of cigarettes do you smoke, any of you?"

A howl of laughter greeted this question. "Once I smoked a grapeleaf one," said Hugsy Goode. "It nearly killed me," and he rolled on the ground, clasping his stomach.

"I happen to smoke 'Muras,'" said Ray Arp. "That's what my father smokes, and so that's what I smoke."

"Could this be one of your butts?" asked Billy.

"Nay," said Ray. "I only smoked one once, and that was New Year's Eve, not Alumni Day."

"All right, then," said Billy Maloon, undaunted. "Now, may I see your hands, your right hand and your left hand, please?" he said. It was clear Billy had something up his sleeve that would clinch everything. "Arp, hold up your hands."

At first Arp hid his hands behind him. A hush settled over the courtroom. Then slowly, first-burglar Arp held up his two bare hands. There were cuts on both. How convenient that he had been chosen to be robber number one! Just yesterday he had cut himself on the top of his fence on the way up to his tree.

"Your Honor," said Billy Maloon triumphantly. "View this piece of curtain. View the bloodstains on it. The bloodstains were put there by the defendant, who had cut himself with his tool named 'Stanley' when he broke down the door. He then dropped his cigarette (he lies, I think, when he says he has smoked only one in his life), and then he placed his bleeding hand on the curtain upstairs in Mr. Ives's dressing room. I charge this man with being the main man of the crime and these four others with being his accomplices, asking Mr. Fabadessa questions about who lives where and being the lookout guys, some across the street and some—one, anyway—in the getaway car . . . probably had his foot over the accelerator all the time, ready to whisk them all away . . ."

"That was me," said Brother Stuart, who was crazy about cars and knew the make of all of them, this year's, last year's, any year's . . . and whether it was a foreign one or what, even an ancient Stutz.

At this moment, much to everybody's disgust, for of course he *would* stop and listen, who should come walking along No-Name Street but Bully Vardeer. He had his *boulevardier* sort of hat on, tipped in his certain way on the back of his head, and he was walking his tan dog named Prince. Instead of walking right on past, as most people had, he stopped to listen and laugh and make soft, sarcastic comments, good-natured but bothersome. Evidently he thought the trial was "cute." Everyone tried to ignore him. Even Billy Maloon, somewhat shy at having an extra in the audience, went staunchly on.

"And, Your Honor," said Billy, "I say the blood on the curtain was from Arp's cut hand . . ."

Just then, on the other side of the fence, on No-Name Street, another person's footsteps came briskly along. Everyone hoped that this person, whoever he was, would not stand and gawk, too, as Bully Vardeer had. And at first, the person went past. But then he stopped short and came back. The smell of his cigarette was wafted into the Alley, into the courtroom scene going on in the Circle. "Mura," whispered Billy Maloon. "Yes," said Ray, the smoker of one cigarette—a Mura. Bully Vardeer was standing exactly where the tall brick wall ended. The new person came and stood beside him, where he could see into the Circle and also be seen by those inside. Connie was sitting on the curb near the end of the brick wall. She couldn't see the new man very well—her back was to him— but she could hear him. She—everybody—heard his rather crisp, well-spoken voice, say, "Hm. Nice dog. What kind is he? Unusual . . ."

Connie's heart felt as though it had turned over. The voice of the man was that of the person who had spoken to her and Mama and Wagsie on the day of de Gaulle; and the words spoken were almost identical. Connie slowly turned into a position so that she could see the man. He was a rather small man with a bullet-shaped head. He was holding his hand out to Prince. "Nice doggie, good doggie," he said to Prince. And to Bully Vardeer he said, "Does this dog bite?"

12

✹ ✹ ✹

BULLY VARDEER AND THE
BULLET-HEAD MAN

"Bite?" Bully Vardeer's low, drawling voice could plainly be heard in the Circle, where silence had fallen. "Does this dog bite? Princey? Eh, Princey? How about it? Do you bite? She's pretty friendly," he said to the man. "But . . ."

Though frozen with terror, Connie caught Billy's attention. She beckoned to him to sit down beside her—even though he was in the middle of proving the pretend bullet-head man, Ray Arp, guilty. "Billy," she said. "See that man talking to Bully Vardeer? Hear him? It is the bullet-head man, the real one, not the Ray Arp one."

Billy Maloon sank to the curbing and sat beside Connie. He was so tense, he was stiff. The rest of the children probably did not suspect that the real-life burglar, one of them, anyway, might be standing this very minute on the other side of the red brick Alley wall. It did not occur to them, probably, that if this new man were one of the burglars, he was talking to Bully Vardeer just to get the low-down on *his* dog, as he had on Wags on the day of de

Gaulle. However, the children suspended their game—the trial—until the big people would go away, because they did not like an audience. They wrote things on the sidewalk, assumed blank expressions, and hoped for the speedy departure of both men.

Out of the corner of her eye, Connie saw the man's foot. Sitting so close to the shoe of the bullet-head man made her quite uneasy. But if she moved, he might notice her— recognize her. "Hm," he might say to himself. "There's that girl who lived in that house I broke into. I didn't realize this was such a tight little Alley, everyone knowing everyone else. Hm. I better keep my eye on her!" And then! If Katy went on with the trial and he heard himself—Ray—being tried, what might he not do? Mow them all down, something!

Billy gave Connie a nudge. "Smell this," he whispered.

He had the old Mura butt in the palm of his hand. Connie smelled it; but it just smelled like any kind of old burnt-out cigarette to her. "Now smell the cigarette smoke from that man," Billy said. Connie sniffed. "Are they the same?" Billy demanded. Connie shrugged. She didn't know.

"Watch the guy," said Billy Maloon, "and see where his cigarette butt lands if he throws it away when he leaves."

Connie nodded. Bully and the bullet-head burglar-man had strolled a few steps down No-Name Street. By just turning her head slightly, Connie could now see both of them plainly and also Princey, who was interested in the man and kept smelling his pocket and wagging his tail. The men were chatting jovially about dogs—what dogs bite and what dogs don't. At any moment, Connie thought she might hear the bullet-head man tell about his little girl—how he had had to get rid of his cocker spaniel because she had bitten his little girl.

Gradually, the other children became aware of the tension in the air. One look at Connie and Billy gave them the impression that they should be smelling a rat. Almost every person in the trial in the Circle cast a glance at Bully Vardeer and the bullet-head man. No one said a word; their faces remained blank. Connie couldn't tell whether or not any of them realized that the man talking to Bully Vardeer might be burglar number one. Who knows? They might all have forgotten the part of the burglar story that dealt with events leading up to the day itself—the loose-stocking lady . . . the beautiful-mansions man, all of it. Anyway, thank goodness, no one—not even Hugsy Goode, who was apt to blurt out whatever comes into his mind—said one common word and spilled the beans to bullet-head that they had his number.

Evidently, Katy, the judge, may have begun to realize a connection. She pretended to be examining her speller. After a while, to throw the bullet-head man off the track so that he would not suspect that, at this very moment, one of them, Ray Arp, was impersonating him and being the burglar, number-one suspect on trial in the Alley, Katy said, "Soon the spelling bee will begin. I want you all to think— just think," she admonished. "Remember, 'i before e except after c.'"

Complete silence met Katy's words. Hugsy, however, had not gotten it clear. "Bee?" he said. "I thought this was a trial."

But Katy stopped him with an awful look. "You want to be put out of the G.G.C.?" she hissed. "Just be quiet, you."

Hugsy—everybody—was quiet. Again words spoken between Bully Vardeer and the bullet-head man could plainly be heard.

"What kind of dog is that?" asked the bullet-head man. His voice had a sort of squeak.

"Oh, just any old kind of dog," said Bully good-naturedly. "Mainly terrier, I think."

"That so? We had a dog once, not too long ago . . . mainly terrier, too. Mainly just dog, ha-ha. Had to get rid of him, though. Bit. Yes, I'm sorry to say he bit my little girl's hand. She was just sitting in her high chair, reaching out to pet him. . . . Of course, we could not keep a dog like that. Had to give him away. Ah, yes. Your dog do a thing like that?"

("Ts," thought Connie. "*Lies* as well as *steals*. First it was a spaniel; now it's any old dog . . . mainly terrier.")

"Princey? Bite? Oh, no," said Bully Vardeer. "Not a member of his family—I don't know about strangers."

The man held out his hand to Princey, open so that Princey could sniff it, get acquainted—get to know it. He even patted Princey's head. "Good dog," he said. "Nice doggie. You like me, don't you?"

Princey wagged his tail. He liked the man very much.

Bully Vardeer said thoughtfully. "I do think, though, that Princey would bite anybody that tried to hurt any of us."

"Ah," said the man smoothly. "You have little ones, and he likes the little ones, eh? Not like my bad little fellow. 'Scrappy' his name was."

"My little one is hardly 'little,'" said Bully. "My son, though only thirteen, is already six feet tall."

"Can you imagine!" thought Connie. "Bully Vardeer is giving away his whole life story, just about, to this man who is—I'm sure he is—the number-one burglar on trial right now in this Alley, Ray Arp." However, she was mesmerized by the conversation. "Am I dreaming?" she asked herself. "Hearing practically the same things said again as were said before to Mama and me, except now his dog's name is 'Scrappy,' not 'Goldy,' and is 'he' not 'her.'"

"Well," said the stranger. "We, as I say, had to get rid of Scrappy. . . . Nice dogs as a rule, though, mongrels are. Bright, oh, very bright. Hard to outwit them."

"The hipe-o-crite!" thought Connie.

Then the bullet-head man drew a milk-bone dog cooky out of his pocket and gave it to Prince. "Oh," thought Connie. "How mean! Deceiving dogs right and left like that." She wanted to say, "Princey! Don't eat it!" She wanted to yell, "Hey! Help! Police! There's a thief here!" But, of course, she did not dare. This burglar-number-one man might kill them all! Anyway, where are the police when you want them? Up in an attic, perhaps, or down in a cellar, looking for things real burglars don't take. Can you trust the police? Of course, usually. But can you trust Sergeant Rattray and Officer Ippolito? Ah. That is what this trial in the Alley was going to prove, if only they could get on with it.

Then Billy gave Connie a nudge and muttered, "Turn around." Turning her head slightly, Connie noticed that the bullet-head man had put his hand casually, as though to rest it a moment, on the wire fence that began where the high brick wall ended. On this hand—it was his right hand— there were fresh, not completely healed scars! Well! Proof piling on proof! This must be the hand that had held the tool named "Stanley" and had broken into her house. Connie was positive . . . she was just as sure about this hand and "Stanley" as her mother had been about seeing her ring through the policeman's pocket.

"If only we could get a sample of his blood," murmured Billy, "and compare it with the curtain evidence."

"How brave Billy is!" Connie marveled. "He trembles, but he is brave. Bright, too, though not in the R. A."

As if in answer to Billy's prayers, the man whose hand

was lightly resting on top of the fence, not realizing how jagged the barbed wire was, gave the fence a sudden shake—perhaps he wanted to test the fence for strength in case of future break-ins—and he gashed his hand. "Ouch!" he exclaimed.

Bully handed him a piece of tissue. "I always have some of this in my pocket. I'm a painter, you know."

The man took it and dabbed at his scratched hand. Then, in spite of the do-not-litter sign, "Keep Our Campus Clean," he threw the tissue away. ("Educated man, hah!" thought Connie. "He thieves, he lies, he litters.")

The tissue began to blow away, but Connie watched it—where it blew. And then—still more luck—the man threw down his cigarette. This started rolling after the tissue in the slight easterly breeze.

"Well," said bullet-head. "Have to chug along now," he said jovially to Bully Vardeer. "Nice talking to you. And nice meeting you, too, puppy—what did you say his name is?"

"Princey," answered Bully in his slurry, slow, sentimental voice. "Just Princey."

"By-by, Princey," said the awful man. Finally he, the bullet-head man, burglar (Connie was sure) number one, disappeared behind the Sholes' house, the last one on the Alley. He was whistling, as he went, "On the Street Where You Live." You could hear him for a long time in the distance.

Bully Vardeer then sauntered away in the other direction with his dog, Princey, in his usual carefree way, hat tipped back, and swaying slightly as though strolling along the banks of the Seine; he was not in the least aware that he had been having a friendly conversation with a burglar.

Well, the fresh clues! Connie was too scared to go out of the Alley to get them—the new cigarette butt and the tissue —to compare with the old clues. But Billy Maloon wasn't scared. "He doesn't know *me*," he said. "I'll go." And he walked, not ran, down the Alley, disappeared around the Carrolls' house, and crawled, probably—they could not see him, of course—under the iron gate. Soon, there he was, standing outside on the other side of the fence on No-Name Street.

Now, the other children in the Circle, who had been waiting and waiting for the two grownups to go away so they could get on with the trial, said, "What's going on, anyway?" No one, except possibly Katy, had taken in the significance of the bullet-head man and his dog questions. They had just thought he was a regular person, not a burglar—a nuisance, standing there talking so long.

Katy said, "Billy! You come right back in here or you can't continue being the main lawyer."

Connie waited for Billy to come back before making the announcement that a burglar had been standing there, and Billy did not bother to answer Katy. He walked slowly up No-Name Street, looking for the new clues. "There they are," Connie said. "There, Billy." She had scarcely taken her eyes off the butt and tissue for one minute, lest they be lost forever. Billy picked them up and came back the way he had gone, taking his time as usual.

"That is the way to build up suspense," thought Connie.

"Take Hugsy! Hugsy would have run every inch and probably lost the clues, the new ones and the old ones—some of them, anyway—so that no one would know which was which."

Everyone gathered around Billy, who sat down next to Connie with his new things. "What's up, anyway?" asked Jonathan, exasperated. "We're playing a game, you know."

"Billy and I think," said Connie, "that that man who was talking to Bully Vardeer was the real number-one burglar . . ."

"Then, who am I?" interrupted Ray Arp.

"You are him," said Billy. "Now we'll compare the evidences, the new and the old," he said.

No breeze was blowing in the Alley, for they were protected by the high brick wall. Billy took his first almost worn-out butt and placed it on the curb beside him.

"See this butt?" he said to Katy and all the others, who were pressing around curiously. "Well," said Billy, "this butt is named 'Mura.' It is a Turkish cigarette, not very well known now, but my father says it was quite common when he was a boy—he used to collect empty Mura boxes because they are very pretty."

"My father smokes them," Ray interrupted.

"Yes," said Billy. "He's the only one I know who does except for you know who. Now, here," he said. "Here's butt number two—the butt that that man who was just talking to Bully Vardeer threw on the ground. We will now see what brand *it* is. M U R A—Mura! That is what *it* is!"

A Mura butt . . . two Mura butts—the old one dating from the day of Connie's burglary and the new one dating from right now, seen by both Connie and Billy first being smoked and then being thrown down by the bullet-head man, asker of the question—they had all heard it— "Does this dog bite?" This bullet-head and the old bullet-head man were the same person—going around asking the same old question.

When Billy with Connie's help explained this, astonishment swept over the children. Confusion burst out. Here they were, holding a make-believe trial in the Alley, and then who should come marching along outside the Alley and outside the game but the real burglar whose part was being played by Ray Arp. Then they all began to feel afraid. Hugsy climbed the Stuarts' catalpa tree to see if the bullet-head man had really gone.

"Oh, come," said Jonathan. "You can't see over the houses on Waldo Place from up there, Hugsy!"

June said, "Well, I'll have to have more proof than this— that that man and Connie's burglar man are the same." You would think she was the judge and not Katy!

"June," said Katy severely. "The trial is not over yet. And you are not supposed to make any comments."

"And, Your Honor," said Billy, paying no attention to the interruptions, "you see this piece of tissue that the man wiped his hand with just now when he scratched it on the bobb wire? And you see this piece of evidence that I've produced in my charge against the first burglar, this bloodstained piece of curtain evidence? Well, I submit, Your Honor, that the blood is the same!"

A murmur ran through the courtroom. "That's not scientifically proven, lawyer," said Judge Starr. "I can't take your word that the blood is the same just because you think it is the same, on account of what you're deducing from Wagsie, and Princey, and Muras, and all. I can't do that, you know. What kind of judge would I be if I did that?"

"A loused-up one," said Hugsy.

"No one asked *you*," said Judge Starr. "So, how are you going to prove it?"

Billy was silent.

But Connie was not. "Under the microscope!" she said. "Under my microscope!" She was excited. She had gotten a microscope for Christmas. With its help, she had made a science project on different types of blood cells—rabbits, mice, chickens—no humans, but does that matter? So she knew how to look at cells. Connie did not like science very much; but she did like making that report on cells and she got an A on it. Still, Mr. Crawley gave her a C in science on her report card—not very good at all. And there! She had spent all of Christmas vacation doing the science report. Connie's mother said that was really not fair—getting an A on her project but a C on her report card. But Connie shrugged it off. She had liked doing the report.

Anyway, she thought that she had had enough experience with examining blood cells to see if the curtain specimen matched the tissue specimen—if she could bear to touch them! She said, "Wait while I go and get my microscope." She would make the comparison right here so all could take a look—all would know that no question of scientific accuracy would be left unanswered.

"All right, Miss Ives, you may go," said the judge.

Like Billy, Connie did not run; she walked with dignity

to her house, went upstairs, and got her microscope and slides. She returned to the court in the Circle and set the microscope on top of the flattest garbage pail. "Only Billy and I can handle this," she said. "Afterwards, you can take turns and look, but not touch it." Some of them might accidentally break the microscope in a second, especially Ray or Hugsy, who moved so quickly always.

Billy tore off a tiny piece of curtain evidence and put it on one slide, and he put a tiny piece of tissue evidence on another slide. Then Connie, squinting, looked in with one eye. "Don't lean all over me, Hugsy," she said. "Get off my back," she said. "And don't breathe down my neck, and don't breathe away the evidence." They all backed off, and Connie studied the two slides.

"Hm-m-m," she said. "Just as I thought. These two bloods are the same. That man that was just here *is* burglar number one. We should warn Bully Vardeer. The bullet-head man might be robbing his house this second!"

Everybody gasped. "Let me take a look at the slides," said Billy Maloon. Naturally, since he was Connie's lawyer he had to know what was what, too. He was no better than Connie in science in school. But outside of school, he was excellent in it. The moon was Billy's specialty, not blood. Still, he scrutinized the specimens coolly and with scientific detachment. "The same!" he said at last, agreeing with Connie, the cell specialist.

"The same! The same!" everybody exclaimed.

Hugsy politely asked to take a look. In science Hugsy concentrated on "insectae" as he called them. "Latina," he said. It might be. Connie hadn't had Latin yet. But then, neither had Hugsy. Connie let him examine the precious slides. "All right, but be careful," she said, remembering how Hugsy accidentally broke almost everything he came in contact with. Then all the children wanted to take a look. "Line up," said Connie. "Line up the way you do to look at the stars through Professor Goode's telescope."

Each one looked, and each one exclaimed, "The same! The same!"

Connie was proud and excited! This was almost as good as the day of the burglary itself. Then, Hugsy—honestly, Hugsy! What do you think he did? He took the new clue, the piece of tissue, and by means of a small magnifying glass that he always carried around with him, he started to burn up this important piece of evidence with the sun's rays!

"Hugsy!" said Billy. "Are you crazy? We need that to show detectives when we have the chance, to prove that this blood and the curtain blood are the same." Fortunately, only a faint fringe of brown had scorched the edges.

"Oh," said Hugsy. "I'm sorry. I thought you had already proved it!"

"I've proved it to us," said Billy, "but not to real detectives. We have to prove it to them if we ever have the chance."

Hugsy was ashamed. He had very good manners. "I'm sorry," he said again huskily. "I thought we were all real."

"Whee-ee." The judge sighed. "This trial is getting out of hand. It's all mixed up. Nobody knows any more whether they are real or not, ever since that real—perhaps— burglar came along. Why did he have to come along, anyway, and spoil a good game? We haven't finished the trial at all; we don't know what to think yet about the diamond ring and seeing through pockets and all. Here we are, holding one trial for one burglary—Connie's—and at the same time a new burglary may be being burglared down at Bully Vardeer's house. The crook policemen . . . if they are crooks . . . may soon be there, too, raking in their haul, their rings and things."

"How?" asked Greggie Goode. "How can I be robbing Bully Vardeer's house and at the same time be on trial here for robbing Connie's house?"

"That's what I mean," agreed Katy. "We're all mixed up, myself as well as you, Sergeant Rattray." ("Ts," thought Connie. "It's awful to have a judge mixed up.") "We'll recess," said Katy, "until after we find out more about what's going on. Let's go down to Bully Vardeer's house."

Everybody, with studied casualness, in case some accomplice of the bullet-head man had his eyes on them from somewhere, meandered with many stops and starts to Bully Vardeer's end of the Alley. They turned the corner of the T, and they reached the iron gate. All were scared, but they crowded to the iron gate, pressed against it and looked right and left as far as they could. They waited and they watched. Billy climbed the catalpa tree in Mr. Bernadette's yard to see if he could see anything. "Nothing doing. No sign of bullet-head," he said, "or of any lookout men—nothing!"

Then, along came Bully Vardeer, back from his walk with Prince, carefree, hat set on the back of his head, jaunty, in the true *boulevardier* fashion. He was completely unaware that he might have been burglarized—or was being considered for a burglary. He said good-naturedly, "Ho-ho! Moved up to my end of the Alley, eh? No bouncing balls now on the wall. I'm going to take a sunbath." And he went into his house with Prince, into their—it must have been—unbroken-into house, for there were no exclamations of shock, surprise, or cries of "Help, help, police!" And he went straight through his house and out the back door and sat down on the top step.

Judy Fabadessa said, "Oo-oo-oh! We should tell Mr. Below—tell him he's been talking to a burglar." Her enormous gray eyes looked larger than ever. All the children agreed that Bully Vardeer must be told that a short time ago he had been talking to burglar number one of the famous Ives's burglary, warn him that the dog conversation he had had with a stranger was the beginning of his house being cased . . as it had been of the Ives's . . . and that the next thing he knew he might be broken into. Yes, he must be told, or they would be as bad as Mrs. Fabadessa in the kitchen or Mr. Fabadessa and the missionaries.

"You're the judge," said Billy. "You have your judge's robe on, Katy, so you tell him."

"No. Connie must," said Katy. "She's the one who knows the burglar."

In the end, Billy, being the lawyer, did the talking.

"Mr. Below," he said. Billy did not like to speak to grownups; but he had the clues, and these gave him courage. "Mr. Below," he said. The children had entered Bully's garden, not boisterously—quietly and in orderly procession.

"Yes, Billy," said Bully Vardeer, opening one eye. He always closed his eyes immediately on going out in order to get every bit of the sun's rays, even on his eyelids.

Billy spoke rapidly in a low, tense monotone. "You know that man," he said, "that you were talking to just now? The man with the round bullet-head who asked you, 'Does this dog bite?' Well, Connie and I think that he is one of the men, the main man, probably, of the bunch of burglars who broke into Connie's house on Alumni Day. He may be casing your house, him, he—and his other guys—men. He may be watching you right now, from somewhere, to see what time of day you go out walking Princey and what time you come in. He wanted to know if your dog is a friendly one or not, just as he did Connie and her mother about Wags. That man said to Connie and her mother the very same words he said to you, 'Does this dog bite?' "

Bully suddenly opened his eyes wide. His pointed, bushy eyebrows went way up on his forehead, and his pointed ears took in every word. He pressed his lips tightly together, which is the way he thought. Unlike some grownups who say "pooh-pooh" and walk off thinking that children do not know what they are talking about, he said, "Oh, yes, Billy? That's terrible!" He showed respect; he listened.

"Yes," said Billy. "We have evidence. You better keep on the watch, and you'd better keep your outer green door locked. Maybe you should have a burglar alarm put on your house—we're going to—and perhaps put a bucket of water over the door . . ."

"You are!" said Bully. "Well . . ." he said. "Thanks for

the tip. I'll be on the lookout." And he closed his eyes again, his eyelids being the only untanned part of him.

It put a damper on the proceedings to see Bully Vardeer go to sleep, so Katy said, "Recess until after lunch. Court dismissed!" she said. She hiked her father's robe up—not to get it any dustier—and she and everyone went home to lunch.

"Mama?" said Connie, going into the kitchen.

"Yes, darling?" said Mama.

"Mama, listen," said Connie. Connie told her mother about the bullet-head man, Bully Vardeer, Princey, the trial —everything.

Mama listened intently. She was very disturbed. *She* didn't close her eyes—go to sleep in the sunshine. Whenever Mama got disturbed over anything, Connie got calm. "Don't worry," she said reassuringly. "We will finish the trial this afternoon and then decide what to do."

"Well, I'll tell your father the minute he gets home and see what *he* wants to do," said Mama. "But," she added, "the minute you see that bullet-head man again, you come and see me. You should have done that this morning."

"We couldn't interrupt the trial," said Connie, pouring catsup on her beans. "Woops!" she said. "Too much!" Then she had some blueberry pie, and then she sat in her little red rocker and had some more conversation with Mama about the microscope and the clues. "You should have gotten A in science," her mother said. It was a wonderful conversation, and Connie regretted that soon she would have to go back outside and finish the trial. But she did—Billy Maloon came for her and they swung until everyone came back out to the Circle.

"Swingers!" said June with a sneer when she came out and saw them. "She has forgotten that we are all friends now," thought Connie, "that the burglary and the trial have made us all friends—big girls and little girls, G.G.C. or not G.G.C., boys . . . all are friends now."

13
↯ ↯ ↯
WINDING UP THE TRIAL

"Recess is over. The trial will now resume," said Katy. "All burglars back to the witness stand, please. Now, as we were saying when Bully Vardeer and the real burglar . . ."

"Sh-sh-sh . . ." said Connie. "He might be coming along again . . ."

"True," said Judge Starr, more than a little scared herself. She lowered her voice and said, "Your witnesses, Mr. Maloon."

"Yes, Your Honor," said Billy. "The defendants have already admitted having been on Story Street at the hour of the burglary, and owning 'Stanley,' and smoking a 'Mura,' and scratching their hands from breaking down the door— all more than enough to send these five men to Sing Sing. I accuse burglar number one, him—he—with the scratches on his hand (yeh, you, Arp) of doing the actual breaking in of the Ives's house." Then, pointing his finger at all five burglars, he said, "Did you or did you not break into the house of these innocent Ives people? Take all their things, suits, antiques, silver dollars, diamond ring?"

The five burglars hung their heads. Though they aimed to look ashamed, they were sniggering. The first one, Ray Arp, was finally able to speak. "True," he said. "We have to confess—the evidence being so exclusive—"

"*Con*clusive!" corrected Laura Fabadessa.

". . . confess that we did, yes we did, break into the house on Story Street, marked on the door Number 175. But we didn't take no . . ."

"Didn't take any . . ." corrected Laura.

"Silence in the courtroom!" said Katy, whamming down her gavel.

"But," Ray went on, "we didn't take *no* diamond ring, and we didn't take *no* antique watches and *no* studs and *no* any such things. I wish we had tooken, but we hadn't tooken them. Sawtooth Pete—he was one of the guys outside, across the street—well, he give the signal that the kid and her maw had been sighted. That's when I got the blood on the curtain, looking out at him, at Sawtooth Pete." (Ray had to repeat the made-up name because it had proved a great success, having been met with howls of mirth, from Hugsy especially.) "Then, Sawtooth, he started whistling, 'Get Me to the Church on Time.' That was the scat signal— skidoo! The O. K., get-ready-to-bust-in signal is, 'On the Street Where You Live.'" Ray tried to whistle the latter. But since Ray could not carry a tune, you would not have known it from "Get Me to the Church on Time."

"No whistling in the courtroom," said the judge.

". . . so all the loot we got was this crummy antique typewriter that we sold for two bucks . . ."

"Two bucks!" exclaimed Connie. "Why, that is the ancient typewriter of my father that he had in college, that he typed all his homework on, his themes, his papers, a poem —all ! He had just given it to me for my own . . ."

"And Mr. Ives's three suits?" Billy suggested coolly.

"Yes," agreed Connie. "And remember, they were brand-new, too, you know. Papa never gets anything for himself; and he always sends back everything that Mama buys for him—says he can get along without this, without that. He has only two pairs of pajamas—he just took *one* pair to Europe with him, said he could wash it out overnight now and then. . . . But one day he just happened to have bought three brand-new suits—they were having a sale at Pete Rogers—we don't know what got into him; he just got them, got three brand-new suits. He hadn't even worn one of them once . . . then, gone!"

"Why didn't he have one of the suits on? On such an important day as Alumni Day under the tents, why didn't he have one of them, at least, on?" asked June Arp crossly.

"Because it would not be seen under an academic robe. Why waste a new suit under a robe?" Connie asked scornfully. She was beginning to be able to stand up to the big girls. How brave the burglary had made her!

"They don't wear suits under robes, anyway, do they?" said Greggie Goode.

"Oh, yes," said Connie. "I think they do. I heard of it somewhere."

"Silence in the courtroom," said Katy again. Turning to Connie, she said, "Complainant, we are trying to recover your possessions for you—at least find out who got what—so please leave Pete Rogers out of this, and all other sidelines. Now, on with the trial-oh! Right, burglars?"

"Aye, aye, sir," said the five burglars. Again everyone was quite mixed up in his speech.

"We got ten bucks each for the suits," said Ray Arp, "because tags, pins, labels, and all them things were still in them. But jewels? We don't know nuttin' about dem jewels. Ask dem dicks dere."

"Dicks" is an underworld word for "cops." Connie knew that. But—what a turn for the trial to be taking! Her burglars were educated ones—not "dese, dem, dat, dere" sort of ones.

"Call the two first policemen to the stand," said Billy.

"Two first policemen to the stand-oh," chanted Judge Starr.

"Heaven's sakes! Now she is being a sailor," thought Connie. "A judge—a sailor!"

Laura Fabadessa and Gregg Goode returned to the stand. They were haughty and tried to look innocent by twiddling their thumbs and scanning the sky. "Your Honor," said Greggie, "this is a disgrace. Two honester policemen can't be found in the entire presink!"

"That may be," said Judge Starr dryly. "But the question today deals with you, you and Officer Ippolito, and not with the 'entire presink.' Did you or did you not take the famous jewels of the Ives family in which family they have reposeth for far longer than thou thinketh, me thinketh. I'll wager ye canst not count back as far as these jewels gothe . . ."

"Gothe?" said Greggie.

"Aye, gothe," said Katy.

"Go-eth," said Laura Fabadessa.

"Go-eth," said Greggie. "But, Your Honor," he said. "I object. No one, not even a judge, can wager in the courtroom. Wagering is betting, and betting is illegal in the presink."

Who would have thought that Greggie Goode, Little Greggie Goode, was so smart? And he wasn't the least bit stuck up. He was embarrassed, almost, by his smartness— didn't run around the Alley, beating his chest, saying, "I got all A's." "He should certainly be put in R. A. when he gets up to grade seven," thought Connie.

"Objection sustained," said Judge Starr.

Billy Maloon put in, "Your Honor. It is the lawyers who make the objections, not the accused."

"Correction sustained," agreed Judge Starr amiably. "I ask you . . ." said Katy, "and mind you—men—you are under oath to tell the truth, the whole truth, and nothing but the truth . . . did you or did you not take the famous Ives jewels? You can be charged with purgatory if you lie."

Laura Fabadessa said coldly, "Perjury."

"Did you take the jewels?" the judge repeated, equally coldly.

Laura and Greggie, defeated, hung their heads. "Aye, aye, sir," they said. (They wanted to go to the Library Park —sit on the cannon—so they had resolved now to admit all and wind up the trial.) "We did."

"You know whereof you speaketh," said the judge. "You will have to go to jail, you knoweth."

"We knoweth whereofeth," said Greggie. He tugged at his signet ring finger to get the ring off. (Wasn't it lucky that Greggie had a ring on? It was a signet ring and it had two capital G's entwining each other on its face, standing for Gregory Goode. He was the only boy in the Alley who owned a ring and it was lucky, though accidental, that he had been selected to play the part of Rattray.) However, hard as he tugged, he could not get the ring off. His mother had said that he would have to go to a blacksmith—if there were any blacksmiths any more—and have it sawed off. Greggie had thought that now, since he was on trial, the ring would come right off. But it didn't. It still stuck.

Then the other policeman, Officer Ippolito (Laura Fabadessa), spoke. She said, "Your Honor. Sergeant Rattray may have stolen the ring. But he lies when he says,

'*We* did. *We* stole it!' I didn't know anything about a ring. I never saw the ring. I never knew there was a ring to steal. I was the one who opened the gift and—what was in it? Soap. I didn't want to smell like lavender and old lace. I didn't see anything worth taking. And I never saw a ring. And, Your Honor, I don't think my partner, Sergeant Rattray, when he stole the pencil, knew he had a ring, too. He thought he only had a pencil. That's my theory, though I am not a detective, just an ordinary cop. It was when Mrs. Ives clutched her heart and said, 'Oh, my ring, my diamond ring!' that he, Ratty, knew he had a hot potato in his pocket."

"That's right," whined Greggie Goode, no longer a proud and bully policeman. "I didn't know I had anything as expensive as a diamond ring. I would never have taken a real ring, Your Honor, only a fake one. I would have putten a real ring right back where I found it, Your Honor. I would only have taken the pencil for my little boy, Danny, for his birthday and putten the ring back. That's all, just for my little Danny boy."

Laura Fabadessa, Officer Ippolito, withered Greggie with her contemptuous stare. "I really didn't know either, Ratty," she said, "that you had a ring. I really didn't know it until the lady screamed, 'My ring, my ring!' Then I had the hunch, just like she did. 'Where was it? Where, where?' I asked. 'On the pencil case,' she uttered. Nearly swooning she was! Shows she really has the knack of seeing through pockets, tell your ma'm," she said in an aside to Connie.

When the laughter subsided, she went on. "And if it

175

hadn't been for the lady spilling the beans that you did have the ring, you would never even have shown it to me—go fifty-fifty, right, Ratty? Right."

"What sayest thee to that, Sergeant Rattray?" asked the judge.

Greggie said, with a modest mien, "I always find the best things, Your Honor. Not to say that Ippolito, Ippy, is stupid, just not so fast at nosing things out as me. In one house that had been broke into right in this neighborhood, too—it was me spotted the new electric razor in the bathroom, passed over by the original burglars, too. But I found it, and I never did say anything to Ippy, no nothing. 'To the victor go the sperls,' I says." Greggie laughed at himself so hard that his skinny little body shook all over.

Laura Fabadessa—Officer Ippolito—gasped at the treachery being unmasked before her.

"Some buddy!" she sneered.

"Strip them of their rank!" ordered the judge. "Let them go to jail like any crooked criminal, they and their sob stories . . . 'didn't mean to do it . . . just thinking of my kiddies!' Defenders of the law! Ha-ha. Some defenders!"

"Defenders of the law! Ha!" echoed Connie, appalled at such wickedness. "He, Ratty, should have given the ring back to Mama, if all he wanted was a pencil for his little Danny boy. But he didn't. He kept it. My!" she said. "You expect real burglars to be wicked—but, *policemen!*"

Billy Maloon put in, "Your Honor, let me remind you that you can't sentence the crooks until the jury says 'Guilty' or 'Not guilty.' "

"You are *right!*" said the judge with a resounding wham of the gavel. "Foreman—head juryman! Step forward!"

Jonathan Stuart stepped forward. He was growing impatient with the whole trial. "Yes, Your Honor?" he said crisply—the way he spoke when he wanted someone to hurry up and make the next move in checkers or chess. "Oh, hurry up!" Trust Jonathan not to get pirate language, medieval language, or any other language mixed up with what he knew was the right language for this occasion, present-day *good* Brooklyn talk—not 'sperl' for 'spoil,' not 'woid' for 'word'—just plain talk.

"See?" said Connie to herself, "what I mean about Jonathan—he is right . . . he is always right . . . alas."

"Foreman," said Katy, "and other gentlemen of the jury . . . and ladies too. I charge you with determining the guilt or the non-guilt of, first, these five burglars, and second, these two policemen, who possibly are common burglars also, but who, worse, masquerade as protectors of the law—come in like scavengers after the real burglars have taken the initial risk of breaking into a house (thus making the job of the policemen easy and enabling them—often—to make off with the best of what's to be had). Weigh the case solemnly," the judge charged the jury, "for justice must be meted and the letter of the law obeyed by hooks or by—*crooks!*" Katy gave a lavish sweep to her grand robe.

Everyone laughed at the pun.

The jury then went into a huddle, which lasted thirty seconds. Jonathan Stuart, the foreman of the jury, jotted down notes in a blue notebook—he always had a pencil—sharp—and a notebook—clean—with him. He stood up, polished his glasses, and then he read the verdict. A hush fell over the whole courtroom in the Circle, even over the little ones crouching at the edge.

"Your Honor," he said. "The verdict is unanimous, and it is . . . *guilty!* The seven, all seven—the five burglars and the two policemen—all, all are guilty! 'Let the punishment fit the crime,'" he said with a squeak and a jump. It was his favorite Gilbert and Sullivan expression. Too bad he didn't have Professor Starr's robe on—he would have looked more comical, Connie thought.

"You have heard the verdict of the jury," said Judge Starr solemnly. "I now impose the sentence. For the first five real burglars—*ten years at hard labor*. For the two despicable policemen—*a stripping of their rank* and *fifteen years at hard labor*."

"Think of our kiddies, of dear Danny boy," said Greggie Goode, the first policeman, throwing himself at the feet of the judge and pretending to be about to swoon.

"You should have thought of dear little Danny boy before you stooped to such a hyena-like crime. Like a vulture, coming in after the kill. Thus didst thou steal, after the house had been broken into. Ah—low, low. How doth the mighty fall, when stoopeth they to vulture-like crime. Now the sentence be imposeth. Now to celleths shall ye goeth. Now ye rippeth what thou sewest . . ."

("Eu*rip*edes, Eum*end*adees," said Billy. It was his favorite saying at this time.)

"Oyez, oyez, oyez," said the judge. "Court is adjourned."

The seven burglars, the five real ones and the two police-men ones, were run off to jail in Hugsy Goode's yard. "Into the pit with you," said Jonathan. It was a tight fit, but the seven fitted. Lucky that at least the only other inmate, Anthony Bigelow, had made a break; he must have had to go to the barber, or else where was he—not spoiling things any more?

"It's like playing 'sardines,'" said Laura with a breath-less giggle as Arnold practically sat on her.

However, they could not stay in jail for long because everybody's parents suddenly, as though they had been given a signal that the trial was over, came to their back stoops and whistled or called for their children to come home for dinner. Usually, everybody had dinner at a different time. "Why don't parents all have dinner at the same time?" Connie frequently wondered. Having dinner early, before the others, was horrible for the early eaters, because the sound of fun outside kept them from eating anything, or else they bolted their food and got hiccups. On the other hand, having dinner late, when everyone else had finished and was back outside, was just as bad or worse. "Haven't you eaten *yet?*" they'd ask at the back door in disgust. "What custooms!" said Hugsy. Anyway, today, all dinners worked out just right.

Before he went in, Billy said to Connie, "Connie, if we could locate your father's pencil, then we would definitely know who was the real burglar of the ring."

"But," said Connie, bewildered. "The policemen were proven guilty, the judge said so, and they're in jail right now, with time out for dinner."

"That was a *make-believe* trial," Billy reminded Connie. "We—you and I—must keep our eyes open for your father's pencil. After all, we spotted the guy who said, 'Does this dog bite?' Now we must try to spot the guy who has your father's pencil."

"That's right," said Connie rather sadly. She had hoped that the trial in the Circle had solved everything. But it hadn't; there was more to be done. They could not yet put the burglary out of their minds—the Alley could not yet be the just plain, beautiful, not being watched by bullet-head man Alley that it used to be.

"See you later," said Billy, and he walked slowly home.

At dinner Connie said, "Papa, did Mama tell you about the bullet-head man and the Muras and Bully Vardeer, and the man asking, 'Does this dog bite?' "

For a while, Papa did not answer. He was morose about the news in the paper. "Trouble," he said. "Trouble everywhere." Finally he said, "What, Connie? What was that?"

"Ts," said Connie desperately. "Can't you ever listen?" She repeated her questions.

"Oh, that," said Papa. "Yes. Yes, your mother did tell me."

"And did you go to the presink?" asked Connie.

"No," said Papa. "They'd just say, 'Child's play.' 'Kids' stuff.' They already think your mother's crazy, seeing through pockets. They'd think me crazy, too, with Muras, and children's trials in the Alley, and a man who asks an innocent question about dogs, a man who probably was miles from our house at the time it was broken into—an innocent lover of dogs, that's all."

"Innocent, hah!" said Connie, disgusted. Even the best adults, like Papa, could be so stupid! It was because he was old, almost fifty . . . forty-eight and one-half, to be exact —that he was so stupid. If only she had a young father who would believe things! A young mother, too, for that matter, like Mrs. Starr, Katy's mother. Katy's mother walked up the Alley with a cup of coffee in her hand, like a movie star . . . stomach thrust forward—beautiful she was—the most beautiful person in the Alley. "The whole family is the most beautiful in the Alley, the most wonderful," thought Connie. "Well . . . that's life," she thought. "I have an old father and an old mother. In their forty-eights."

After dinner Billy appeared at the back door. "I have to go to my grandmother's now; I'm spending the night there. But don't worry. These burglars don't work at night, you notice, when everybody is home. They work in the daytime, and mainly during the lunch hour. I figured it out. At least around here they do. So, we'll get on the job tomorrow."

"What job?" asked Connie.

"Casing," said Billy.

"What are we going to case?" asked Connie.

"Case the casers," he answered with assurance. "You know they're after Joe Below's house now."

"What a boy Billy is!" thought Connie. "He doesn't give up and let bullet-head men make off with a whole Alley! A whole beautiful, formerly safe Alley!"

"So long!" said Billy.

"So long," said Connie. She went to the back door and watched him go. It had begun to rain. No one was out.

Connie couldn't swing, so she sat down in her little red rocker, and while Mama was cutting up the kidneys for the cats, Connie asked her if she would like to be read to. "Yes," said Mama.

Papa had stretched out on the divan in the living room and was snoring slightly, the awful newspaper, with its awful news, billowing on his stomach as he breathed. Wags lay on the floor beside him. The two cats crouched together in the doorway between the kitchen and the dining room; they did not take their eyes off Mama, and they kept twitching their noses in patient anticipation. The kitchen was quiet and peaceful. "Are you listening?" Connie asked Mama.

"Yes, Connie," Mama answered.

Outside the rain pattered gently against the window-panes. Lights came on here and there in the Alley. The little train went briskly by. "Hello, Connie. Good-by, Connie," it said as usual. Connie sighed happily. "What a life," she thought. "What a life!" And happily she began to read.

14

✹ ✹ ✹

CASING—JUST IN CASE

Casing the casers did not prove to be as scary or as interesting as Connie thought it would be. The next afternoon she and Billy Maloon went down the Alley toward Bully Vardeer's house. None of the children of their age were out—only little ones. Probably Katy, Ray, all the others had gone to the movies. Today Connie and Billy didn't care; they had so much to do. They had to case casers.

Connie's heart began to hammer very fast; probably Billy's did, too, because, although brave, he was frightened a great deal of the time. They stood at Bully Vardeer's end of the Alley, and they looked to right and to left toward both gates. Thoughts of the bullet-head man yesterday made them cautious. His famous words, "Does this dog bite?" echoed in their ears, especially in Connie's, for this was the second time in her life that she had heard the same remark uttered by the selfsame man in the selfsame, identical, high-pitched, brisk tone of voice. It was only the first time in his life for Billy.

They turned the corner at Bully's garden and slowly made their way toward the gate next to his house. On the way past Bully Vardeer's garden, they noticed that Bully was not sitting in it. He had fixed his yard up like a Japanese garden, on the order, though small, of the beautiful one in the Botanical Gardens. Sometimes he sat on his back stoop, sunning himself, dressed only in shorts. His eyes would be closed so that even his eyelids would get the benefit of the sun's rays. Princey would be asleep at his feet; but now neither was out.

"Walking Princey probably," Billy deduced. "All the more chance that casing is going on, if not the actual breaking in," said Billy.

"Oo-ooh!" said Connie. They were now in the shade of Bully Vardeer's house, which was on their right. On their left were the gardens of the houses that faced Larrabee. In Billy's yard, back a few houses, his dog, Atlas, set up a great howling and yowling, all kinds of remarks expressing distress and anguish because Billy was out and he had to stay in the yard. He couldn't bear it and spoke of his despair and jealousy in many octaves. But—"No dogs out in the Alley!" That was the rule. And it was fair, for even the nicest dogs sometimes do bite. They are especially apt to bite babies who, not knowing the danger and not walking well yet, lurch at them with outstretched hands and gurgle, "Ah-goo, ah-goo."

Connie and Billy tried to ignore Atlas, and proceeded to the end of the Alley. "*Be nonlachont*," Connie instructed

Billy. Billy already was nonchalant. They looked out the iron gate and saw no one. So they sat down on the curbing beside Mr. Bernadette's garden, the end one on Larrabee, and the site of an ancient, years-ago burglary. Opposite it was Bully Vardeer's tiny little front patch of crab-grass lawn facing on Waldo Place. They sat and they waited; but nothing happened, no one appeared. There was no whistling. "Remember," said Connie to Billy encouragingly, "it was many days after the bullet-head man asked Mama and me, 'Does this dog bite?' that he burglared our house."

Billy nodded. Suddenly he pinched Connie's arm. "Sh-sh-sh," he said. "I think I hear something."

Terrified, Connie whispered, "What?"

Billy whispered something back, but Connie did not catch what he said. They sat close together on the curb and waited. Soon they heard footsteps, then the jingle of a dog's license. Ah! Just Bully Vardeer and his dog, Princey. The artist spotted Connie and Billy. "Hello," he said gaily. "Trial over? No game today?" He pushed his hat back to a still better Bully Vardeer angle—it was a habit he had whenever he saw anyone to make sure his hat was set at the right jaunty angle. Not waiting for an answer, he said, "Come on, Princey—dinner!" And he went up his steps and into his house. Billy and Connie listened. They heard only one of Bully's doors close—the inside one. People, people! There are some people who never can get things through their heads. Connie and Billy had warned Bully only yesterday to be sure and close his outside green door—yet in he had gone and left the green door open! "Maybe as a

trap, though," said Connie to Billy. "You know—'invitation to the burglars'—and then bop them over the head. I wonder if he has a Tiffany vase? He's probably in there now waiting for them to come."

The two children sat in silence for a while on the lookout for the bullet-head man or to hear the sound of whistling—something, anything, to make casing worthwhile. "Knock wood that nothing does happen," thought Connie, and she knocked Billy's head, a custom in the Alley, to knock on a head and bring good luck.

Then Billy said, "Well, this casing is getting boring, us sitting here, not being able to see very far out to case, anyway. I could climb Mr. Bernadette's tree for a better view. But you know him. He'd think I was a Gregory Avenue kid and bellow at me."

"What is wrong with the Gregory Avenue kids?" said Connie.

"Nothing. Except that they are Gregory Avenue kids, not Alley kids, that's all. Not that he is exactly crazy about Alley kids either."

Connie and Billy discussed which grownups in the Alley liked children and which ones didn't. Then they remembered what they were supposed to be doing, and they realized they were getting tired of doing it. "Connie," said Billy. "How about my getting my express wagon and we go outside? I can pull you sometimes, then you pull me—we can go around the block, go along Gregory Avenue, keep our eyes peeled. We might hear them set the date of the next robbery."

But Connie said, "No. No, Billy, no," she said. "Mama wouldn't let me do that."

Sometimes Billy made the world outside the Alley sound wonderful. Sometimes he would crawl under the gate and go on an expedition on foot. Sometimes he'd just go out the front door with his express wagon. His dog, Atlas, also had the same fondness for the world outside. Sometimes Atlas squeezed under the Alley gate and made a successful getaway. Once when the Maloons were coming home across the Brooklyn Bridge, they saw a black and brown Irish terrier dodging in and out between the cars and trucks, loping along briskly, returning assuredly from a trip somewhere in Manhattan, his tongue hanging out thirstily but happily. "Is that Atlas?" they said. "Yes, it's Atlas!" They couldn't stop in all the traffic to open the car door and let him in—he probably would have refused the invitation, anyway, enjoying his jaunt and resenting the interruption.

"You know," said Connie. "I really admire a dog like Atlas. Think of Wagsie, dear, scared old Wagsie. I would never want her out with the cars and trucks on Brooklyn Bridge alone. She'd be too frightened to enjoy the view." And she, Connie, would be too frightened to go outside the Alley to case. All right to case from in here, safe—but outside? No. "No, Billy," she said again. "I'm not going outside the Alley."

"O.K.," said Billy. He sounded relieved. Who would want to go out with five real burglars and two possible policemen burglars at loose somewhere outside the gates, they didn't know where?

After a little more casing from the curbing under the catalpa tree, waiting for something to happen, Connie and Billy grew really tired of this game. Billy said, "Oh, let's go and play now. I'll get my new Dinky Toy—it's a police car."

"Hm-m-m," said Connie. "Fits in with things, doesn't it?"

"Fits," agreed Billy.

They stood up. They pressed their heads against the pretty iron gate for one last look around at whatever there might be to be seen. They saw nothing. Well, when Connie and Billy had decided to case the casers, they really had not expected to see anything . . . they just had thought that they should case, just plain case, in case. . . . Someone should case, they thought, after the second appearance of the bullet-head man and the same old question. But why they? they asked themselves now. Why not Bully Vardeer himself—owner of the dog now being studied, inhabitant of the—probably—next house to be robbed?

Having heard nothing, seen nothing of importance, Connie and Billy crawled on their stomachs, sticking close to the curbing, to Connie's back gate. This was a rehearsal of what they had decided to do in case they ever did see the bullet-head man while they were casing. They would crawl away and give the alarm, probably to Bully Vardeer in his Japanese garden, and then crawl on home.

"Crawl flat," Billy instructed Connie. "Stay five feet behind me the way cars do in the Holland Tunnel—they have to stay a certain number of feet behind the car ahead. Keep your distance. Then, if one of us gets killed, the other might not."

"Oo-oo-ooh," said Connie.

Thus they crawled inch by inch down the Alley. "If only," prayed Connie, "Ray and June Arp don't come out and say, 'Whatcha doin'?'" But there was still no sign of the Arps in the Alley or of any of the other children their age.

Keeping five feet apart, and with no one in the Alley to observe them, they reached Bully Vardeer's garden gate. There he sat, on his top step again, his eyes closed, lids and all, not to miss one wan ray of pale sunbeam; even his arms were outstretched behind his head to burn his furry armpits. Billy and Connie crawled past him to her garden, went in, and closed the gate.

"Isn't that something," said Billy in disgust. "Just sits and suns, with burglars asking about his dog! He should sit behind the curtains and be on the lookout. He's been warned! We warned him."

"I know," said Connie. "But he may be right. Why watch now? The burglars waited a long time between the day they asked Mama and me, 'Does this dog bite?' and the day they broke in. They probably wouldn't come to Bully Vardeer's house the very next day—that is, to break in. Maybe they are just casing it for a while, keeping in touch —when Bully goes in, when he comes out, getting everything down pat about his house."

"Yeah," agreed Billy. "Maybe they even saw Bully come in just then with Princey, knew he was home. They couldn't tell that he had stripped off his shirt, come right out the back door, gone into sunbathing, and wouldn't be able to hear them; they couldn't tell that, with Bully sunning, it's as good a time for a break-in as with Bully away."

"No," said Connie. "They can't see through solid. Anyway, Princey would have heard them and barked. They would know that that type of dog barks."

"True," said Billy.

"Anyway, they may be waiting for another Alumni Day," said Connie.

"There's only one a year," said Billy.

"Well, some other day of importance," said Connie. "When everybody is somewhere else."

"True," said Billy.

Billy and Connie got on the swings and swung and thought in silence for a while—until around four o'clock when the other children their age trooped out of the Arps' house, singing "It's Howdy-Doody Time." Katy stopped long enough to take a look at them. "The swingers," she said.

"Yeah," said Billy. "Well, Eu*rip*edes, Eum*end*adees."

"Plee-a-dees," said Connie. And they swung high.

They were both very nonchalant.

15

THE FOUND NICKEL

About a week passed with, thank goodness, no unusual happenings. Connie had to just plain live as well as case and so did Billy, though he preferred casing to schoolwork. But he had to visit his grandmother often and do his homework —put out the trash—everything! Having done their main job—warned Bully Vardeer—and also having told their parents all they knew, they went on with just life. One thing Connie had to do in just plain life was to take piano lessons.

Today, about a week since the trial in the Circle, the main happening was that Nanny had come home . . . happy-looking. She had played lots of bridge, visited lots of dearly loved friends; then she had begun to miss Connie, and so, here she was again, home in Brooklyn. Not that Brooklyn was really "home" to Nanny, the South was really "home" still to her; but, "I have to go back to my children now," she'd tell the people in the South, meaning Papa, Mama, and Connie. To Connie she often said, "Brooklyn? Child!" she said. "They laugh about Brooklyn in the South. 'Jupe!' (my nickname) they say to me—'You don't mean to say you live in Brooklyn?' You know, child—Brooklyn is supposed to be a place you laugh at, not live in, in the South . . ."

"They don't know how beautiful it is or they wouldn't say that. They don't know about the Alley—probably never even heard of it—if you can imagine such a thing!" said Connie.

Connie had been practicing the piano, "Indian Drum Song" and "Dancing Marionettes." When she finished, she went into the kitchen and sat down in the little red rocker. It was good to have Nanny back. Connie loved to sit, and talk to her, and hear about her trip on the Augusta Special. Nanny was polishing and counting her silver, the forks, the spoons . . . everything. "I have to make sure that those thieves didn't get something."

Connie thought, "If Nanny had never gone away, the burglary might not have occurred. Or, if it had been bound to occur, anyway, it was too bad that she had missed it; for Nanny loved excitement." Nanny had the news on every hour on the hour and sometimes in between to get the latest. She also listened to *all* the baseball games—she was for the Dodgers. When Nanny was listening to a big league game, you had to tiptoe in this house. She would get really cross, say that she would go back down South if you made noise while the game was going on.

Connie had written Nanny the entire story of the burglary, of course, and when Nanny came back, she had retold it to her in every detail, even told her about the trial in the Alley, the clues, Bully Vardeer, and casing.

"Ts! Child!" Nanny had said over and over in a very satisfying way. Connie's usual feeling of peace and contentment stole over her now as she sat rocking. Today at school an extraordinary thing had happened, and with Mama away for the day, she was going to tell it to Nanny, first. She loved talking to Nanny. "Nanny?" Connie would say. And Nanny would say, "Yes, darling?" in such a loving voice. If Connie had a wish for all children everywhere, it would be that every child had a grandmother like Nanny.

Nanny was little and round; her shoulders were bent over because of her arthritis—she was quite stooped. As Connie grew taller, Nanny seemed to grow shorter. Connie was already as tall as Nanny. Imagine being as tall as a grandmother! In good weather when Nanny walked Wagsie to the green grass near the athletic field, she took a cane with her—it was made by the mountain folk in the

South, of pine. Wagsie would follow her or race ahead of her; then would come mother Mittens and lastly daughter Punk. The four looked like a picture out of a folk tale, meandering up the street and then slowly, taking their time, meandering home again. Wagsie liked to frisk and gambol despite her stoutness, and sometimes she would find a stick and implore Nanny to throw it. But Nanny would never throw sticks or do anything of that sort. She just walked the animals, talking with them all the way, amiably, or scolding them. "Drop that awful-looking thing!" she would say to Wags, who ate anything. The cats would lurk behind, play games, hide under cars, and then spring out at Nanny to surprise her. "I see you," Nanny would say to give them joy. How the animals loved Nanny! No wonder! She cut up kidneys for them, and liver, fixed dishes that looked tempting enough for Connie to eat—saved delicate little morsels for them, like bits of shrimp. She let Wagsie, shaking in fear, get on her bed in a thunderstorm and lay her head on her pillow.

"What a grandmother!" Connie thought with a sigh of happiness as she settled herself again in the little red rocker. Now Nanny began to cook . . . something good—perhaps a soup. Nanny prepared delicious soups. "Don't throw that away," she'd say of some left-over. "It will go into the soup." And what soups!

"Nanny?" said Connie. She wanted to tell her grandmother about an extraordinary thing at school today. She had found a nickel—the nickel was in the palm of her hand now—and tell her, too, about a pencil she had seen and held, a very important pencil.

"Yes, darling?" said Nanny.

"Nanny? See this nickel?" said Connie. She held a nickel up for her grandmother to see.

"Yes, darling. What about it?" said Nanny.

"Well, I found this nickel, Nanny," said Connie.

"Found it!" exclaimed Nanny. "Where, darling?"

Connie could always count on Nanny to respond in exactly the right way. She was always interested in everything. She always said, "O-o-oh?" in an interested way. She was a great listener and a great storyteller, too—great. She inherited the ability to tell stories from her father, who was a great after-dinner speaker. So was Papa. It came straight down the line, the ability to tell stories, from Great-Grandfather, to Nanny, to Papa.

"Yes, darling?" Nanny repeated. "Where did you find the nickel?"

"Well," said Connie. "Did I ever tell you, Nanny, I may have long ago, about a nickel that was stuck in the middle of Morrison Avenue—imbedded in the hard tar—right in front of Morrison School? Everybody in school knew about that nickel, and nobody knew how long it had been there. Georgie Genung—he is a boy in my class—he said his mother, who had also gone to Morrison School, remembers that nickel from when she went to school; it may have been there, stuck in the street, for as long as Morrison School has been there, and that is ninety-four years—like Mrs. Harrington. Or—did they have nickels then? Perhaps they just had pennies?"

"Well, I'm not ninety-four, but I *think* they had nickels then," said Nanny. "Buffalo nickels, I think . . ."

"Buffalo nickels!" said Connie.

"Yes, buffaloes," said Nanny. "That's what they had, buffaloes."

Connie examined her nickel. "You're right, Nanny—this is a buffalo nickel! It's an antique buffalo nickel, and it has been stuck in the street there from buffalo days."

Nanny wiped her hands on her apron and examined the nickel, holding it close to her eyes. Nanny needed new glasses, but she just wouldn't go to the oculist—she kept putting it off. So now, she tilted her head back and peered down at the nickel through the bottom part of her eyeglasses. Her mouth was open and her upper jaw overhung her lower one. At last she said, "Yes, Connie. This *is* a buffalo nickel, the kind we had—I remember them now —when I was a little girl. Now, how did you get this nickel out of where it has been stuck for so many years?"

"Well, Nanny, I'll tell you if you don't run the water . . ."

"Not any more than I can help," said Nanny.

"Well, Nanny. Today in school there was a fire drill; at least, we thought it was a fire drill. But it wasn't a fire drill at all—it was a bomb scare. Somebody said, 'A bomb is going to go off.' So the whole school was emptied out, and all the classes had to stand along the street and wait for the bomb scare to be over. The street was roped off, and only the fire engines and a police car were allowed in. So our class, grade five, was standing on Morrison Avenue, and I happened to be standing right near where the nickel was, still in its old worn-down place where it has always been.

"Well, Nanny, we were supposed to stay in line. If we

didn't, we would get detention. Anyway, I saw the nickel, still there all right. Now, Nanny, I suppose you wonder why no one has ever gotten the nickel out of the street before—some poor bum like they have over on the Bowery, who needed a nickel badly? But the reason is—well now, Nanny, really, you know that no one can chip a nickel out of the middle of the street in the daytime with all that much traffic. And buses! And in the nighttime no one would know about the nickel—no one would see it. So, there it lay."

"Yes, darling," said Nanny. "So how did you get it out, having to stand in line and all—not to get detention? And in a bomb scare?"

"Well," said Connie, "we were all lined up outside, and fire engines and a police car were there . . . a police car from Presink 9999. And you know what presink *that* is, don't you, Nanny? Well, it is *our* presink and the presink of the policemen, the two first policemen whose pockets Mama said she saw through—saw her ring on its pencil clip . . ."

"Yes?" said Nanny, pausing while stirring the soup to show she was trying to take it all in.

"Well, what do you think, Nanny?" said Connie. "The two policemen parked in the police car marked 9999, our presink, were *our two policemen*, Nanny. I recconized them! Why shouldn't I? They were in our house for such a long time. Well, I hoped they would not recconize me, because they knew that Mama thought they might have taken her ring. I was afraid they might arrest me for having

a mama like that . . . and the trial in the Alley proved they
had taken it . . . so I did not stare."

"No, darling, you did not stare," said Nanny.

"Well. They were parked right by the nickel. And they
saw it. 'Look, Ippy, there's a nickel there,' said Sergeant
Rattray, and he got out of the car and he tried to pick the
nickel up. Imagine! He thought he could just pick up that
nickel! But of course he couldn't! Been stuck in the street
too long, see, Nanny?"

"Too long," Nanny echoed.

"So . . . I pretended to be talking to Judy, my best
friend at school, hoping Ratty and Ippy—"

"Ratty and Ippy?" said Nanny in astonishment. "Who
are they?"

"I thought you were listening, Nanny. They are the
policemen with the pockets! Sergeant Rattray is Ratty and
Officer Ippolito is Ippy. Ratty and Ippy. Anyway, I hoped
they would not recconize me, but I kept keeping my eye on
them, and see—doesn't this prove, Nanny, once a thief,
always a thief? They had stolen—perhaps—Mama's diamond ring; and now they were trying to steal a nickel that
really belonged to the street? Anyway, they gave up, and
Sergeant Rattray, Ratty, got back in the car. After all," said
Connie sarcastically, "they did not have a screwdriver
named 'Stanley' with them the way real, right burglars do.
They are like vultures, these two, birds of prey, and pick
the bones that the real, right burglars leave behind. Understand, Nanny?"

"Yes, darling . . . bones."

"So, after a while," said Connie, "me and Judy got tired of standing in line while the firemen ran in and out of school and up on the roof. So I said to Judy, 'Hey, Judy,' I said. 'Let's try to bounce our tennis balls on the nickel.' We happened to have our balls with us because we were in gym when the alarm rang . . . we had never had a chance to bounce a ball on the nickel before because of all the traffic. 'Walk on the green, not in between.' And at other times, cars would come racing around the corner. But now, the street was closed off in both directions, so I suggested, I made the suggestion—'Let's bounce the balls on the nickel.'

"Judy said, 'O.K.' So we bounced. Now—are you listening, Nanny? I was bouncing my tennis ball at the nickel, trying to hit it, and sometimes I did hit it, and sometimes I didn't. You know, Nanny, I don't get A in P. E. (that's phiz-ed)—just B—not good, not bad—and this is like a dream really. I hit the nickel lots of times. (Judy didn't, and she's better than I am in P. E.—gets A!) Well, I don't know what happened, but out popped the nickel! And—here it is!

"All these years nobody could get the nickel out, not even these two policemen of Presink 9999, and suddenly, like a tiddlywink, it popped out for me! All the kids hurrayed. They said the nickel was mine. I got it out. And they said—the kids said—that it was lucky a kid from Morrison School had gotten it out, because it might have been any old person, not connected with Morrison School, who would get it out, like those two policemen, Ratty and Ippy. And after all, Nanny, it was in front of *our* school;

and it was best that a person, you know, a student, a child there—well, *me*—should get it out. Don't you think so, Nanny?"

"Yes, darling. *You*," said Nanny.

"So, I was the one who got it out. Somehow my ball got it out. Now, Nanny. You know those policemen—they might have said it was *theirs*. 'We saw it first,' they might have said. They wouldn't know that everybody in Morrison School had seen it before. They might have said, 'That's our nickel.' This time they did not come in for the kill—me doing the work, they getting the reward."

"Ts," said Nanny. "What will my friends, Lottie and Miss Annie Hempstead, think about this latest happening in Brooklyn? Ts," she said.

"Oh, they'll be very interested," said Connie. "Anyway, *now*, Nanny, this is *my* nickel. Everybody said, even Judy Fabadessa said, it was mine. In the beginning it belonged to the street. But it was *my* tennis ball that popped it out. So everybody said I should have it. And you can't divide a nickel into four hundred parts (that's how many children there are in Morrison School), for all to share it. So now it belongs to me.

"I took a good look at the policemen, Nanny, and they were looking straight ahead—they were not looking at me. So I put the nickel in my pocket. Then, along came Mr. Leep, my teacher. He is the nicest teacher I ever had. You know that that is saying a lot, don't you, Nanny? Because I only ever had one teacher I really didn't like, and that was Miss Crane in grade three? She screamed . . .

"Anyway . . . the nickel. I thought I should ask Mr.

Leep if it was really all right for me to have the nickel as my own found nickel . . . he knew the nickel, you see, he had seen it often . . . and I asked him if I should keep it. I told him, and Judy, she kept interrupting and saying, 'And that is right, Mr. Leep, and that is right!' I told him how the nickel had popped up out of the street—my tennis ball had made it pop—even though it had been bedded there for centuries. A buffalo—I wish I had told him that. Anyway, he smiled. He has the nicest smile, Nanny . . . even though I only got B, not A, in arithmetic; he likes arithmetic the best of everything . . . he still smiled at me. He said, 'Connie. I think that this nickel is yours and that having it pop out at you is a sign that you will get 100 per cent on your test this afternoon—if we ever get back into school.' And he walked away then to keep order in the lines."

"Yes, child?" said Nanny. "Order in the lines?"

Connie could see that Nanny was enthralled. And she went on. "So," she said, "I brought the buffalo nickel home. Here it is. I am going to put it with all my other found money. It's a wonder the burglars didn't find *that*, too—the found money. Well, it's in my wooden Dutch shoe, hanging on my wall, that's why. Of course, burglars would not think to look in a wooden Dutch shoe, hanging on a wall. They look mainly in old socks and under mattresses. That's the way some old people hide their money. Not you, Nanny, I don't mean you. You put your money in the bank, don't you?"

"When I have any," said Nanny.

"Well, you do have a lot of money sometimes, Nanny.

You are always giving me a dollar. Every chance you get, you give me a dollar, even on Valentine's Day. So you must have quite a lot of dollars. And Uncle Laudy gives you some money sometimes, doesn't he, Nanny?"

"Yes, darling," said Nanny. "He certainly does. Search the world over, you will never find as high-principled a man as Laudy."

"Well, I was glad that Mr. Leep did not get mad at me for popping a nickel out of the pavement where it had been for centuries. He likes things to stay where they always were. Once I broke off a great big icicle that was hanging outside our classroom window. He pretended to get mad at me. 'Oh, my nice icicle!' he said. 'Gone!' he said. 'Shattered!'"

"He did?" said Nanny.

"Yes," said Connie. "It was a very cold and bright clear day. The temperature had been way down, way way down below zero for days. Well, this made a huge icicle grow on the ledge outside the window of our classroom. Well, I didn't know that Mr. Leep was fond of this icicle and that all the kids called it, 'Mr. Leep's icicle.' I just hadn't happened to have heard the story. So, I opened the window and I knocked it off. I just couldn't resist it; I just happen to like to knock icicles off places, hear them crash—and did it crash! Crash it went!"

"Yes?" said Nanny.

Connie saw that Nanny, although still interested, was beginning to cast glances at the clock. "Oh, of course," thought Connie. "Soon time for Lyle Van and the four o'clock news." No one else in this house ever knew what was going on in the world and had to ask Nanny what was. The rest of the people didn't even know that the Russians had seen the other side of the moon until Nanny told them. They never knew the weather—or even what time it was.

One thing about Connie, she did not like to hurry. But she realized that she would have to wind up the story of the nickel and the icicle, for there were just two minutes to go before Lyle Van. She would not be able to go into the pencil part of the story, which was very important, too, until after the news. On she went, rapidly.

". . . so, Mr. Leep, well, he was pretending, Nanny, to be angry about his icicle—he was not *really* angry. 'Oh,' he groaned when he came back into the room. 'My icicle! My great big icicle! I've been watching it every day to see how big it would grow,' he said, 'and to see rainbows in it. And now it is gone! Who did it?' he asked sternly. You know, Nanny, he was not really angry—he was just pretending.

"I had to say, 'Me—I did it.' I almost cried because I thought he might, just might, be really mad. But he wasn't, Nanny. Not at all."

"Not at all," said Nanny.

"Yes. No. Anyway, Nanny, his saying that I could keep the nickel and not saying one word about it being his nice nickel that he could look at whenever he came in or out of school, or that it belonged to the street, where he could watch it, made it all right that my tennis ball had popped it out. That is why, Nanny, I have this nickel now. He was not mad about the nickel, and he had not—he really had not—been mad about his icicle. Did you think he had been mad, Nanny? Oh no, he just wanted to see, probably, whether it would reach all the way down to the ground, three stories down, like a stalectite, or stagelite—which is it, Nanny?—that comes down from above?"

"Land, child. It's years since I went to school. Or been in caves."

"Oh. So, I said to Mr. Leep, 'Mr. Leep, should I keep it— the nickel—or should I put it back . . . glue it in?' "

"Glue it in?" said Nanny.

"The street. Yes. But, 'Keep it, Connie,' he said. 'You might get one hundred on the test . . .' and he went on up the line to look at Vinnie Free, who had started sneezing again. She sneezes every second. It is so distracting. Vinnie is going to the hospital to find out why she sneezes. Anyway, now, in line, she had begun to sneeze. So Mr. Leep had to go and see if she would faint—she did once."

"Faint . . ." said Nanny. And she went to the radio and turned it on. "Connie," she said. "That was a very interesting day you had. And now I must listen to Lyle Van. Do excuse me, please, darling."

"No time for the pencil part," thought Connie—the most important part. She settled herself in the little red rocker to read, while Nanny listened to the news. Connie opened her book. It was *Floating Island*, which she was reading for about the tenth time. "I love you, book," she had written in the front of this book along with a picture she had drawn. She always drew a picture in the front of the books she loved. She sighed contentedly. How peaceful it was here in the kitchen! Despite Nanny's comments about the latest calamities, even though they were the same calamities she had heard on the radio an hour ago—nothing new—no new crash or quake somewhere, and with Nanny saying often, "Ts, ts," or "Uh-umm!" in pleasurable horror—despite these kitchen sounds, Connie became lost in her book.

Suddenly, someone arriving at the back door jogged her out of her book. Billy Maloon at the back screen door, looking scared, the way he always did when he saw Nanny in the kitchen! Connie beckoned to him to come in, silently, not to interrupt Lyle Van. Billy tried to open the screen door noiselessly and gulped when it did squeak a little. Then, giving as wide a berth as was possible in the crowded kitchen—Wags and the cats were there, too—to Nanny, who glowered at him all the same as though he might have been responsible for the potatoes sticking, Billy reached the dining room. There he stood, out of sight of Nanny. Even so, "Don't touch my newspapers, my Chester papers," she sternly warned him.

"Oh, he won't, Nanny," said Connie impatiently. She put her marker in her book and joined Billy where he was lurking.

"Can you come out?" he said. His eyes were wide and bright. He knew something, that was certain.

"Nanny," said Connie. "I'm going out."

"All right," said Nanny sweetly. "Better put your sweater on, darling; there's a little wind."

Connie got her sweater and followed Billy out. Both had news. But since this was Connie's yard, Billy said she should talk first. That was fair. First Connie swiftly told Billy the story of the found nickel—after all it was the second telling of the day, and she wound it up in a hurry to get on to part two, the pencil part of the story. "And then, Billy," she said.

"You know what I saw in Sergeant Rattray's—Ratty's—hand?"

"The ring?" asked quiet Billy Maloon.

"Not the ring, Billy, no. You're warm, though. After all, Mama's ring is a lady's ring, you know. In the first place, it wouldn't fit on a policeman's big hand, and in the second place—well, did you ever see a diamond ring on the hand of an everyday policeman?"

"No," said Billy, sheepish over the mistake.

"Well, what I did see, Billy, and it is as important as the ring, was the . . ."

"The pencil case!" said Billy excitedly.

"Warmer," said Connie.

"The pencil itself!" said Billy.

"Yes!" said Connie. She was proud of this electrifying news and of its effect on Billy. Why not? The pencil was as important a clue in proving whether or not there had been a policeman burglary as the Mura butt, the screwdriver named "Stanley," and the piece of curtain were in the case of the five real burglars. "Yes," Connie repeated. "The pencil itself! The J. I. pencil—Papa's pencil!"

"Tell!" said Billy.

16

↓↓↓

THE J. I. PENCIL

"Tell it," said Billy. "You say you saw the pencil. How did you know that the pencil you saw . . . and, anyway, how did you see it? How did you get so close up to a policeman that you could see his pencil? And how did you know that it was your father's pencil, the one that your mother saw as in a vision through the policeman's pants' pocket?"

"I'll tell you, *I'll tell you*," said Connie. "If you'll only listen!" she screamed. Why did no one ever listen? Why did they always keep interrupting? After Billy had been silent for a couple of seconds, she said, "Billy. You know that after, I say *after*, the policemen saw me pop the nickel out of the street and heard Mr. Leep say it was all right for me to keep it—it was mine now—they began to study me. Every time I looked at them, they were studying me. They were studying me and I was studying them. Only it's a funny thing about grownups. You can always tell, *always*, when a grownup is studying *you*. But grownups never know when *you* are studying *them*."

208

"Dopes," said Billy. "That's why."

"Well, the way I studied them without their knowing it was this: I went close up to their police car, bouncing my tennis ball near and all around it . . ."

"That was brave of you, Connie, since they may be robber policemen—we don't know yet—and probably they were trying to remember where they had seen you before. It was *very* brave of you."

Connie's heart nearly exploded with love for Billy. What praise! "Well, Billy. On one of my bounces around the car . . . and I kept my eyes on the policemen—and yet *not* on them. Sidewise, I looked at them . . . like this." Connie showed him. She got off the swing and gave a sidewise example . . .

"That is the way to do," he said.

"Yes," said Connie, getting back on the swing. "So," she said, "while I was bouncing my ball and looking sidewise out of my eyes, I noticed that the policeman at the driver's wheel, that is Officer Ippolito, Ippy, had taken a little notebook out of his pocket, and he began to write in it. I couldn't help noticing the pencil he was writing with because it was not a regular yellow wood one, but a silver one. Well, naturally, since the pencil that had Mama's diamond ring on it is one of the most important . . ."

". . . *the* most important," corrected Billy.

"Yes, *the* most important clue that we don't have but that we'd like to have to go on about the two policemen—that is, to know whether they were burglars or not— I bounced my ball a little closer and sidewise myself, and with my eyes sidewise, sidewise I looked . . . still bouncing and with the found nickel still in my pocket (it may be lucky, though I did not get one hundred on the arithmetic test; still I did get eighty-eight . . . very good for me, very good). Well, with a found nickel in my pocket to give me luck, I had the courage to get closer and closer, and I did, slantwise but accurately, see the pencil that Officer Ippolito, Ippy, was holding. This pencil was marked with the initials J. I. And what does J. I. stand for? John Ives. And that is Papa. J-John. I-Ives."

Billy's jaw hung open. "Yikes," he said, gulping.

"It was a Christmas present from the people who work for him. Papa said a boss should not expect presents or—take them. That's probably why he hadn't used the pencil yet . . . had left it in his drawer. Embarrassed."

For a while Connie and Billy swung high. Then, slowing down again, Billy said, "Connie. How did you get close enough to a pencil that a policeman was writing with to see initials on it?"

"Well, Billy. You remember why we were all out there in the street in the first place? A fire alarm that turned out to be a bomb scare. So the policeman, Ippolito (we might as well call him Ippy from now on) was making notes about it all with my father's pencil when along came Mr. Leep talking to another teacher, saying, 'Ts, ts—a bomb scare . . .' (There really wasn't a bomb, but they thought there might be.) And off they went. They hadn't been able to stop Vinnie Free's sneezing either . . . you could still hear her up the street—'Tschoo! Tschoo!' —another worry for poor Mr. Leep . . . bombs, sneezes."

"Once I read about someone dying from sneezing. . . .

Oh no, that was the hiccups," Billy put in. "Or was it laughing?"

"Well, when Ippy was reminded of the 'bomb,' he said, 'Bomb! Yikes!' Nervous, see? Shows what a coward he is! And he dropped the pencil in the street right where I was bouncing; it rolled right over to me. I picked it up, and, bless Maud (that's what Papa always says—he says, 'Bless Maud') it had the initials J. I. on it. The initials are engraved in scroll—you know what that is, don't you, Billy?"

Billy nodded. "Yes," he said. "Heigh-ho gryphics."

"Oh," said Connie. "Anyway, it was a little silver pencil like the one Papa had had and had shown Mama and me the night before it was stolen, the night Papa and Mama went to the alumni ball, the night Mama said to Papa, 'By the way, John. Where *is* my diamond ring?' And Papa had shown it to us on the clip of the pencil in its little case in his wardrobe."

"Wowie!" said Billy.

"I handed the policeman the pencil—I should have kep' it; it's Papa's."

"Did they give you a piercing glance?" asked Billy.

"No," said Connie, "nothing. I let my ball roll away, and I ran after it to get away from them. How do I know? They may have said to themselves, 'Hm. I remember that girl now. What's she doing watching us? Hm. Now she knows we have her pencil.'"

"Yes," agreed Billy. "You know, Connie, those policemen must have stolen the pencil, and so, of course, they got the ring that was on it. And if they knew that you knew that they had taken it—and your kind of knowing is real knowing; it's not like having a voice say to you that the pencil is in a certain policeman's pocket, the way your mother knew (although that was the most important *first* knowing . . . otherwise, no one would have thought that anybody but the burglars had gotten the ring and the pencil!)—well, you know those policemen might just plain have arrested you?"

"Arrested *me!*" exclaimed Connie. "They're the ones should be arrested. How could they arrest me?"

"Say you took a nickel belonged to the street."

"Ah-h," said Connie in somber recognition of the perils.

"Well, go on," said Billy. "When you rolled away . . ."

"I didn't roll away," Connie said. "I let the ball roll away."

"Well, anyway," said Billy, smiling appreciatively. "What comes next?"

"Well, then the bell rang, and we all went in . . ."

"Had there been a bomb?"

"No. Some stupid joke. A boy was expelled. He can't ever come back. Has to spend his life in jail, probably . . . real jail. Not a hidy-hole jail."

"And the police?"

"The last thing I saw was the two policemen riding off in their Presink 9999 car."

"Did they look at you, give you a piercing glance as they drove off? Do you think they took it in that you recognized the J. I. pencil as the pencil of your father?"

"I don't know. My knees were shaking. My hands, too. I could hardly make it up the stairs to the third floor, but I did."

"M-m-m," said Billy. "Well, did you tell your mother and father that you saw your father's pencil in the hand of Ippolito?"

"Ippy. No, not yet. I was going to tell Nanny, but it was time for Lyle Van with the four o'clock news. When Mama comes home, I'll tell her. She'll be glad to know she is right about voices telling her what's in pockets. And think! Those detectives telling Papa—and Papa almost agreeing with *them*—that Mama only had high sterricks. High sterricks, ha! *I* knew Mama was right. *I* know Mama! When Mama knows something, she *knows*. This proves it."

"You don't think there are lots of pencils with J. I.'s on them, the way there are lots of screwdrivers with 'Stanley' on them?" asked Billy. "We have to be sure of everything."

"No-o," said Connie hesitantly. How could she be sure? Then a dreadful thought occurred to her. "Oh, Billy. You know what? The name of one of the policemen is Ippolito.

His first name might be *John*. John Ippolito, same initials as Papa's—J. I."

"Yes," said Billy. "Or Joseph."

"M-m-m," said Connie. "Then we can never prove anything. Well, that's life. Ts. Oh, well . . . what happened to you today?" she said.

"Well," said Billy. "Mine's good, too. I was going to take Atlas for a walk. We're trying to keep him on the leash all the time so he won't go away. He just loves to go across Brooklyn Bridge! Someone else saw him trotting along yesterday over the Brooklyn Bridge. He'll get killed yet. So, I had just gone out the front door with Atlas, and I had stopped a minute to make sure the doors were locked. Then —I smelled Muras! I know the smell of Muras by now, all right, my stubs—the old one and the new one. So, I stopped and looked out from under my eyelids . . . this way . . ." Billy showed Connie how he looked out from under his eyelids so that no one would know he was looking at them. He had very long sweeping eyelashes, and this helped to throw people off the track. Billy's glance of deception was on the order of Connie's sidewise look. Both were excellent.

"And," said Billy, "coming up the street—he was about in front of Arnold's house—there was the . . ."

"Bullet-head man!" Connie could not help but interrupt.

Billy did not mind the interruption. "Yes!" he said. "The bullet-head man!"

Connie gasped. She was speechless! Imagine! Her over there on Morrison Avenue with the second pair of robbers, the policemen pair! And Billy over here on Larrabee with a real, right original robber, the chief caser, the *brain* probably! "That's even scarier than my day," she said at last.

"Both are scarey," said Billy. "Well, he was headed *away* from me, going toward Gregory. But when he heard Atlas's chain and license jingling, 'A dog!' he probably thought. 'A dog to find out about.' And he stopped dead in his tracks. He scratched his head as if to say, 'Oh, darn! I forgot something,' and he wheeled around and came toward me."

"Yikes!" said Connie.

"So, I went slowly down the steps and walked toward him . . . I wouldn't want to have my back to him, you know . . . I walked toward him and he came toward me. We met . . . we passed . . . we walked a step or two—he in his direction, I in mine. He stopped again . . . he turned around . . . so did I . . . and he said (he spoke in good English, the way he always does) . . . he said . . ."

"Oh, no," gasped Connie.

"Yes," said Billy. "He said, 'Does this dog bite?'

"I said, 'Yes, he is vicious. I'm on my way to get a muzzle for him now.' I gave Atlas a tug on the leash. He knows what that means—Growl! Bare teeth!"

"Good old Atlas," said Connie. "Think of Wags! She would have been . . . she *was* scared of the man."

"But the man," said Billy, "was not scared of Atlas. He gave a smile, and he said he could make friends with any dog, including vicious ones. Then he held out his hand, the right way, you know, for making friends with a dog, and he said, 'Nice doggie.' "

"Gosh!" said Connie, overwhelmed at the nerve of the man.

"I yanked Atlas back, and I said, in a menacing way, 'Better not pet this one; he might have rabies. He was bit by a rat in the churchyard.' And I began to back up the street. He took a little dog biscuit out of his pocket . . ."

"Must have quite a supply," put in Connie.

"And he said, 'Oh,' he said. 'Some day he'll be my friend. Won't you, puppy?' he said. And, 'What's his name?' he said. I didn't want to tell him 'Atlas' because . . ."

"The nerve! I mean it!" said Connie.

"So I said . . . the first thing that come into my head . . . 'His name is Agamemnon.' "

"Agamemnon!" screamed Connie. "Imagine little Atlas with a big name like that!" Still, there was no denying Atlas was brave. A heart like Agamemnon's, that's what he had— heart of a hero.

Connie and Billy couldn't help laughing. "Here, Agamemnon, here, Agamemnon," Connie said. "Can you imagine calling him with a name like that? Worse than, 'Here, Heathie.' "

"He'd be over the bridge before we got it all out," said Billy. "Anyway, the guy said, 'H-m-m, a rather unusual name for a dog. What does it mean—Hercules?' "

"Not as educated as we thought," said Connie.

"A coincidence that he would say that, though," said Billy. "Because Hercules took the weight of the world off Atlas's (my dog's) shoulders. Anyway, he lighted another Mura, and he went down the street, the other way from the way he was going in the beginning. He began to whistle. And you know what he was whistling?"

"Oh. Oh, no! Not—'On the Street Where You Live,'" said Connie.

"Right," said Billy triumphantly.

"Oh-oh-oh," said Connie. "So now we know that both your house and Bully Vardeer's house are being cased by the main caser. Mama and Papa should call the police."

"No sense in that. The man's gone, and the police would just laugh if we told them our suspicions. Anyway, you don't arrest a man because you *think* he's going to rob you and whistle 'On the Street Where You Live' before he does rob you."

"But we know he robbed our house," said Connie.

"Pretty certain. But . . . Connie . . . have you ever thought how it would feel for you and me to be the ones to catch the burglars in the act somehow?"

"Ourselves?" said Connie. "Hey, yeah," she said. "I often dream," she said, "not dream, *imagine*, that I would catch a burglar. Think what Katy would say to that! She has never caught a burglar!"

"Well, Connie," said Billy. "We must think of a trap to catch this bullet-head man. Then the case will crack . . ."

"Will what?" asked Connie. Sometimes she did not understand Billy's language. Billy watched "The Defenders," as well as Perry Mason, and knew a great deal of burglar language.

"Crack . . . be solved!" he explained.

"Ah," said Connie. "It's already solved," she said.

"Yes, but now we have to think of a way to trap this fresh guy, him and his dogs and his love of all dogs, vicious or not!"

"That's right," said Connie with a sigh. "We have to prevent the two future burglaries, yours and Bully's."

"That's right," said Billy. "So think."

He and she swung quietly for a while, thinking. But it's a funny thing about plans. They really have to come to you; you can't always just think one up when you need one. They thought of a few, and they were either too dangerous or too simple. They hit on nothing. Then Connie had to go in to dinner, and Billy said he would see her later. He went home to case from the front window of his second story; his burglar alarm was all set, and he had a paper bag to fill with water and drop on any suspect. But he saw no suspect and he smelled no Mura.

After dinner, Connie practiced the piano until Mama came home. Then Connie told her the story of the buffalo nickel and the pencil. She ended up with what had happened to Billy that day. Mama could hardly chop up the onions—she was preparing a rare and fancy recipe for tomorrow—she was so interested. She cried from the onions, and she cried from fear. She said that if Connie or Billy saw anything suspicious, they must come and tell her right away and she would telephone Papa and de Gaulle. De Gaulle might as well be good for something besides chasing imaginary little boys off great big ball fields. That was what Mama said indignantly. "And she's right," thought Connie.

For a number of days after that great one, nothing happened in regard to burglaries, dog lovers, casing. Connie began to forget about it all.

"After all, Billy," she said. "You know we wouldn't have had a burglary if we hadn't had an Alumni Day, and there isn't going to be another Alumni Day for one year. They only really like to burgle—*these* burglars, anyway—on a day of importance. And what day of importance is coming up soon? None. Just plain none." That's what Connie thought and said.

17
⇂⇂⇂

ALLEY CONSERVATORY OF MUSIC

The warm days of early June dawdled along to vacation time. Connie spent a great deal of time practicing the piano —she loved playing the piano and she liked to practice. But she neither loved nor liked taking lessons. Nor did she like piano recitals. Her teacher gave three little recitals a year, so that each pupil could see how the others were faring—not to laugh at them but to be heartened knowing that others make mistakes, too. So far, Connie had been in two recitals this year. Another was coming soon. That recital would end up the lessons for this year—at least that was something— and there would be Dixie Cups for those who liked them, and cookies and lemonade.

Connie had been taking lessons for a year and a half. Her teacher, Miss Fannie Moore, still gave her little pieces— "Indian Drum Song," for example, and said that Connie was not ready for "The Moonlight Sonata," not quite yet. Ts. One day, while practicing, Connie thought, "Here I am— practicing the piano, wasting my time *practicing*, when I should be *giving* piano lessons!" Connie had been *taking* lessons for a year and a half; she could play the piano now. "Why take lessons when you can play?" she asked herself. "Why not *give* lessons, instead."

In the Alley there was no piano teacher, no music teacher, not one. The Alley needed a music teacher. She might as well be it—Connie Ives, the music teacher of the Alley, the way Bully Vardeer was its portrait painter. Some children might like to take lessons but couldn't, because there was no teacher. Consider the Carrolls. Four children in the same family and not one taking lessons. How much should she charge for a lesson? Connie's father often said, "Professors are not made of money." Well, she, Connie, would not charge as much as Miss Fannie Moore did for a lesson—four dollars! She would charge only twenty-five cents. Mama, when asked, had suggested five.

"Five!" exclaimed Connie. "You think a piano lesson is not worth any more than a popsicle?"

"Oh, do excuse me, darling," said Mama. "Of course. You are right."

"Now to round up the pupils," said Connie, going out. Fifteen minutes for each lesson would be enough, she thought. Hers lasted a half an hour, though they seemed an hour. The four little Carrolls were all in their yard, playing, yelling, screaming. Connie knew that they would all be very musical, every one of them, even the littlest—Notesy. Look at their mother! The lady from Nebraska! She could play any musical instrument, the piano, the recorder, the organ, and how she wanted to own bagpipes! (Her mother stemmed from the Scots.) "If you ever go to Europe," she said to Connie's mother, "please bring me home some bagpipes." She also played taps on an ancient bugle when it was time for her four children to come in.

But Connie decided not to ask the Carrolls first. She was somewhat afraid of Mrs. Carroll and had to muster courage. She decided to ask Winifred first. Winifred was a new girl in the Alley, and if anyone needed piano lessons, it would probably be she, for she was very musical. Billy needed them, too, but he was too busy casing. He didn't want to stop casing a minute, scarcely even to eat or sleep. He crawled around the Alley on his stomach all the time and wormed his way into Bully Vardeer's Japanese garden; and he climbed up the Bernadette's tree. He didn't care about Mr. Bernadette's bellowing at him—he just went anywhere in the Alley, just so it was casing.

"The trouble with people," Billy said to Connie—and Connie felt he meant her—"is that they let a case drop. They forget to be on guard."

"That's right," Connie agreed. "Billy, you go on casing, and you let me know when you need me. Otherwise, I have to give piano lessons. And that is going to keep me pretty busy."

"Give!" he exclaimed. "Lessons?"

"Yes," said Connie. "Yes. How would you like to take?" she asked.

"From who?" he asked.

"Me," said Connie. "Me." She blushed. Billy was looking at her with admiration. That was the way with Billy Maloon. He thought that everything Connie did was fine.

And she thought that everything he did was fine. That was fair.

"No, thanks," he said. "Some other year. Right now I have too much to do."

"O.K., Billy," said Connie. "See you later. By."

"By," said Billy. He crawled off.

Connie could see that Billy was a little dejected, because she wasn't coming casing with him. Casing is a lonely life. But he had chosen it. She, Connie, just could not case every minute. Life had to go on—piano lessons . . . giving them and taking them . . . reading, drawing, swinging, everything—casing or no. She planned to give a recital in a few weeks, less . . . in days, if her pupils did well. There was a great deal to do. She hadn't even asked anybody to take lessons yet, and here she was planning the recital—the recital of her pupils! "What pupils?" she asked herself sarcastically.

As things turned out, Connie had no trouble rounding up pupils. The new girl, Winifred, a very pretty girl with black glossy hair and deep dark eyes, accepted with alacrity. She was coming at four o'clock for a lesson. Connie got out some of her old pieces. How easy they were! Winifred should soon be able to do these.

The piano was in the dining room, a funny place for a piano, perhaps, but the only place where it would fit in their little house. Anyway, Connie liked having the piano there because Mama could hear her from there while she was at the stove, cooking. And so could Nanny, when it was Nanny who was doing the cooking . . . if Connie could get the lesson in before Lyle Van.

"You know, Mama," said Connie, "that Winifred is a very timid and shy girl—very, very. She is afraid of many things. I'll teach her to play the piano, and that will be one thing that she will be able to do. She won't ever climb to the top of the jungle gym, says she is scared of high places."

"Lots of people are scared of high places," Mama said.

"That's no excuse. I'll teach her to *not* be afraid. I taught Hugsy to walk the fence. He used to be scared to walk the fence. But now, he *can* walk it. Why? I gave him courage, that's why. He used to manage to get up on the fence, but then he would crouch down, be afraid to stand up. 'Stand up,' I'd say to Hugsy. 'Stand. First just learn to stand up straight. Then, take a step or two. Go easy. You can always jump off if you think you are about to fall.' That's what I said to Hugsy."

"Yes?" said Mama.

" 'Uh-uh,' he'd say to me when he would be standing— almost straight—his legs wobbling. 'Connie! Help, help! I'm falling!' he'd say. 'Just stand still,' I'd say to him. 'Be calm. That is the way to learn. Make yourself stand all the way up, now. Don't half crouch. That's the first thing. Don't half crouch.'

" 'They, the people who run this place, won't like it,' he'd plead. 'Get me off of here. Mama! Help! There's a rule, Connie, not to get up on the fences.' 'That is just an excuse,' I told him, 'for you not to learn to walk the fence! Now, you are up. Now, take one step, just one step. See, Hugsy? (I'd hold my arms up to him as though to catch him.) I am right here, Hugsy. You are safe.' "

"Yes?" said Mama. "And did he learn? He is right, though, about rules and fences."

"Well," said Connie. "It is more important for Hugsy to get over being afraid to stand on the fence than what a rule like that is—that is an unimportant rule. Anyway, by the end of the day, Mama, he had learned to walk the fence. And by the end of this day, today, Winifred will have learned to play the piano—anyway, the C scale," Connie concluded, swinging around again on the piano stool. "She'll be here in a few minutes for lesson one."

Connie was getting a little anxious. She told herself this was natural. After all, this was the first piano lesson that she had ever given. Who wouldn't be a little anxious at such a time? On the dot of four—the church bells were ringing— Winifred appeared. She did not look at Connie's mother and she did not look at Connie. She looked into air. But she was here.

The two girls went into the dining room immediately, went right to the piano, seriously, not giggling the way Judy, and probably even Katy, would have. "Ahem . . ." Katy would probably have said. But Connie and Winifred were serious, as one should be about serious things. Laugh when something is funny; don't laugh when it isn't. That was a good rule to go by, and Connie tried to go by it. Of course, everybody has to laugh at the wrong time sometimes —in school, in church—that's life.

"Now," said Connie, plunging right into lesson one, not to lose any time. "You see these gold letters in the middle of the piano? They say, 'Ludlow.' Now, middle C is just a little bit to the left of the center of these gold letters. That is the way to find C, the most important note of the piano. If you have that, you have everything. Now, I will play the scale of C major."

Connie played the scale of C major. She decided that she might be a piano teacher when she grew up, because she enjoyed teaching so much. "Now," she said. "You must notice which fingers I use. You must learn to use the right fingers, or you are lost. If you use the wrong fingers, you will never become a great player, or even a just plain regular player. Now, every note must sound like a round thing. It must be strong and round and clear and firm. My mother taught me that—not my teacher, Miss Fannie Moore. Now, you play the great scale of C major."

After a few bad starts, Winifred played the C scale.

"Very good," said Connie. "They may be boring, scales;

but if you don't know them, you can't play anything. Now, you got the fingers right. Very, very good. Now, play it once more . . . loud and strong and deep. The piano does not bite. Then we will go on with the music. Scales are for music what being able to draw a perfect circle is to art," she said. "You heard about the great artist who drew just a circle, a perfect circle, for the pope when he was asked for a sample of his work?"

Winifred looked miserable. Connie could not blame her. "She *is* timid," thought Connie. She could see that Winifred had already lost track of where C was and how to begin. She was probably thinking, "Is C a little to the right or a little to the left of the gold letters?" Connie gave her a gentle reminder. "A little to the left of the middle of the gold Ludlow letters in the center of the piano, Winifred," she said.

Winifred played the scale again; and she did better, much better. "That's good, Winnie, very good," said Connie, and she meant it. "Now, look at that!" she said to herself. "If I can teach, why should I, a teacher, take lessons?"

So now, already, Winifred could play the C scale, and after she had gotten up it and down it three times, Connie said, "There, that will be enough of that. Now, for music." She got out her little book of first pieces. "I think," she said thoughtfully. "That I will start you on the very first piece in the book, 'On the Sand.' First, I'll play it. You must think of little grains of sand falling between your toes on the beach on a hot and sunny day. Now, wasn't that nice? Now . . . you."

Winifred cautiously struck the first note. "Right!"

exclaimed Connie. But from then on, the going was not smooth. Beads of perspiration bedewed Winifred's brow as she struggled with "On the Sand."

"Don't lose middle C!" Connie reminded Winifred. "If you keep that in mind, you will never get lost."

Winifred tried to smile. She wanted to stop, Connie could see, but Connie would not let her give up. "Are you thinking of sand in your toes?" she asked kindly. "It helps."

"It just gets me mixed up to be thinking of my toes when I am looking at my fingers," said Winifred.

"Well, you must try not to look at your fingers; look only at the music, once you get into position," said Connie. "Then it will be easier for you to think of sand in your toes and get expression into it—feeling. Otherwise, you are just playing notes—the way Ray Arp does—and not music. You must think what the music *means*."

"I'll try," said Winifred with a sad sigh.

Connie knew what was in Winifred's head. Winifred had the idea that since she was not very good at gym, she probably was not going to be good at the piano either. "Winifred," said Connie, "you may not be good at basketball; but that does not mean that you will not be good at the piano. For all you know, you may be the best in the Alley at the piano. Now, again, find Middle C."

Connie had meant for the lesson to be only fifteen minutes. But it had ended up being twenty-five. A penny a minute, that was fair. By the end of these twenty-five minutes, Winifred could find all the notes of "On the Sand."

"You have done very well," said Connie. "And you may

come in every afternoon at four to practice, since you don't have a piano."

A startled look swept over Winifred's face, but she said, "O. K." And the two of them stepped over Wags, asleep in the doorway between the dining room and the kitchen— Winifred to go home and Connie to swing and rest and think. What a great deal to have accomplished! On a Saturday afternoon in June, she had given a piano lesson to a person who had never been given one before.

"Now," thought Connie. "Who else to have for piano pupils? You are not a real teacher if you have only one," she thought. "You can't call yourself an Alley Conservatory of Music for just Winifred." From her swing, she looked to see who was out—what likely pupils there might be, ready to be rounded up.

Some of the little ones were doing really hard things. Notesy was pulling a big wooden box that her brother had tied a rope to. It was heavy. Even so, she tried pulling it with Nicky in it. That was hard. "It's a sleigh," she said to Connie. Greggie Goode had put his express wagon on top of the back trailer attached to his odd-looking special sort of a three-wheeled bike. He was pulling all of that. Katy Starr was riding Brother Stuart's tiny three-wheeler. She was not sitting on the seat, she was sitting on the back axle between the wheels, where usually an extra person could stand. She looked like a frog. After all, she was eleven and large for that vehicle. Her sharp voice directed traffic and life in general, whenever it needed direction.

Connie jumped off the swing and stood at the gate to get

a close view of life in the Alley. A baby doll, rubber and naked, lay in a puddle made by Bully Vardeer's hose. Sometimes, as he sat sunning, Bully Vardeer liked to water his Japanese garden. He had made a miniature little pool in his garden with a tiny fountain, too, cool-sounding on a hot and humid day.

"Some people can't wait for the little ones to get into bed to water," said Mrs. Carroll in annoyance, and loudly so the whole Alley could hear. The little doll lay there, wet and muddy but smiling. Her eyes were a startling blue, fixed on the sky. Along came Nicky Carroll, and he amiably stepped on her, and then he jumped on her.

"Why do you step on that baby doll, Nicky?" asked Connie.

"I always step on baby dolls," he affirmed matter-of-factly.

"Want to take piano lessons? From me? And stop stepping on dolls and cats, be nice?" asked Connie.

"Sure," said Nicky.

"Ask Bang-bang-your-daid Danny when you see him," said Connie. "You can come together."

"Su-ure," said Nicky.

They were awfully little, but it is never too early to begin.

Greggie Goode, tired out from his lugging, came back and asked to swing. Connie let him, and she got back on the swing, too. All the mothers had told their children not to let Greggie bite them because last week he was bitten by a rat in the churchyard, and he was being carefully watched for signs of rabies. The waiting time was nearly over. But Greggie was a gentle boy. He would never bite anyone, anyway—not like Anthony Bigelow, who often bit, no matter what, and despite the Katy law against it.

Anthony even tried to get Greggie to bite the little ones. Every time he saw Greggie, "He's mad, he's mad," he'd say and roll on the grass and writhe, predicting what might lie ahead for Greggie. Anthony came along now as Connie and Greggie were swinging, and he said, "He'll give you rabies, and you will writhe, like this." He writhed. Greggie's lower lip quivered. He muttered to himself about Anthony Bigelow and the rat.

"Go away, Anthony," said Connie. "That's not nice." And to Greggie she said, "Never mind him, Greggie. You won't get rabies. That was a nice rat, I'm sure, since it lived in a churchyard. Would you like to take piano lessons? I'll give them to you."

Greggie quickly said he would, so now there were two pupils. "Registration growing . . . blooming," thought Connie happily. "Five cents for you," she said. She had decided Mama was right, at least for children under ten. For them, lessons would be five cents. Connie wondered where Billy was. Casing somewhere, probably. She knew he would not mind that she was not casing when he heard that she had earned twenty-five cents. And that she had Winifred, Greggie, and probably Nicky and Danny already as pupils for the conservatory. Sometimes Billy earned money—shoveling snow, sweeping sidewalks. Why shouldn't she, casing or not? That was fair. Wouldn't Billy be surprised at the size of her class! She would have them play in a recital in just about a week—if they did well. What an important day in the Alley that would be—the day of the recital.

Little Jane with the sweet high voice, so high she sounded like a little pipe organ, came to the gate. "Can I swing?" she asked.

"Not right now, but—would you like to take piano lessons?" asked Connie.

"O.K., when?" asked Jane.

"Tomorrow," said Connie.

"O.K.," said Jane.

"They're five cents," said Connie.

"O.K.," said Jane. Jane was pretty small for lessons, some might think. Connie would not agree. Jane carried a tune perfectly, though only three. "Do you think three too young for piano lessons?" Connie asked herself. "Not at all," she replied. "Mozart could compose music at the age of five." And so had she, Connie—"The Teddy Bear Song."

Well, let's see. Who else for pupils? Connie jumped out of the swing, got on her bike, and slowly rode up the Alley. Many Frankensteins were in the Alley now . . . the four Carrolls with cardboard cartons on over their heads, walking jerkily and frighteningly (their mother had painted the terrifying mouths on the square heads, and the tiny ones hoped they would not dream about it all). Stephen Carroll was being the main Frankenstein . . . Connie recognized him by the size.

"Frankensteins," Connie said politely—it gave her courage not to see their real faces—"how would you all like to take piano lessons from me?"

"Pianner, pianner," said Nicky in a Frankenstein mechanical voice. "I already said I'd tooken," and he stopped his stiff-legged trip up the Alley long enough to pretend to play a piano in a Frankenstein frightening way.

"Sure," said Stephen. "I'll come." Notesy and Star, from inside their box heads, gave splendid imitations of the head-man Frankenstein man. "We'll come tomorrow," they said. They jerked their horrible heads to right and left.

"You can be on scholarships," said Connie. "No charge for you." She knew that schools give out scholarships. The Carrolls, certain to be talented, could be her scholarship people. "So," she said, "I'll see you tomorrow."

Just then, Bang-bang-you're-daid Danny came along, having at last found a suitable Frankenstein box for his head, too. Confusing for the moment the courtesy of the invitation with the fact that he was being Frankenstein, he asked if the piano lessons were only for Frankensteins and should he wear his head?

"No," Connie said. "Come as you usually are . . . just you. You and Nicky can come together."

When news of Connie's music studio got around—the Alley Conservatory of Music—she had lots of eager applicants. One problem—it was for them to solve, not her —was how earn the nickel for the lesson? You can't have everybody on scholarships. The school would fall apart. She suggested that Bang-bang-you're-daid Danny might carry messages, be the messenger boy of the Alley. And she suggested that Danny, since his lesson was going to be at the same time as Nicky's, play the xylophone instead. Imagine a duet of xylophone and piano by children aged three! Their

233

mothers would sink with pride. Happy? Connie was very happy with all her plans going along so nicely.

Billy came in. Silently he got up on the other swing. Silently they swung. Then Billy said, "Connie."

"Yes," said Connie.

"Nothing doing today—no smell of Muras, no man asking, 'Does this dog bite?', no sound of 'On the Street Where You Live.' Casing was dull. There has been nothing doing for a long time . . ."

"Ah, Billy. Too bad, too bad," said Connie. She had had a wonderful day, rounding up piano pupils, creating a music conservatory, much better than a day, another dull day, of casing with nothing happening. Fine to case when you see something. But it tries your patience when you don't. "But you know, Billy," she added, "a watched pot never boils. Why not stop for a while, take piano instead?"

"Well," said Billy. "I'll case for one more week . . . just one more week . . . just in case." Billy and Connie both smiled at this smart thing to say. "Then," said Billy, "if there is no smell of Muras . . . no whistling . . . nothing . . . I quit!"

"They . . . the burglars, are apt to come only when something important is going on," said Connie. "Something like Alumni Day, not an ordinary everyday day . . . something really important so they have a clear coast."

"There are no rules for burglaries," said Billy morosely.

"I know," said Connie. "That's life. Billy, soon I have to go in and look for the music for all my pupils. Eight at least! They can't all play 'On the Sand.' There has to be some other tune."

Then, some children streamed out of the Arps' cellar, next door. Katy didn't know yet about the Alley Conservatory of Music or that casing was still being done to keep the Alley safe. "Swingers!" she shouted as she ran out of the Arps' yard.

Billy and Connie were facing the other way swinging. Billy half turned his head toward the Arps' yard. "Yeah? So what?" he said. For a few minutes longer they swung. Then Billy hopped down. "So long," he said. And he went crawling . . . it was his habit now . . . up the Alley, past Bully Vardeer's garden, where he lonesomely took up his position. "Why did Connie have to go in for piano lessons and conservatories," he wondered, "with so much casing still to be done?"

18
♵ ♵ ♵
A DAY OF IMPORTANCE

At last it was the day of the recital. It dawned sunny, bright, and hot. There was no casing going on, for Billy was sick with a cold, and he had to stay in his bedroom. For some days Billy had had to stay in because of his cold. Connie had been able to concentrate on her pupils—all were coming along fine—without her conscience bothering her about whether or not she should join Billy in casing. Everyone could now play "Indian Drum Song" and "Mary Had a Little Lamb." Some could play "On the Sand" or "The Burly, Burly Bear." All the pupils had been very interested in the idea of a recital. "Poor things," Connie thought. "They don't know how awful recitals are."

During the week, the little boys, Danny and Nicky especially, had wanted to come every half hour or so to play the piano. But Nanny sometimes would not let them in. "Not now," she'd say. "Shoo!" Off they'd run, saying, "Bang-bang-you're-daid!" Then back they'd come as soon as they could, saying, "Bang-bang-you're-daid," or, "Heigh-ho,

Silver!" Danny always fired his gun at Connie or into the air as he came into the yard . . . an unusual way for coming to piano lessons, but his way. Nicky was always, these days, dressed in his Zorro cape. He always carried a little rope in his hand. He even swung with this small piece of rope clutched tightly in his moist left hand, and he climbed with it likewise. Probably he did not put it down even at mealtime. Perhaps he slept with it. Almost all the time both he and Danny had on their Heigh-ho Silver cowboy boots. Usually, Danny was dressed in a blend of costumes . . . a fireman's hat with an Indian feather in it and, like Nicky, the cape part of his Zorro uniform. He could answer the roll call of any famous character, in life or fiction, on the plains, in the city, on a pirate ship, in space. He had his gun with him always, clicking it, saying, "Bang-bang-you're daid." Mama did not like this. She said in her family no one had been allowed to own a toy gun, and especially they had not been allowed to point a gun at anyone if they did get hold of one. Despite this, Danny was a great favorite in the Alley with mothers and fathers, and even with Mama.

The two Zorros . . . Danny and Nicky . . . were the most eager pupils that Connie had. The only trouble was—Nicky would not let his rope out of his hand. At first this bothered Connie. She'd say, "You must put your rope here on the table."

"Oh, no," he'd say.

"But," said Connie. "It is not possible to play the piano with a rope in your hand."

"I can," he always said. And he did. Well, it was true, he could! He needed only one hand for "The Burly, Burly

Bear." That was his piece . . . and that was what he was going to play today at the recital. It had five notes for one hand only . . . perfect for a boy who always carried a rope in the other.

Before their lessons, Connie always let Nicky and Danny warm up a minute. (Her teacher had always—though impatiently and only for a minute or two—let her play "Chopsticks" or "Heart and Soul" before her lesson.) Nicky could not play "Chopsticks" or "Heart and Soul," but he played loudly and with expression something he made up.

"You have a very good ear," said Connie.

"Yes," he said. "I can wiggle it." Every time Connie praised him, he wiggled his ear.

"He's probably a genius," thought Connie. "His mother should get him a piano as soon as possible. You cannot begin too soon with these little fellows; think of Mozart." Connie thought of Mozart, tiptoeing down the stairs in the middle of the night, when all was still and everyone was sleeping, and of him in his nightshirt, composing a lovely thing. She was convinced that Nicky Carroll was a genius, too.

"You do very nicely, Nicky," said Connie to him. "You may be a genius."

"Zorro," he corrected her. Then, flushed with pleasure over the praise, he would sit politely at the edge of a big chair and wait while Danny had his xylophone lesson. Danny did much better on the xylophone than on the piano, and since Connie called her studio, "Alley Conservatory of Music," any instrument could be included if she knew how to play it and teach it. She could only play the piano and the xylophone. Therefore, so far, that was all she could teach.

Connie's great Aunt Beasie had given her this xylophone for Christmas when she was five. It was a good two-octave xylophone and fine for "My Country 'Tis of Thee," which required a lower note for the " 'Tis" than some xylophones, and harmonicas, too, have. Danny had learned "The Burly, Burly Bear" very quickly, so perhaps he was a musical genius, too—on the xylophone, not the piano. That made two musical geniuses in the Alley—rare, but possible, and this did not count Katy Starr, who was practically a genius at everything.

"What a pleasure," thought Connie, "to teach little children on the order of Nicky and Danny. They were so interested, with their ropes and costumes and large round eyes. So, now the training period was over; now was the great day itself. If only her pupils did as well for the recital as they had for plain lessons! And too bad that Billy could not attend as part of the audience. It would be nice to have an audience of one, at least—because probably none of the mothers would come. Mama always came to Connie's recitals; but these mothers with their cups of coffee and their strolling up and down the Alley, chatting, first with one person, then with another, would probably not even know there was a recital—let alone come. Oh, if only Billy was well! He'd come. She knew he'd come, unless he had to case. But there he was—in bed!

If you had to stay in a bedroom in the Alley, you could not be in a better one than in Billy's, for it looked straight down the Alley to the Circle. Also, from its window you could see to the left and to the right to both the iron gates on the top ends of the T. Although Billy was supposed to be staying in bed with his hacking cough, often Connie glimpsed his pale face at the window. Sometimes he wanly waved to Connie as she swung. Today, early, to cheer him up and show him that he was missed, she went to his gate, called up to him, and said, "Billy, today is the day of my recital, I mean my pupils' recital. We're having it at eleven o'clock. Mama's going to serve lunch in the garden afterwards. I'm sorry you can't be in the audience and can't have lunch . . . probably hot dogs . . . I'll get one to you somehow. At first I was going to have it at three o'clock, but the little ones wouldn't be able to wait that long. So— eleven o'clock is the hour."

"Oh-ho," said Billy. "It's an *important* day, isn't it?"

The meaningful way in which he said "important" reminded Connie that important days, days such as Alumni Days under big tops, were the kind of days on which bullet-head burglars broke into Alley houses. But how could burglars have heard about her recital? They couldn't have . . . she hadn't put it in the paper, not even in news of the Campus, and there was no green tent in her yard. In this way, Connie reassured herself. But she had not counted on parents. She had not invited the parents because she had not thought they would want to take time out from their coffee and their chatting up and down the Alley. Just pupils and friends of pupils were what she expected. But the parents came, and it was their coming that made this an important day, a day like under the big top on the campus, a day that burglars, casing, would immediately know was important, seeing one parent after another leave her own little house in the Alley and go into Connie's . . . all congregate there. They probably even knew that Billy, their counter-caser, was sick in bed—supposed to be—with an awful cold.

The day had dawned bright and clear and hot. Danny and Nicky had arrived for the first time very early in the morning, about seven-thirty, their faces shining, their hair wet and brushed down. Connie hadn't even gotten out of bed yet, but she had heard the back door bell ring, had guessed who it was, and had raced down in her robe before Nanny could holler at them—say they were waking up the whole family and, besides, that she was listening to the seven-thirty news and had now missed the most important thing, they always gave the most important thing first. Scare them she would (though they were not so scared of Nanny as Billy and Hugsy were because of their costumes, ropes, guns, and trappings, and could always holler back, "Bang-bang-you're-daid." However, today, in their best clothes . . . Nicky only had his rope . . . they might be frightened.) and they might not come back for the recital.

"Hello," said Connie to them sweetly, to counteract the effect of Nanny's scowls.

"Here's we," said Danny.

"I see," said Connie. "You look so nice. And, Nicky, I see you have your rope." The two tried to come in. "Oh, dear," thought Connie. "I should have had the recital at nine o'clock instead of eleven. How can they wait so long?" Out loud she said, "Nicky? Danny? I haven't had my breakfast yet. And, anyway, the recital is at eleven o'clock. O. K.?"

Danny and Nicky left cheerfully. They asked to swing, instead, and tried not to go too high. From then on they came to the back door every fifteen minutes or so the whole morning, asking when it was going to be time.

Then, finally, it was time. At about a quarter to eleven, Greggie Goode, the other Carrolls, little Jane, all the other members of the Alley Conservatory of Music came, including Winifred. All had their good, not their Alley, clothes on, except Winifred, who had on her Alley purple slacks. Quickly, seeing the others, she realized the mistake in her costume and raced home to change. Imagine at the age of three, Danny and Nicky knowing to wear best suits to recitals and not Alley clothes . . . not Zorro costumes or cowboy clothes, and to wear ties besides! During the morning, Nicky's mother had bellowed at him, "Nicky!"

"What?" he bellowed back.

"Don't get your suit dirty, or you can't be in the recital."

Well, back came Winifred in a skirt and blouse. Connie asked her if her mother were coming, and she said she didn't know. "Can you imagine," thought Connie, "*my* mother not coming to a recital of *mine* that I was in? But," she thought, "that's life." Anyway, to her surprise, Mrs. Carroll, Nicky's mother, arrived. She came with Mrs. Most, Danny's mother, a fine musician herself. You would think that Danny's mother, not Connie, would have thought of the Alley Conservatory of Music, since she had gone to the Boston one. But she hadn't. Bang-bang-you're-daid Danny was probably all that she could manage to do in one lifetime. You couldn't expect the mother of Danny Most to have the time to give piano lessons . . . luckily for Connie and her conservatory. There couldn't be two conservatories in the Alley.

Then came other mothers of other performers. Greggie Goode's mother came. As usual, she looked startled. For some reason, Mrs. Goode always looked startled. Then came Brother Stuart's mother. Brother Stuart was not a student of Connie's, but Mrs. Stuart was one of the sweetest mothers in the Alley, and she just had to come, she said. She had on pretty clothes, too . . . a white skirt and a flowered blouse . . . whereas, Mrs. Carroll had her Alley slacks on . . . she always wore slacks. Connie had never seen her in a dress except at one New Year's Eve party that she gave in her house, when she wore a white flapper dress of the nineteen-twenties. It had fringe on the bottom, and her husband had bought it for her at the Good Will Industries as a joke. Mrs. Carroll looked cute and funny in it. She should wear dresses more often, Connie thought, real dresses of nowadays, not costume dresses of the flapper days. Mrs. Most was likewise dressed in slacks, though she often wore dresses. Then, mother after mother after mother arrived, including mothers without children in the conservatory. All the children in the Alley filed in—Judy Fabadessa, Katy Starr, the Arps, all. How had they heard about the recital? "Well, that's life," thought Connie. News gets around in the Alley of something important . . . like a pot-luck supper or a recital. News of this sort also gets around outside the Alley, too. Practically everybody, mothers and children, were congregating in Connie's house, even Arnold, who said music made him sick. But the fathers were not there. Being Friday, all fathers were at work; they were at one of the regular Friday faculty luncheons, which had to be attended by each and every professor-father of the children.

Connie had not put up signs in the Alley, the way Ray Arp and Hugsy—Brother Stuart, too—did, on every gate, when they were going to have a sale of old soldiers, toys, and comics in their back yard. She had put up just one sign on her own gate, which said, "Please do not ring the bell and ask to swing because there is a piano recital going on, (signed) Connie Ives." Now, that is not exactly an invitation to a recital, is it? It is simply a request for there to be no interruptions, no bell ringing, while a recital went on. But the children all came, anyway, and the mothers—invitation or not.

Connie's heart sank. Katy, June, Judy, Laura, everybody! All the big and all the little children. All the lovers of the swing and all the non-lovers, or rather, the one non-lover of the swing—Katy. At the sight of Katy coming into the yard, Connie became really scared. Goose flesh popped out all over her. Yet, why should it? *She* wasn't going to play. She was just going to be the teacher, looking on, giving smiles of encouragement, her hands folded calmly over her stomach. Now Connie knew what her piano teacher, Miss Fannie Moore, must go through every time she gave a recital for her pupils. Ts! Connie had always thought that it was only *they*, the ones who were in the recital, who got scared, not the teacher. Not so. *She* the *teacher* was the most scared. Her knees wobbled, but she found chairs . . . Mama helped . . . for the mothers. Connie did not mind the mothers. But the sight of the entire child population of the Alley—approximately thirty-three, not counting babies in laps—rather unnerved her. However, they made themselves at home on the floor; they had to—there were not that many chairs in this house, and no one could sit on the George Washington chair, unroped off though it was.

Nicky was the first to perform. Connie had meant the pupils to perform according to age, but Notesy would not come out from under the table. So Nicky was first. Connie wound the piano stool up higher and higher. Katy said, "Oh, how cute!" What a relief! Had Katy said, "Ugh! How boring!" that would have been the end of the recital. Everyone would have left with a whoop and a holler.

"It wobbles," said Nicky of the stool.

"Never mind," said Connie. "Wobbling sometimes helps music."

Nicky was anxious to get over with "The Burly, Burly Bear," and also "On the Sand," which he had gotten in his head from listening to Winifred. He played well. Some might not think this easy, either, with his rope in his left hand. But he did very well. He concentrated on where C was, a little to the left of the gold letters, and since he played only with his right hand, why shouldn't he have a rope in his left? It did not interfere much and gave confidence. He was through in about one minute.

Danny was next—on the xylophone. After their solos, Connie had hoped that the two boys would play a duet, Nicky on the piano, Danny on the xylophone. She now had little hope of this, though, for the boys could see by this time how terrible recitals were. Danny was in a black mood —he had not liked the clapping and he longed for his gun.

Nicky held his head in his hands. He had not liked the clapping, either. Well, neither had Connie ever liked clapping or bravos. (Who does like clapping and bravos? "Only great prima donnas," she thought. They are the only people who love clapping and stamping, whistling plain or whistling through the fingers. They—some of these great people—even employ—*pay*—people to come and clap, they like it so much. Connie's father had told her this . . . her mother also. It must be so.) However, Nicky, slowly unfolding his head from his hands, surprised her. He said, "Now for the duet."

It would be hard to name the duet that Nicky and Danny played . . . he on the piano, Danny on the xylophone. It was a blend, but they played it thoughtfully. It lasted forty seconds, and they received some more loud applause.

"Really," thought Connie. "Mrs. Goode should be more quiet. That laugh!" Then the two little boys sat down on a big, tall dark-red armchair with petit-point embroidery all over it. This chair was known as Uncle Ham's chair. Unlike the George Washington chair, it could be sat on. The boys were being very good, and the chair, though weak, did not break.

Next on the program came Winifred. She was supposed to be last, but she asked to be next—get it over with—and Connie let her. Since Winifred did not want to talk, Connie announced her first piece. "On the Sand," Connie said. By mistake, Winifred played "The Burly, Burly Bear" first. Then she played "On the Sand." She played both of them as fast as she could, not making any error other than getting the wrong piece first and playing them skippity-skip instead of burlily (for "The Burly, Burly Bear") and pensively (for "On the Sand"). And since she was in a hurry to get through, and since she did get through, everybody clapped and said, "Yay-o-o-oh!" The audience was not tired of hearing the same pieces played by everybody in the conservatory because everybody played them differently, and they sounded like different music. Winifred looked pleased. Her shining face was pretty, and she sat down on the big armchair next to Hugsy, who said she had been the best yet; his husky voice really meant it.

After all the other pupils had played, the big girls, Laura, Katy, and June, who had not said "boring" once, all asked if, even though they were not pupils of the Alley Conservatory of Music, they could play something. Connie was not sure that this was the right thing to do, for non-pupils to play at a recital given just by real pupils. Still, it was very nice of them . . . especially as the whole real part of the recital, the eight-pupil part, had lasted all told only ten minutes. Later, Mama said she thought it had been fine, everybody joining in and having a good time.

Connie said, "You're not supposed to be having a good time. You're supposed to be having a recital."

"Excuse me," said Mama.

Still, in the main, Connie agreed with her mother. Join in. Naturally you would not do this if you were in a big hall and listening to a great player. Then, naturally it would not be the thing to do . . . join in, say, may I do something now? But it was all right here, and Mama was right. It stretched things out . . . perhaps, today, it had stretched things out too long.

June and Katy and Laura each played "Heart and Soul" also "Chopsticks." This was not the sort of music that Connie taught her pupils. But what could she do? Then Laura played "Nearer My God to Thee," and Katy played the "Fifth Symphony" of Beethoven by ear. June played a piece that she had been practicing ever since she had moved into the house next door. It may not have been so tiresome to the audience as it was to Connie, who had heard it for three years. Then the people, big and little, said that Connie, the teacher, should play something now. Connie really didn't want to . . . not at her first recital. It is strain enough to be in charge of a recital, let alone playing a selection besides. She considered giving the sort of little speech her piano teacher, Miss Fannie Moore, gave at the end of her recitals—before the cookies and the Dixie Cups. Miss Fannie Moore always said, her hands clasped neatly over her stomach to depict relaxation, "Well, it's true some of us made some little mistake or other, didn't we? But after all, we are all human, aren't we? And we all make some little mistake sometime or other, don't we? And the important thing, the most important thing, is that we did, each and every one of us did, reach the end of our piece; and that was the important thing, to reach the end, wasn't it?"

Ah, Connie couldn't say it. Vividly though she remembered her teacher's after-recital speech, she could not say it. So she neither played anything nor said anything, and everybody went out into the garden, where Mama was spreading the picnic table, borrowed from Mrs. Carroll. Papa, of course, was still at the faculty luncheon. Nanny had gone next door to Mrs. Harrington's to play bridge. Tired from her exertions, Connie stretched out on a long garden chair, unable to eat anything. It was as though in a dream that she noticed Bully Vardeer and Princey on No-Name Street. In Connie's yard, everybody was having a wonderful time, talking, laughing. The gaiety really and truly made this day a day as important as the day of the alumni lunch under the tent. People were all sitting around, eating, talking about the recital, chatting about this and that, and then suddenly, just like on that other famous day, Alumni Day, the unexpected happened.

Who should appear at the back gate but Bully Vardeer! He looked haggard; but he spoke quietly, even more so than usual, the way a person does when he is tense and trying to hold back his excitement. Connie knew in a second what had happened. No one had to tell her. Look at the time. Twenty minutes after twelve, the perfect time of the day for robberies . . . the perfect time, the perfect day . . . the day of the recital of the Alley Conservatory of Music, with all the people here, not in their own homes, and the chief, the main counter-caser, Billy Maloon, sick in bed with a cold. What day could be more perfect for burglars to make a burglary than a day like this with the chief counter-caser of the casers sick?

"Could I use your phone?" asked Bully Vardeer. "To call the police? My phone is out of order. My house has been broken into."

"Oh, gracious!" cried Mama. "Certainly, go right in!"

The people crowded around to hear Bully's story. "What happened? What happened?" everybody asked when Bully came back out. Mama made the announcement; in dramatic tones she said, "The house of Joe Below has just been broken into."

Connie was the first out of the gate. She was going to be the first to tell Billy Maloon. Poor Billy! To miss first of all the recital and then the breaking in of Bully Vardeer's house that he and she had been trying to protect for days. All their watching, all their warning, their casing, all for nothing! She should not have had a recital. Then there would have been no burglary. But, pshaw! Life has to go on, burglaries or not. She ran to Billy's back gate. She couldn't get in. It was padlocked as usual. She looked up at Billy's window; it was wide open. Its bright yellow curtains were blowing in the breeze. Something told Connie that behind those bright yellow curtains Billy was not there.

"Billy," she called.

There was no answer; there was certainly no answer. Where, then, was Billy Maloon?

19
♭ ♭ ♭
WHERE BILLY MALOON WAS

Getting no answer from Billy Maloon, Connie had to just guess where he might be. Since he wasn't anywhere in the Alley where he could be seen, he must be up in Mr. Bernadette's catalpa tree. He certainly would not have gone out of the Alley—would he?—not with burglars loose in the world and him with a cough.

People of the Alley were slowly leaving Connie's garden, some still nibbling on their hot dogs, wiping the mustard off their fingers. They made their way toward Bully's gate and excitedly discussed this latest Alley outrage, asking questions about how it had happened and reminiscing about all the burglaries they might ever have had or heard about. Connie was rather sorry that this burglary had been in someone else's house, not hers. She heard Bully say, "Well, I must hurry back into the house—the police will soon be here." He strode through his garden and up his back stoop and into his back door. His lips were pressed grimly together; his strong chest was thrust out; he was ready to fight burglars if he found any. "A brave man, Bully Vardeer," thought Connie. She hurried down the Alley to Mr. Bernadette's house, the very last end one on the top of the T of the Alley. There she hoped to discover Billy Maloon in the Bernadette lookout tree.

She did. She saw his bright-eyed excited face peering down at her through the thick early summer foliage.

"Hurry!" he said. "I thought you'd never come," he said impatiently. "You and your old music! On the very day of a burglary, you have to go and give an old piano recital."

Connie was grieved. "Well, Billy," she said. "It was really the other way around. No recital, no burglary. Then where would you be?" Being a good climber, she swung herself up the steep wall on the Waldo Place side of Mr. Bernadette's garden. Only the end houses had these pretty red brick walls. Then she swung herself up beside Billy inside the

dense deep tree called catalpa. Billy lost no time giving her the details.

"I was lying in bed, Connie," Billy said, "trying to get over my cold when suddenly, Connie, I heard the tune; you know, *the tune*, the tune of the bullet-head man . . ."

" 'On the Street Where You Live,' " Connie said.

"Yes," said Billy. "So I grabbed my camera, put it around my neck . . . it has a long strap, you know . . . and I climbed out my window and onto the little roof over the back stoop. I jumped into Mrs. Orr's yard, not ours, and landed on her honeysuckle bush. Thank goodness, I missed the roses, and I crawled across her yard . . . not to be seen by the whistler . . . and I got over her fence and into the twins' yard, and then across it . . . the same way . . . and up and over their fence, sticking close to the houses all the while . . . and, thank goodness, no one saw me . . ."

"Of course not . . . everyone was at my house. Now they're all coming up the Alley to the gate here to watch for the police . . . see what was taken . . . the whole thing. So whisper—unless you want them to know we are up here."

"Well, let me finish. I didn't mean I hoped no *Alley people would see me* . . . I meant *burglar* people see me. . . . I finally made my way up here, into the tree. And, Connie, it was not easy to get up here without busting my camera. But I did, luckily . . . you'll see . . ."

"Oh!" gasped Connie. "Billy, you are brilliant!" She could see what was coming next.

"So," said Billy. "Sure enough. Soon, along comes our friend ("Friend, hah!" interrupted Connie, enjoying the sarcasm), the bullet-head man. Walking briskly, he was, and whistling his tune. And he trots right up Bully Vardeer's steps as if Bully were expecting him ("Bully probably would like to paint him, likes to paint everybody," Connie put in), stood a moment, looking toward Larrabee . . . where his cronies were . . . and I snapped a picture of him! He was smoking a Mura; I could smell it. Then he whistled faster, and one of his cronies . . . I don't know how many he had, but this other guy . . . Sawtooth Pete, I suppose ("Just like Mr. Fabadessa said," Connie put in) . . . swiftly joined him, and I snapped a picture of him . . . this sawtooth guy, too. Bullet-head gave the door a big push—that was all it needed apparently. Bully Vardeer . . . ts, ts . . . in spite of all our warnings, when he took Princey out for a walk, did not close the outer green door. So there they were inside the little vestibule. I heard a cracking noise. Door being busted in, I thought . . ."

"Just like ours," said Connie.

"Then in they stepped, I suppose. But they were not in there long, just a few minutes, when some guy out on Larrabee began whistling, 'Get Me to the Church on Time.' You know, it must be their signal to beat it . . . they must have seen Bully coming home . . . and the two inside guys came out. I snapped another picture . . . of the two of them together. They had . . ."

"The Olivetti typewriter," said Connie.

"A typewriter," said Billy. "Naturally I did not know the make."

"Olivetti," said Connie. "Brand-new. Bully saw it was

gone from the desk in the hall where it had just been delivered . . . that's all he knows about . . ."

"Well, and so they strode swiftly away. I heard a car start off in a rush. I snapped a picture of it when it came in view beside the tennis court, but it will probably be a blur. Of course, the license plates wouldn't show up . . . but, anyway, the more pictures the better," said Billy.

"True," said Connie. "But where are the police? They sure got to our broke-in house faster than this."

"Slow-pokes," said Billy.

At this moment they heard the police siren. "Here they come," whispered Billy. The police car sounded as though it had come into Waldo Place on two wheels, and it stopped suddenly, with a screech. Two policemen hopped out of the car, drew their pistols, just as they had in front of Connie's house, rushed to the front door, and said, "Come out or we'll shoot. We have you covered." And into the house they went!

"Dum-de-dum-dum," said Connie. She was so scared that she thought she would fall out of the tree. "Did you see those two policemen?" she asked Billy.

"Yes," said Billy. "Yes, so?"

"Well," said Connie, trying to hold her voice steady, "they are the two policemen, the two first policemen that Mama said she could see her diamond ring on my father's pencil case through the pockets of! And that were in the presink car the day of the bomb scare with the pencil marked J. I."

"Oh," said Billy. "My gosh! Ratty and Ippy?"

"Ratty and Ippy," said Connie, dazed. "It's as though it has all happened before."

"It has," said Billy.

Now, since Bully Vardeer had strode through his back door and was inside his house when the two policemen entered, there was little chance of their getting diamond rings on pencil clasps or anything else. Brave Bully followed them every step of the way upstairs—(Had the burglars touched his great paintings? No.)—downstairs (Had they bothered the organ? No.). Sometimes burglars just break things for the sake of breaking things, but there had not been time for this. Soon everybody came out and congregated in front of Bully's house. What a day! First a recital and then a burglary! It was not as great a burglary as Connie's. Just the typewriter gone—the Olivetti. Not a burglary inside a burglary. No hunches needed here, since Bully accompanied the policemen through the house. But— this was the important thing—one of the policemen, the tall one named Officer Ippolito, took out his notebook, and he took out his pencil to write up the burglary. He put his notebook on the top of the red brick wall just two feet under where Connie and Billy were lying, clinging to the thick branch of the catalpa tree. Connie nudged Billy. He took in immediately what she wanted him to . . . that Officer Ippolito was making notes with a shiny, silvery-looking pencil, not the sort of ordinary pencil that you would expect a policeman to use, not a plain yellow wooden one.

Then Connie, seeing all her friends and the Alley people below her, felt brave, and she did a very brave thing. It is true she did not have Nanny's tall green glass Tiffany vase to drop on this . . . suspected . . . burglar-policeman's head. Even if she had had the vase, it was unlikely that she would have dropped it on his or anyone else's head. Connie was just not the bopping-on-the-head sort of girl. Quiet, she was, quiet and gentle. But she said out loud, in her reasonable, calm little voice, "You know, Billy, my father once had a pencil exactly like that."

The policeman, Ippy, hearing a voice from out of the tree above him, was very startled, naturally, and he looked up.

"He did?" said Billy. "Hm-m-m."

"Yes," said Connie. "The pencil my father had—that was like the one this nice policeman has—is where he used to keep my mother's diamond ring, on its clasp, that's where. But that's gone now—the pencil—and the ring's gone with it."

"Gone?" said Billy.

"Yes, gone," said Connie. "Some burglars took it . . . well, we *think* burg . . ." Connie paused meaningfully.

Officer Ippolito cast a searching glance up at Connie through the leaves. Did he or didn't he recognize this girl as an inhabitant of the house around the corner that he and Sergeant Rattray had investigated a few weeks ago? His hand was shaking a little as he wrote down the facts. He said he and Sergeant Rattray would report to headquarters. And since there was nothing more to do, they'd go. ("How disappointing this burglary must be to these two compared to ours," thought Connie.) However, as he was about to leave, Sergeant Rattray accidentally nudged Officer Ippolito's arm, and the shiny pencil fell. It fell over Mr. Bernadette's wall and down into the hidy-hole in Mr. Bernadette's yard, all covered over with ivy and heavy creeping squash vines.

"Oh!" said Officer Ippolito. "I must get that pencil." And he started to climb over the red-brick wall.

"Isn't that a lot of trouble to go to . . . just for a pencil?" asked Bully Vardeer in his soft, deliberate voice. "I'll get you another one."

"I want that one," said the policeman. "My wife gave it to me on my birthday." ("What a liar!" thought Connie.) He was puffing . . . in quite a heat—as he tried to swing himself up and over Mr. Bernadette's wall.

"Oh, well . . ." said Bully in his quiet voice. "It's a special pencil then. I'll get it for you." And he scaled Mr. Bernadette's wall—he was quite athletic, and all the sunning that he did added to his strength. He strode across Mr. Bernadette's garden—he was now barefoot, having kicked off his moccasins. ("Good for the feet," he often said, "to go barefoot.") Then he climbed down into the hidy-hole. He looked like half a man to Connie . . . like a statue in a museum, cut off at the waist.

Bully then felt around in the hidy-hole for the pencil with his hands.

Connie saw Mama standing in the Alley, outside Mr. Bernadette's wall, and she swung herself down out of the tree. "Mama," she whispered. "Those are the same two policemen who came to our house . . . that you saw through the pockets of . . ."

"Sh-sh-sh," said Mama. "I see they are, darling."

"And the pencil they are looking for in the hidy-hole is Papa's pencil with the J. I. letters on it."

"You saw it?" asked Mama.

"Yes," said Connie.

There were a lot of people swarming around now, even little fellows from the recital, and they had hopped down into the hidy-hole with Bully Vardeer, hoping to be the one to find the important pencil of the policeman. By this time, even Officer Ippolito had climbed over the fence and was in there feeling around with his long arm. He looked like a man in swimming, trying to find a lost something or a shell on the bottom of the sea.

Mama came into the yard—by now somebody had opened the Bernadettes' gate, and she said, "I've always been good at finding things. I always have a sort of hunch as to where things are, in pockets—or hidy-holes. You all get out and let me try to find the pencil. I have a sort of hunch. I know this pencil well."

When Officer Ippolito saw Mama, of course, he must have remembered her from the day of her famous burglary. His already red face turned even redder. He stood up, looked at Connie's mother and at Connie, and their burglary probably all came back to him. Connie said to her mother in a voice that all could hear, "No wonder, Mama, he wants his pencil back. It is such a pretty one, just like Papa's new one that the ladies of his department gave him for Christmas with J.I. on it and your ring on it."

Silence fell over everybody as they tried to recall the details . . . something about a pencil, they remem-

bered . . . about Mr. Ives's pencil and ring and robbery . . . something . . . everything. Officer Ippolito
picked himself up, brushed himself off, gave a disagreeable
sort of a snort, and said, "Oh, well, what's a little pencil
more or less in the world? Come on, Ratty. We might as
well go. No sense spending any more time on this case with
important robberies going on all over the city probably. Let
me know if you find anything besides the typewriter
missing," he said to Bully, who was still standing in the
hidy-hole, as though rooted there in the ivy and vines. The
two policemen then got into their police car, and they
turned around practically on two wheels and tore out to
Larrabee Street and up it and around Gregory Avenue
with brakes screeching.

"Phew! They were in a hurry," said Bully Vardeer.

The two little fellows, Danny and Nicky, still in their
recital clothes . . . their best . . . got lifted out of the
hidy-hole by Bully Vardeer. "We couldn't find the pencil," they said.

"No," said Bully, "because I am stepping on it, that's
why. The minute I stepped down here, my bare feet felt
something slippery and cold, and I knew it was the pencil;
and I knew that there must be something special and peculiar about that pencil, so I didn't let on."

Bully stooped down and picked up the pencil and
climbed out himself. "Now," he said. "What *is* there so
peculiar about this pencil?"

Connie's mother said, "May I see it, please? Yes," she said.
"Connie is right. I think this is John's pencil. See? There are
his initials. J. I. Connie, you're a great detective."

"It's Billy," said Connie, "not me, who's the brains. He . . ."

Billy climbed down out of the tree. "Sh-sh-sh," he said. "You were the brave one who said, 'My father had a pencil exactly like that . . .'"

"But you took pictures of the other, the real, burglars, with your camera, and . . ."

"What's this? What's this?" Everybody clambered around Billy and Connie, trying to take everything in at once, old burglaries, new burglaries, pictures having been snapped, a ring—where was it? The pencil. How could anyone prove that the policeman had the ring even if he had the pencil, and, now that he was gone, how could anyone prove that he had had this pencil in the first place? Too many fingerprints on it now. Well, all these questions had to be answered. In a lull, the excited voices of Nanny, "O-o-oh, child," and of Papa, "Hey! Hey!" could be heard as they came up the Alley. "Ah, now! If anyone would know how to tackle the police, Presink number 9999, it would be Papa," thought Connie proudly.

Billy said he was going into his house to develop his pictures.

"What bright children there are here in the Alley," said Nanny.

"Billy probably has an I. Q. of 180," said Connie proudly.

"Not quite," said Billy. He ran to get away from the praise and to see the negatives. Whether it could ever be proved or not, everyone felt that one-half of the original burglary of Mrs. Ives's house had been solved, the half about who had got the ring . . . the burglars or the policemen.

The policemen, of course, since they had the pencil. And that showed how good Connie Ives's mother was at seeing through things. Everyone agreed to this and wished the same could be said about them. Even Connie's father agreed to this. "It surely does," he said, and he gave Mama a hug and kiss right in front of everybody. Connie didn't know whether to be happy or embarrassed.

While Billy was in his house developing his pictures, downstairs in his father's darkroom, and quite nervous he was, too, about whether they would turn out or not . . . if they didn't, he would be left with the same old clues—a Mura butt; the question, "Does this dog bite?"; the screwdriver named "Stanley"; and the bloodstained bit of curtain . . . all the other people were still standing around in the Alley. It was a lovely day to be out, anyway, and let the dishes wait, thought and said all the mothers, talking about this burglary and the Ives's old burglary . . . or any old burglary they had ever read about or had had.

Connie's mother had to give the details of hers over and over in every detail; and Bully Vardeer the details of his. "Imagine!" he said. "I had just stepped out for a few minutes! Imagine how they must have been watching my every move! I had only walked Princey over to Library Park, across the Mall, that's all. And they came, they broke in . . . they took my Olivetti—it is brand-new, you know. And we don't know yet what all they took, we don't know —probably little things of Dolly's, though they were not in there very long. Still, they work fast . . ."

And Connie said, "Mr. Below, I wonder if they left a screwdriver in your house named 'Stanley,' too."

"That's right," he said, "I wonder." Many followed him back into his house to see if they could find "Stanley" or any other interesting clue.

Clues. The most important clue of the solving of Connie's own original burglary was now in the hands of Connie's mother—the silver pencil of Connie's father, given to him by his ladies, with the scrolled J. I. on it. She had it, the burglars had not gotten it, and if they had not gotten it, then they had not gotten the ring. The policemen had had the pencil all along, and they must have had the ring, too. Now, let anyone say, "Hysterical lady!" about Mama and her hunches about seeing through pockets, thought Connie with great pride.

Then Billy came back out. Connie had never seen anyone look so excited and triumphant. After all, he had lived through this whole new burglary, while all she, his casing partner, had been doing was giving a piano recital! That had been nerve-wracking, too, but not *as* nerve-wracking as being in a tree at the scene of a crime and unraveling not only this crime, but also the old crime, proving all over again what the children in the Alley had previously proven in the trial in the Circle—that the bullet-head dog man was Connie's main burglar, and now, also, was Bully Vardeer's main burglar, and that casing had not been in vain. Billy showed the pictures first of all to Connie. "Wowie!" said Connie. "Honestly, Billy, you should be a whee-gee news photographer, the pictures are so good."

There in picture number one was the bullet-head man, coming along whistling . . . you saw him side-view; there in picture number two was his lookout man, Sawtooth Pete, his helper in breaking down doors; next a picture of the bullet-head man coming out of Bully Vardeer's house with the Olivetti typewriter. There it was in the burglar's hand. Also there was a picture of the two of them . . . bullet-head man and Sawtooth Pete together. And finally there were two pictures, blurry, but still they did show something, of the escape car driving them off. "It's a beat-up Pontiac," said Billy.

"You know, Billy," said Connie, "you and me solved this burglary, and we solved the other one, we really did. Wouldn't I like to take these pictures over to the police station and say, 'There! Catch your robbers that you never seem to be able to catch!' "

"Hey, let's," said Billy. But this was not to be. Connie's father and Mr. Fabadessa, home from his class in "phiz-ed" were studying Billy's snapshots. "Why!" exclaimed Mr. Fabadessa. "That is one of the men, I'm sure it is, who rang our bell the day of your burglary, John, the day we had the missionaries here from India; the others—let me see—yes, I'm sure they are all the same people."

Connie's father said, "Well, I'll be gol-darned."

And Mama said, "Billy Maloon, you are a genius and a brave boy besides."

Nanny said, "Bless Maud!" Connie hoped this meant Nanny would never more speak crossly to Billy.

Wagsie, not liking the excitement, clung closely to the back of Papa's legs, hanging her head, looking dejected. The cats, Mittens and Punk, were sitting behind a rose bush.

They enjoyed the excitement. Still, their twitching tails were meant to say to Mama, "Where are our kidneys? It is time to eat."

Though they were the heroes of the day, Connie and Billy were not going to be allowed to go over to the police station with all the clues and the pictures. Mr. Fabadessa and Mr. Ives were going to do that; also Bully Vardeer, the latest victim. Off the three men went, and gradually, sorry that everything was over . . . piano recital, burglary, piecing things together, examinations of snapshots, people wracking their brains to try to remember if they, too, had ever seen these men . . . gradually one by one, people went home, the mothers wondering what to have for dinner —no one was in the mood for cooking. Billy and Connie went into her yard to swing. No casing to do now, they thought. No more piano lessons to give . . . the recital was over. "What a day!" they thought.

All the other children of their age congregated in Ray Arp's yard. Many asked, and got permission from him, to get up in his tree. From there they watched Connie and Billy swinging. Nobody said anything. With blank expressions, they just watched the two gifted, swinging detectives.

"The swingers," said Ray Arp once, with a sort of wonderment in his voice.

20

✸✸✸

ALL SOLVED

The view from the swing included a view of the police station on Gregory Avenue across the athletic field. It was one of the few attractive buildings in the Grandby College neighborhood aside from those on the campus. It looked like an old castle . . . something that you might see on a picture post card sent from abroad, and it had a round tower. Connie and Billy did not watch the children in the next yard who were watching them. They were watching Gregory Avenue, hoping for a view of Connie's father, Mr. Fabadessa, and Bully Vardeer coming out of the police station.

At last, there they were, Connie's father talking as usual with great excitement and waving his arms around. You could even hear his voice, the wind was in that direction, though not what he was saying. The three men walked along the athletic field and soon would be coming down Larrabee. When they could no longer be seen, because of the little houses on Waldo shutting out the view, Billy and

267

Connie jumped down and went into the house to watch for her father from the living-room window. Soon, here he came. Bully Vardeer was not with him—he had gone home —but Mr. Fabadessa was, and he and Connie's father stopped outside the house and went over and over things.

Mama went to the front door. "John," she said. "Sh-sh-sh! You're talking so loudly, everybody in the world will be able to hear you."

"That was the way with Papa," thought Connie. Shouted. Got so excited; shouted into the phone besides. But then, so did his mother, Nanny. When they spoke on the telephone, you would think every person they talked to was stone deaf. ("They soon would be," said Connie's mother, a non-shouter.) It must be a family trait, like crunching on ice. Papa loved to crunch ice—did it whether there was company or not. Connie was beginning to crunch ice, too . . . the habit stemmed from Nanny down to Papa and now to Connie. No one knew about Papa's grandfather, whether he had crunched ice or not.

At last Papa wound up his animated conversation with Mr. Fabadessa and came in to report to Connie and Mama and Billy.

"What happened? What happened?" asked Connie.

"Well!" exclaimed Papa. "Just you wait!" He stomped back into the kitchen for a long glass of cold water, drank it down without stopping, and then he stomped back into the living room, followed in both directions by impatient Connie and Billy. "Well!" he repeated and sank to the couch. He wiped his brow with his handkerchief. His legs were sprawled out straight in front of him, stiff. Despair

clouded his face, the way it did when a bill he favored did not pass in Congress. "What is the world coming to, I wonder? Those two policemen!"

"Tell it, Papa. Papa, tell it," pleaded Connie, "and from the beginning."

"Well," said Papa. "We got there, Joe and Fab and I, and it was exactly at police changing time, that is—many officers were coming in to go on their beats, and others were about to go off, finished for the day. There, standing in a corner, were our two policemen, our two splendid—I must say—officers of the law, Rattray and Ippolito!" (Papa could be withering in his scorn sometimes, and he was always dramatic. It ran in Papa's family to be dramatic . . . stemmed from Grandfather Jonas. Nanny was, too.) "Well! They didn't notice us coming in . . . they were having a little argument it seems between themselves. I went up behind them (they had not noticed me), and this is what I heard! 'Wise guy, eh? You never told me, Ippy, that you got a ring in that haul.' The answer: 'I tell you, Ratty—now you know me, Ratty—the rule is the small things we keep, but the big things we share. Well, I never knew there was a ring on the pencil. In fact, there wasn't. Those loonies . . . you know they're eggheads— just must have *thought* there was! But there wasn't.' 'Ho-ho-ho! I thought so!' said the other one. ("Fighting among themselves," said Connie, "the way thieves always do," she said. "Yeah," said Billy.) And I," said Papa, "had heard enough. I just walked over to the captain, and I slammed all my cards on the table . . ."

"Clues, you mean," said Connie. She could just envision her father over there. He was very peppery . . . red peppery.

"Clues, pictures, the pencil, everything. 'Chief,' I said to the chief. 'Arrest those two policemen. They finished up, tied it up very nicely, very nicely indeed, after the real burglary, and there's the proof. This pencil is the proof. The one known as Ippy had my pencil today when he arrived at the burglarized house of my friend here, Professor Below. He dropped the pencil in the garden. He was most anxious to retrieve it—and why not? Such damaging evidence as that! I demand to know, sir, where is the diamond ring that was on this pencil? See my initials on it? J. I.? John Ives. Me.'

"The two policemen, hearing me, quickly buttoned up their coats to leave. But the chief said, 'Stay a moment, officers.' So they stayed. The chief questioned them. He showed them the pencil. They denied having ever seen it before, despite the proof, all the witnesses, to prove he had dropped it in Mr. Bernadette's hidy-hole. Then Officer Ippolito said, 'Anyway,' he said, 'my name begins with an I.' 'And what is your first name?' asked Papa, not waiting for the chief to ask. The man said, 'Joseph!' "

"Wasn't that unlucky . . . I mean for us?" said Mama.

"Then of course, more denials, and of course, they had no logical answer as to why they had stayed upstairs so long in our house. Anyway, the upshot of that was that they are going to be questioned by the police commissioner himself, who is on an inspection tour of all precincts, I understand, so we can only wait and see what he finds out. It's too bad his initials had to be J. I. like mine. But, Jane, I am now as sure as you were that those two policemen are dishonest and that they did have your ring."

Mama glowed with pride. Praise from Papa was a very great privilege.

"It's like having many screwdrivers named 'Stanley' to have two pencils named J. I.," said Connie.

"Then," said Papa. "We got on to the burglary clues, the original burglary clues . . . and I must say, Connie and Billy, the chief was really impressed with all your casing and your deductions, and especially with the pictures. He rang the bell. Four sergeants answered. He showed them the snapshots and said, 'Go forth and find these men. ("Sounds like King Arthur," Billy murmured to Connie.) They probably live in the neighborhood or they would not have so much time to case the little college houses; and if we catch *them*, we can clean up this whole neighborhood.'

Well, the four sergeants went out, and they came back in fifteen minutes with the bullet-head man handcuffed to them, and, likewise, a man with sawed-off teeth. They didn't have a leg to stand on—with the snapshots, of course —and confessed to everything . . . Joe Below's burglary (they had been trying to sell the Olivetti in Pete's Pawn Shop on Myrtle Avenue when they were caught)—and they confessed to our burglary, also Bernadettes' and others in the neighborhood. But they denied having taken any diamond ring or pencil. 'Never saw the pencil before,' they said. And so that proves, too . . ."

"Proves I am right about hunches," said Mama, laughing.

"It certainly does," said Papa, giving Mama another kiss and a squeeze. "Anyway, they confessed to lots of burglaries around here, and this is the end of their activities, I guess. Phew-ee!" Papa sank back on the couch again, mopped his brow again.

"Why should he be tired?" Connie wondered. "Billy is the one to be tired, and with a cold and all!" She and Billy went back outdoors to talk and to swing. Papa went over to Bully Vardeer's garden to discuss everything. You could hear his indignant voice. "They'll never do anything, you'll see," he said. "Not one thing will they do," he said hotly, "about these two officers." He was off on a new tack . . . how there would be an investigation, how it would be dragged out, and how in the end nothing would be done.

The children couldn't hear Bully's voice. It was low and smooth, but he was agreeing with Papa . . . that they could gather. "You know," said Connie. "They, the two policemen, might kill the whole bunch of us. Our entire family might be wiped out by them."

"Me, too. Mine, also. Because they know I am your friend and was in the tree with you. I wonder who would move into your house?" said Billy.

"Billy!" exclaimed Connie in horror. She had expected to be reassured, not agreed with. "You don't really think they will, do you, kill all of us?"

Billy shrugged. "Who knows?" he said lugubriously. He was going to miss the casing. What would he do without casing—and without swinging, since Connie had a job now, running a music school?

Connie, reading his thoughts, said, "Billy . . . you know, don't you, the recital is over? That means no more lessons till fall. Ts! What will I do?"

Billy smiled and swung.

That night Billy, cold or not, and Connie stayed up until twelve o'clock. It was like New Year's Eve, the only other night so far when Connie had been allowed to stay up that late. In every yard clusters of neighbors gathered filling in the chinks and cracks and crannies of the two solved burglaries. Various people up and down the Alley served cold drinks in their gardens. There were a great many people in Connie's yard . . . laughing, talking. Little by little, people drifted away. There was a translucent, pearl-like moon just over being full. It was more like a waft of a cloud, and one could imagine seeing right through it. Sometimes an airplane, lighted and serene, held steady on its course to La-Guardia Airport. Connie and Billy could not believe that they did not have to go to bed. Expecting any minute that they would be called, they did not enjoy themselves as they should. Why didn't their parents once and for all simply say, "We'll forget about bed for tonight, until you really and truly want to go there, you yourselves. Otherwise, stay up." But the parents didn't say this, and thus they kept the children on edge. Just wait until the parents wanted to go to bed, then they'd say crossly, "What! You children still up!"

Mrs. Goode came and got Hugsy. Mrs. Goode made the remark that if only Connie had to go to bed, she would have no trouble persuading Hugsy to go home and go to bed. Then she made a remark about how Mrs. Ives had practically invited the burglars in in the first place, having told them that Wagsie didn't bite!

"Uh! She always gets everything all wrong, all backward," said Connie to Billy. "Because that is the opposite of what Mama did say."

"You don't have to tell me," said Billy. "Grownups! That kind of grownups!"

Finally all the neighbors left. Just Billy and Connie were in the yard. "Come in," said Mama.

"Oh, please," said Connie. "Just five more minutes."

"All right," said Mama. "Then . . . really and truly . . . in!" And to Papa, Mama explained, "They have been through such a lot . . . and the night is such a lovely one!"

Billy and Connie swung and swung and did not mind the squeak in the swing. The little train went briskly along Myrtle Avenue; and from Mrs. Carroll's yard came her voice: "You kids still up? I'll have to fix that squeak in the morning." Mrs. Carroll always fixed things that went wrong in the Alley—broken gates she mended, squeaks she oiled. Finally Connie's mother came to the back door and said, "Well, now, you really do have to come in." So Connie went in. "S'long," she said. "See you later . . ."

"Alligator," said Billy.

"What a day, what a marvelous, glorious day!" thought Connie.

And then, after a few days, it was as though it had never happened . . . their burglary, their trial in the Circle, their casing; also Bully Vardeer's burglary, Billy's hoarding of the clues, his snapshots, the solving—all, all was as though read about in some book, some other life than theirs.

But, one day soon afterwards, at lunchtime, Connie's father burst into the house excitedly. He always came in excitedly, but this time there was really something to be excited about, more than seeing that somebody had picked his crocuses. "There you are! There! You see that, Connie? Jane, see that?" He banged the newspaper on the table. "See that? There is some justice, after all."

"Hush, darling," said Mama. She couldn't stand noise . . . shouting, water faucets running, people speaking loudly or crossly. "Let's see," she said.

Papa didn't lower his voice. He couldn't help talking excitedly—it was his nature, like Nanny's, and came down in their family, through the generations. "There we have it!" he said.

"Have what?" asked Connie. Papa pointed to an article on page one.

"That!" he said.

275

Mama and Connie examined the newspaper. There, right on page one of the *Brooklyn Eagle* was a picture of their two policemen, Sergeant Rattray and Officer Ippolito. "Precinct number 9999 cleaned up," said the paper. The news account gave the details of how these two officers of the law had been accused of petty thieving—they had done in some other house the same thing that they had done in Connie's house. But there they had been caught in the act, stuffing jewels in their pockets whilst pretending to search the house for, possibly, hiding burglars. In *that* house the lady had not seen through their pockets, as Mama had. The lady saw the policeman, just plain saw him . . . no hunches . . . pick up a ruby ring and drop it in his pocket. "Hah!" thought Connie. "What could be more damaging than that?"

"Well," said Mama. "Isn't that wonderful? Caught! Caught, that Ippy and Ratty!"

"Papa," said Connie. "Will you get back your ancestral cuff links, Mama's ring, and the watch?"

"I'm afraid not," said Papa. "I've already been over to the precinct. But of course the men deny having taken our things, and we really have no proof. We . . ."

"No proof!" exclaimed Connie. "What about the pencil?"

"Well, the two of them say the pencil we brought over there was not the pencil they were looking for, and they still say they never saw the ring. But, anyway, plenty of other charges have been made against them, and they're in real hot water."

"And, anyway, now," said Connie, "even though we don't have our things back, now we can trust policemen again. We can always trust them again, since the two wicked ones, the only two wicked ones there are and probably ever will be, or have been, are 'spelled from the police force and have been put in jail. *Now*, if we call the police to help us, we know that *good* policemen, not burglars in disguise, will come and *help* us, not *steal* the few little things the real burglars did not have time to take . . . or find."

"Yes, at least that," agreed Billy Maloon. And he and Connie went outdoors to swing. After a while Billy said sadly, "Connie, tomorrow I am going to camp for the whole, entire summer. I have to go home, soon, to pack."

"Pack!" echoed Connie in dismay.

"Yes," said Billy. He turned his face toward Connie. "Yes, I'm going to camp. I don't know whether I'll like it or not. I hear there's something about the bunks—the making of the bunks—I hope I'll know how."

"Oh," said Connie. Her heart was sinking. All the long days of playing with Billy Maloon were over . . . the Dinky Toys, swinging, casing, talking, building cities and tunnels and tracks and everything—all this was going to be over and right now—tomorrow! Then she thought of Billy in the woods, in a camp, swimming, making bunks, and he was so little! And she knew Billy, and she knew that he was a very brave boy—who else could catch robbers, smell Muras a mile away, and take pictures on his camera of a real honest-to-goodness going-on-right-then burglary? But

—but he might be lonesome; at night he might, he just might, with the lights out . . . cry.

"Billy," said Connie. "You'll like it there—I know you will. And if you don't, you can telephone me from camp. I'm an old hand on the phone, now. I answer it all the time."

"O. K.," said Billy. He jumped off the swing. He stood in front of Connie for a moment; he didn't say anything; he just looked at her; his eyes looked like deep dark pools. Then he said, "Well, by."

"By," said Connie.

"It's Camp Pineside," said Billy. "Vermont. Write."

"I will," said Connie.

"Well, by," he said.

"By," said Connie.

Connie's father came to the back door. He handed Billy his box of clues. "Billy," he said. "The police returned these clues to you. They don't need them any more. Your evidence was completely conclusive, they said. So, here they are . . . your mementos."

"Thanks," said Billy.

Connie said she would like to keep the screwdriver named "Stanley," if Billy didn't mind. Billy said, "O. K." He was going to bury the others in his yard. "If Atlas doesn't dig them up," he said, "centuries from now, someone, a member of an expedition, might dig them up. 'H-m-m, what's this?' they would say, and wonder what they meant."

Then Billy really went, he went in to pack. Connie, with a lonely heart, as she swung, turned toward Billy's house, at his end of the Alley. Soon a light came on in his room. He didn't pull down the shade. His yellow curtains fluttered in the breeze. It was very late when finally he put out his light.

"By, Billy," said Connie softly.

By, Billy. Now . . . what?

21

✡ ✡ ✡

MAY I COME IN?

Now, Billy Maloon was gone. The long hot days of June melted together, and it was hard to remember what day of the week it was, much less day of the month. Connie read to her mother a great deal—a picture post card from Billy of Camp Pineside with an X showing where his cabin and room were was her bookmark; and she read to herself a great deal. Or, sitting in the little red rocker, she just talked to Mama or Nanny, who said the South might be hot, but you did not have this humidity there. Connie did not mind the long days that began empty and ended up full. Oh, the wonderful and long days of summer! Just to hold a whole day in your hand and have it and think that it was empty to begin with but that each moment could, would, contain so much. She didn't even miss Billy too much—at first.

A great deal of the time, as usual, she swung. And, as usual, quite often one of the big girls, June or Katy or Laura, as they passed by, watched her swinging. Often Judy or June or Laura came in to swing. Once in a while Katy

said, "Boring." But Connie kept her eyes glued to the far end of the Alley, the Circle end, to the view of the Circle. Sometimes Katy came in. She never asked. She just opened the gate, left it open, came in, swung a while, jumped down in a moment or two, and walked off as though to say, "How boring!" which indeed she did say now and then, but in a dispirited, lifeless sort of way, a warm, summer-sort-of-day way of talking. Usually, in fact never, did she bother to close the gate, though Wags could get out.

Quite often, however, Connie did miss Billy acutely. The wonderful days they had had together . . . building towns and villages, camps, motels, highways for the Dinky Toys, their garages, or having the cars travel along the little roads on the patterns of the rug. She recalled the first day that

Billy Maloon had come to play with her. "Can Connie play?" he had asked Mama. Connie really now could not help feeling lonesome for him. He and she were such good friends. Neither one of them ever said anything mean to the other! They just liked each other the way they were. They never had to think what to say to each other. They never minded if they never said anything. Or, sometimes, they talked for hours. And how was Billy making out with the bunks, Connie wondered. She could not help a tear weaving down her smooth, tanned cheek. Where'd that come from, she wondered. She almost never cried. "Such a brave girl!" her mother always said. "And such a 'mart girl, too," Connie would always add, recalling a baby expression.

Connie brushed the tear away. She wondered where Hugsy was; he was next best to Billy in the Alley. Oh, yes, she remembered. He and his whole family—Greggie, Susie, Mother and Father, all of them—had gone off on a camping trip in the Catskills. Well, should she be really lonesome? Another tear swelled up and out of her eyes. Well, she was not the crying type, and she brushed that one off, too. So . . . she would go in and read to her mother. A few more swings, touch the bottom branch of Mrs. Harrington's tree with her bare toe, and then out she would hop.

At this moment, Katy Starr came to her back gate again. Katy was all alone—the other girls were not with her. They were still down at the Circle. She stood at the gate a moment. "Now," thought Connie. "She will walk right in again, swing for a second or two, then hop off, shake her shoulders, and go back out, saying, 'How boring!' Well, that's life," thought Connie neither sadly nor not sadly. Still, she was not in the mood for this. Why not have Katy stay out of her yard once and for all? Or at least obey the rules posted on the tree . . . to ask, just plain ask to come in.

But Katy did not follow her same old pattern. She stayed at the gate, and from the gate—which you remember was always kept closed, always, because of Wagsie—she said to Connie, "Connie? May I come in?"

ELEANOR ESTES (1906–1988) grew up in West Haven, Connecticut, which she renamed Cranbury for her classic stories about the Moffat and Pye families. A children's librarian for many years, she launched her writing career with the publication of *The Moffats* in 1941. Two of her outstanding books about the Moffats—*Rufus M.* and *The Middle Moffat*—were awarded Newbery Honors, as was her short novel *The Hundred Dresses*. She won the Newbery Medal for *Ginger Pye* in 1952.